"A real page turner filled with flawed, conflicted, but lovable characters. I knew nothing about harness racing but was completely pulled into this fast paced, gritty story of love and the admirable gumption of the main character, Bucky Whalen. Once I started reading, I couldn't put it down."

–Richard Taylor, author of *House Inside the Waves: Domesticity, Art and the Surfing* Life

THE ENDLESS
MILE

ANDREW C. F. HORLICK

 iUniverse®

THE ENDLESS MILE

iUniverse books may be ordered through booksellers or by contacting:

iUniverse
1663 Liberty Drive
Bloomington, IN 47403
www.iuniverse.com
1-800-Authors (1-800-288-4677)

ISBN: 978-1-5320-4473-1 (sc)
ISBN: 978-1-5320-4474-8 (hc)
ISBN: 978-1-5320-4475-5 (e)

Library of Congress Control Number: 2018902992

Print information available on the last page.

iUniverse rev. date: 01/28/2019

For my Mishpucha

CHAPTER 1

The sound of a car outside drew Bucky Whalen away from the kitchen table. He looked out the window and saw his uncle, Max, pull into the farmyard in his burgundy Cutlass Supreme. He watched as Max parked next to his father Carl's truck, which was covered in snow, and then trundle his way up the lane in his unzipped boots, baggy trousers, and oversize coat. In the distance Bucky could see their standardbred racehorse, Roundaboutway, trot over to the fence to spy the new visitor to the farm. He was a dark brown colt, and his coat was speckled with the snow that was falling lightly in the air. Bucky watched as the colt pawed the snow and hung his head over the fence to get Max's attention. But Max ignored Roundaboutway. For a moment Bucky thought that the farm looked pristine under the fresh blanket of snow. There were one hundred hectares of rolling knolls that looked like windswept tundra, and the branches of the evergreens along the distant tree line were covered with snow. Bucky thought that in many ways the farm looked prettier in winter, with the horse's breath huffing in the cold air and the outside world only a muffled interference. When he was young, there had been sleigh rides, snow angels, and Christmas parties, but not anymore. Now it was as if he and his dad were in their own little snow globe, their picturesque land in the middle of nothing and nowhere. At least that's how it felt sometimes for Bucky.

"Just Max," Bucky said to Carl, who was engrossed in the *Harrington Journal*, and then he sat back down at the table. Moments later Max walked in. Bucky watched as he shook himself off, stomped his boots on the mat, and then put his coat on the rack beside the door. At sixty-five, Max bore the stains of time in his pockmarked cheeks and drinker's nose. He had a bushy mustache and a large forehead, with a receding mop of dark curly hair. He carried a lot of extra weight on his six-foot frame, mostly around his stomach. Bucky wondered if at times he wore shirts that were intentionally too small, like today, with his physique marvelously on display beneath his tight wool sweater.

"Nice to see you as always, kid," Max said to Bucky, who didn't acknowledge him. Bucky's birth name was Johnny, but when he was a boy, he fell off a stepladder while changing a light bulb and smashed his front tooth on one of its wooden steps. The result was a crooked dead front tooth that he'd never gotten fixed and a nickname that had all but extinguished his given name. In fact, he couldn't remember the last time he had been called Johnny—perhaps by his mother, Delores, on the day she died, killed by an errant golf ball that had flown over the pine trees lining the fairway and over the safety net, splattering into her windshield like a bird flying into a glass pane. The shock had caused her to swerve into oncoming traffic. She died instantly in a head-on collision. It was a violent and unnecessary death, one that Carl and Bucky would never fully accept.

Bucky had thick brown hair that covered his ears and eyebrows, and at five foot six and three-quarters—or five eight, as he told most people—he had what could almost be deemed a slightly stunted stature. When Bucky was a teenager, Carl often told him that his growth spurt would be coming any day. Bucky waited and waited, but now, just past thirty, it was clear to him that it would never come.

"Brother," Max said to Carl, who didn't bother looking up from the paper.

"Glad you're okay, Max. Ever think of calling?"

"My cell phone died, there was a storm, I was out of town, and there was this girl …"

"Don't worry about it." Carl waved him off. Bucky could tell that his father didn't want to hear it. The mud was just too deep with his adopted brother. It had been three weeks since they'd heard from him, and for all they'd known he was dead or on his way to being dead, most likely facedown in a ditch somewhere.

Without hesitation, Max rifled through the empty cupboards like a rabid animal looking for food. Carl continued to read the paper. After a minute, he finally looked up from the paper and announced that eggs were on sale at Acme Market.

No one said anything.

"Also a great deal on milk," he added, but this still wasn't enough to inspire anyone's excitement.

Bucky watched as Max opened the refrigerator and sighed at the barren shelves. Carl, with his head back in the paper, mumbled, "These savings are tremendous," and licked his finger and turned to the next page.

Max poured himself some coffee and took his place at the table. Even from a distance, Bucky could smell Max. It was that same briny stink he remembered that emanated through Max's pores and trailed him around wherever he went. Max took a deep wheezy breath that turned into a coughing fit. Everything always seemed to be a struggle for Max, even breathing. His presence annoyed Bucky to no end during these quieter moments. Max hadn't shaved for days, and his curly hair was awry. His eyes, like usual, were tired, groggy deceitful-looking things. Bucky was sure that if he were to ask where Max had been, he would get a lie in return.

Max lit a cigarette and slurped his coffee. Bucky could tell he wanted to talk and was doing his best to ignore him.

Noon was the brightest time of day in the farmhouse. The sun shone through the kitchen window over the sink and spread across the table. On the wall that separated the kitchen from the living room was a green telephone with a long cord that nearly touched the floor. There was an outdated horse calendar from 1996, which was three years ago, and a blank to-do list. Outside in the hallway there was a credenza where they kept a couple of lanterns, keys, and loose change. There was a mirror with a wooden frame, and beside that was a small canvas painting of the homestead. Other than that, there was barely any aesthetic. When Delores died, so did any semblance of her woman's touch that had once added color to the farmhouse. For a while, Carl had tried to maintain the place by watering the plants, dusting, and the like, but eventually he gave up. Now, the only thing that might pass as decorative were the empty whisky bottles that lined the top of the green kitchen cabinets.

In the sunlight, each exhalation of Max's cigarette smoke took its own shape, lingering like a summer-morning fog over the farm. He blew rings and thin streams of smoke that eventually broke into little clouds. He watched them rise to the top of the room, squinting his tired eyes against the sunlight.

There was usually an uncomfortable reassimilation period when Max returned after an extended absence. Bucky felt that that's what was happening now. Carl never said much, but Bucky wondered to himself who this guy was who could just show up, eat, drink, sleep, and never have to explain himself. Just when Bucky thought that maybe Max's presence wouldn't be so bad and that it would shake up the monotony on the farm, he'd quickly change his mind after Max showed up and acted like he hadn't been gone a day. Max was probably back this time, Bucky mused, because he was broke and needed a lifeline.

"Bernie put you and Bucky in the same race next week at Speedway," Carl said, folding the paper, and putting it neatly by his side. "You going to be ready? We need you to start winning some races so we can start paying the bills around here. Things are bad."

Max took a moment to relish the question. Bucky knew Max loved the fact that he was actually needed. The Callaghans' farm in Harrington, Delaware, was a small one. To have any chance of digging themselves out of the perpetual financial pit, they needed both Bucky and Max to be harness racing, while Carl handled the entries and the business end. When Max didn't show up for weeks at a time, the whole enterprise was threatened, as they lived and died by the purse money. Without knowing if Max would be around—or if he was even alive—made it nearly impossible for Carl to plan.

"Speedway?" Max said. "Next week? Yeah, I'll be ready. How's Voltrain doing, anyway? You settle him down yet? I got no taste for eating shit these days."

"He's really come along," Bucky said. "Clarence thinks he should be able to pay his way this year, and then some."

"Well, that's good news. Carl, you hear that? We're gonna have a winner this season, and thank God for that," Max said. He looked to Bucky. "You get him ready tomorrow. I'll ride him out first thing."

Max's optimism heartened Bucky and Carl, but only a little. They had heard this all before, only to be disappointed. They recognized the familiar tones and promises, and had come to see them as fleeting glints of hope, like a bluebird or sparrow that briefly lands on your windowsill, just to fly away moments later.

The night before their race at Speedway in New York, Carl, Bucky, and the old black horse trainer, Clarence Holladay, met at a restaurant called Duffy's Buffet. It was a popular spot near the stadium. Many drivers had their regular booths or tables where they would sit with their families and friends. There was a buffet in the middle, so if the juicy rib eye didn't satisfy you, there were chicken wings, onion rings, and a whole smorgasbord of items. The oval booths were spread along the outside of the room, and the seats were covered with orange vinyl upholstery.

When they walked in, they saw that Max was already in a booth. He was saying goodbye to a friend of his whom Bucky recognized from the track. The man gave Carl and Clarence a friendly greeting and threw Bucky a wink as he parted.

"What was that all about, Max?" Clarence asked.

"Oh, nothing," Max said. He got up and started showing Bucky an unusual amount of affection, leading him into the booth to take the seat of his choice.

"How are ya, boy?" Max asked, trying sit closer to him. Bucky shifted away.

"Fine, Max. Doing fine."

"Well, that's good. Just dandy."

Carl got in on the other side, and Clarence sat on the end, the farthest possible distance away from Max.

"Word on the street's that Peter Dexter's the one to beat tomorrow," Carl said to Bucky. "Driving a horse from Hanover, and he's on a hot streak. I don't know, Son. Roundaboutway looks good, but not like Dexter's colt. He's been winning on all the cold-weather tracks this season."

"Don't worry about that, Dad," Bucky said. "His horse races inside, and he spooks if anyone is trailing. I'm gonna follow, and I'm gonna follow, and then I'm going to give him all the line he needs right at the end." Bucky demonstrated with his hands just how it would happen.

"Sure you are, kid, sure you are," Max said, still apparently trying to prove to Bucky that he was with him all the way.

"Let's go to the buffet, Bucky," Max said. Then he looked at the others. "We're going to the buffet," he reiterated.

Bucky and Max stood beside each other at the buffet. While scooping mashed potatoes onto his plate, Max leaned over and whispered into Bucky's ear.

"I need you to blow it in the third tomorrow. I made an arrangement."

"Is that a joke, Max?"

"Does it sound like a joke, kid? I racked up some serious debt playing cards, and if I don't pay up, these guys are going to fuck me up good."

"Yeah, well, one thing you can do is actually win for a change. That's one way to make some money—money that can go back into the farm. But you don't care much about that, do you, Max?"

"So I guess I'll take that as a no?" Max said, moving on to the lasagna.

"Take it however you want, Max. You're lucky you still have a stake in the farm. If not for that, we'd have cut you loose a long time ago."

Bucky then turned around and returned quickly to the table, intending to tell Carl and Clarence what had just happened. Carl only nodded. By his dad's rote response, Bucky knew that he wouldn't even bring up the issue with Max. Carl had been bailing Max out his whole life. Bucky knew his father felt obligated to care for Max. It'd been like that since the sunny summer day in 1941 when a black Ford sedan pulled up to the farm and the pretty social worker dragged Max out of the car to introduce him to the family. He was seven years old at the time; Carl had just turned fifteen.

"This is your new brother," Carl's mother said to him as he looked at the dirty scamp before him. "You're to take care of him and treat him like he's your own blood. One day, you'll both own this farm and will have to look out for each other."

Now, many years later, with his own ownership in the farm to protect, as well as his reputation, Bucky needed to keep Max at a safe distance. If it were ever proven that he helped him in any way on the track it could tarnish his reputation and maybe even get him banned from the sport.

Unlike with Carl, Bucky could tell that Clarence resented Max's untoward request. As they sat in the booth and began eating, Clarence's lip quivered ever so slightly and his nostrils flared. He sat with fists clenched on the table. It took a lot to excite Clarence, but when you did, it was best not to stick around to see what would happen next. A former boxer, Clarence had a face that had as many dents as a rusted bumper on an old car. Most noticeable was the straight line across the bridge of his nose, caused in a twelve-round decision that had almost killed him. Beneath his left eye was a black patch of skin, and both of his ears were cauliflowered. His hair was short, thick, and sprinkled with gray. If you couldn't tell he was an ex-boxer by his face, you would almost certainly be able to tell by his hands. They were as large and as coarse as a baseball glove. Given their size and strength, it was a wonder he was so gentle with the horses.

When Max came back to the table, Clarence stood up. He puffed his chest out at Max, but before he could do anything, Carl pulled him down by his brown leather jacket.

"Not worth it, Clarence."

"The hell it's not," he said and yanked his coat back from Carl.

"If he's injured, he can't drive anyway," Bucky said, making it clear that was his only objection.

"What's everybody all in a huff about over here?" Max said, putting his tray down on the table.

"I guess you're even dumber than you look," Clarence said, leaning across the table. "Do you know what we've got riding on this? Do you? Why don't you tell him, Carl?"

"Those horses cost a lot of money," Carl said matter-of-factly. "A lot of money," he repeated, just as calm. By looking at his dad's eyes, Bucky could tell that something had been sacrificed. There was always something sacrificed when you got a good horse. Bucky was aware of Carl's penchant for taking risks and had come to accept it as part of the business. It wasn't like Carl was a degenerate gambler like Max was. Nor was he dishonest. He was a gentleman gambler and wasn't too different from anyone else in the industry who won or lost thousands of dollars at a time.

"Let's just say if these horses don't earn, it's going to be a long, cold winter," Carl said calmly. The other men waited for him to explain what he meant, but he didn't. Was the farm on the brink of collapse? Had Carl thrown the last nugget from the family coffers into Roundaboutway and Voltrain? He had done it and lost before. Bucky recalled the sting of their first bankruptcy when he was a kid; bankers and lawyers had come by, then the auction people and moving people. They even took away his favorite horse. Everyone wanted a piece, but it never happened thanks to a filly named Angela. Carl had picked her up with their last three grand at a sale, and she won her first race at Kent Raceway. The next day, the trucks rolled back with the furniture, and even the horse was brought back. It was a small victory, but it left an impression on Bucky, showing him how easily you could lose it all.

The next night at Speedway in New York was cold and icy. The racetrack was lit up like a birthday cake, with the lights surrounding the oval planted into the snow like candles in a layer of icing. The city bus pulled up on the road outside the stadium. Gamblers and desperados—who, in some cases, had traveled hours just to try their luck with the ponies—shuffled off expressionless into the harsh glitter of the night.

Post time was 7:10, so Bucky, Carl, and Clarence lingered around the paddock area, going through all their prerace preparations. While they checked the equipment and got their pacer, Roundaboutway, ready to go, they also chatted with some of the other grooms, trainers, and drivers who bustled around in the ammonia-smelling stables. There were some familiar faces from Harrington and Dover, but for the most part, racing at Speedway was a whole other experience. It lacked the hominess of the Delaware tracks. And just as Max was protective of ship-in drivers to Delaware, the New York drivers didn't like seeing outsiders on their home turf.

Max, however, felt right at home at Speedway. Like an old deli, the New York racing scene was short on civility, but long enough in character to keep the fans and drivers coming back. There was a bawdy quality to it. Whether that was manifest in the facility or in the fans themselves was difficult to say. It wasn't as modern as Dover, nor was it as majestic as the Coliseum in East Rutherford. Stripped down, the racing was more like a street fight than a boxing match. There was less loyalty, fewer friendships, and lots more greed when it came to snatching up the purses. Besides the old Grand Circuit, where there were festivals and parades welcoming the horses and drivers into town, this was where Max had achieved most of his success as a driver. He was known by the track officials and had garnered a villainous reputation, as evidenced by the fans who jeered him during his warm-up scores and the post parade.

When they were set to go for the third race, Carl sent Bucky to look for Max. There had been some confusion in the paddock because the racing officials were considering calling off the races on account of the track being too icy. But if the races were on, Max would need to be ready on short notice.

Bucky opened the door to the drivers' lounge, and there was Max, playing cards with the racing secretary, Bernie Katz; the horseman's bookkeeper, Charlie Baker; and another driver, Joe "Jo Jo" Stevens. In the middle of a hand, they all looked up when they heard Bucky enter the room.

"You guys know my nephew, Bucky Whalen?" Max said.

"Of course. Good to see you," said the old man, Bernie Katz. He peered at Bucky through eyes set deep in his seventy-year-old skull. His enormous Adam's apple bobbed and seemed to travel the whole length of his neck when he took a swallow of his drink. Using the back of his hand, he wiped away the spittle that had collected in the corners of his mouth, exposing the underside of his arm, which was as white as a shark's belly. "They call me the Big Macher around here, don't they, boys? For some reason, the drivers think I wield some sort of magic stick."

"Be nice to him, Bucky," Max quickly interjected. The others vehemently nodded in agreement.

"You need to get ready, Max," Bucky said, doing his best to remain calm so as not to cause a scene in the lounge. The reason that Max, or anyone else really, wanted to be in favor of Bernie Katz, a.k.a. the Big Macher, was that Bernie knew everyone in the industry. If Bernie Katz had it out for you, then you were sure to get clipped by a wheel, or blocked in by colluding drivers. Bernie had his ways, and Bucky knew by Max's reverence for the old man that he must be just as crooked, so it was best just to keep quiet—for now.

The horseman's bookkeeper, Charlie Baker, was Bernie's closest friend and his confidant around the track. He had slick black hair and long muttonchop sideburns. His arms bore jailhouse tattoos that ran into each other in pools of blue ink, as if they had just been smudged together carelessly on his arm. He was the one who cut checks made out to the race winners and handled the claimers. He also had a tax business on the side to help out the drivers. Even though he was thirty years younger than Bernie, he'd worked at almost every track in upstate New York.

"Queens over jacks, Jo Jo," Max said after they'd opened up their hands on the table.

"Asshole," Jo Jo said. He ran his hand through his wavy blond hair and teased his light brown mustache. His shirt was wide open at the top, revealing his thick chest hair and a gold chain. Jo Jo was one of Max's allies on the track. The two of them gambled, drank, and cheated together regularly. Of the three, Bucky knew Jo Jo the best because sometimes he dropped in at the farm and joined Max and whomever else might have shown up to play poker at the kitchen table until morning.

"Well … yeah, that's what most people been calling me lately." Max pulled the pot over to himself.

None of them should have been playing at that time—or with each other, for that matter. Two officials playing cards with two drivers could be seen as suspect to anyone who happened to walk into the lounge. They were, however, gambling buddies, and the game that had started at four o'clock that afternoon was finally winding down.

Sensing that Max had no intention of leaving his card game until he was ready, Bucky left the lounge and went back into the paddock area.

Besides the colt that Carl had warned Bucky about, there weren't too many standout horses or drivers in the third race. It was just the type of race that came down to pure driving skill, especially on a half-mile track. Bucky liked his chances even more because he had drawn the inside post. Also, he was going up against Easy Money Eddy, who hadn't posted a win in over three months; Gerry Phillips, who had shipped in from Chicago; and a few other subpar drivers who had entered. And of course there was Max. Bucky hated racing against Max more than anyone.

As the horses from the last race clomped back down the ramp into the paddock, Bucky talked strategy with Carl and Clarence. Then he pulled his gloves on tight, zipped up his jacket, and hopped up into the sulky.

Max was still in the drivers' lounge playing cards. When he saw that most of the other horses were already heading out, he chugged his drink, butted out his cigarette, and told Bernie not to worry—the arrangement had been made; it was all taken care of. Bernie seemed satisfied with Max's reassurance. Max made for the track in the driver's seat of Voltrain, who was listed at 13–1 on the tote board.

When Max got onto the track, Jo Jo pulled up beside him and gave him a knowing wink. Max then took a few warm-up scores. When his name was announced over the speaker, he could hear the boos from the grandstand.

"They love you out here, Maxi," one of the other, honest drivers said while driving beside him.

"That's why I keep coming back," Max said, unfazed, even proud.

The race itself was a $13,000 one-mile pace. By all accounts, it wasn't an important competition. Most of the better horses were still on winter break, or were racing and training down south.

Max tried to catch up to Bucky before they were called to the gate.

"Remember our chat last night, Bucky?" Max said to him.

"Whatever, Max," Bucky said, rearing up so Max would ride right by him.

"That's why I love ya, kid," Max called back to him. He then swung out right to his post position on the outside, as the mobile gate started to move. The equipment on all of the horses began to jingle even louder as they moved into position, and the two-wheel discs on the bottom of the carts that towed the drivers began to whirl with more velocity.

Max was a good three feet behind the gate. Bucky's horse, Roundaboutway, was breathing on the bars. As the horses picked up speed and got into a better starting position, Max yelled out to all the drivers, "Hey, boys, Dexter needs a new washing machine, so let's give it to him, the poor son of a bitch."

"Up yours, Max!" and "Go to hell!" were the immediate responses, and then the gate opened and they were off. Dexter led the pack early, followed by Bucky, Easy Money Eddy, Max, and two other horses. The horse in last place had already broken and was driving off to the side.

Max wasn't too concerned about his position because he wasn't racing to win. He just had to stay close to the pack and try to block anyone from moving up on Dexter and Bucky so that he and Bernie could cash in on the side bets they'd made.

After the first two quarters, everything seemed to be going to plan. Dexter was still leading, while Bucky was undercover in the pocket. Easy Money Eddy had drifted to the back, like everyone knew he would, and Max led the pack of dogs, already strung out by five lengths behind the leaders. Apart from some movement in the back, things stayed pretty much the same around the backstretch. Then, as the horses headed for home, Bucky made his move. It was Peter and Bucky, and then Bucky and Peter, down the stretch. Max, seeing that he might even be able to show—and also knowing that it never hurt to make things look believable—started to whip Voltrain as hard as he could.

When it was announced over the loudspeaker that it was Peter Dexter's Wind Runner by a nose over Roundaboutway, two of the other drivers started yelling at Max, knowing that it was the outcome he had desired. First, it was Gerry Phillips who drove by and said, "After all this time, you're still a bag of shit, Max."

"Much obliged," Max said politely.

Then, the usually reserved Lenny Irving said, "I could use a washer too, Maxi, and a fuckin' dryer. I don't know what you got going on here, but you're lucky you're still driving."

After the tenth race, Bucky walked into the drivers' lounge with Carl and Clarence. A swarm of people had formed around Max in the drivers' lounge as he bought drinks and regaled his listeners with tales about the good old days, when there were packed houses and Roosevelt Raceway on Long Island was the height of fashion and high society. Max called them over, but Bucky wanted nothing to do with him. Instead, he, his father, and Clarence sat at a table tucked away on the other side of the room. But even from there, they could hear Max clearly. He was telling a story about how one horse had died on him when he was coming down the stretch at Saratoga, and about the time he'd caught Rocco "the Rat" trying to give his horse cocaine with a straw. Max had a million stories, and Bucky had heard them all.

"Can you believe him over there?" Bucky said.

"Funny thing is, I can," Carl said. "You know, as much of a slug as he is, in a way he can still be credited with getting you on a horse."

"C'mon, Pops. I would have done that anyway," Bucky protested. "You know it was just a matter of time."

"Well, I guess, but he believed in you. He saw your potential right away. Without him buzzing in my ear, a lot of things wouldn't have happened the way they did."

"Clarence had more to do with it, Dad," Bucky said. "Max just wanted to put me on a horse so he could make money off of me. He's a liar and a crook."

"Well, whatever he is, he's my brother and your uncle, and there's no getting around that."

"I guess," Bucky said, looking across at Max, who must have said something offensive or else stopped buying drinks, as the crowd around him was starting to peel away. There were a few people left in the lounge who didn't seem to be paying any attention to Max. And so Max, finding himself alone, picked up his drink and waddled over to Bucky's table.

"Bucky," Max said, "I want to thank you for coming second in that race. You've finally proven yourself to be a real team player, a family guy—someone who comes through when the chips are down." He paused to take a sip from his drink. "When I saw Dexter going all out and you right there with him, I had my doubts. How did you do it? Didn't look like you pulled up or anything. My guess is you made your brush too early, knowing he wouldn't have much left at the wire. Well, whatever you did, you're in good with the Big Macher—for a while, anyway—*and* me. Now here, take this." He pulled out a wad of cash from his pants pocket and peeled off a few hundred-dollar bills, which he threw down on the table.

"It's your share—well, just about your share. You know how it is, superstar."

Carl looked at Bucky as if to say, *Calm down, Son. It's what we just talked about.*

"I didn't come in second because of you, Max," Bucky said. "I came in second because I lost."

"Right, you 'lost,' kid," Max said, making quotation marks in the air with his fingers. "Well, thanks again."

"Just get out of here, Max, okay? And take your money. You make me sick."

"I ain't taking the money, kid. It's yours. And don't worry—I know you. I've known you since you been yay big," he said, making a small parcel with his hands. "You did the right thing out there today, trust me." And with that, he tripped his way out the door.

CHAPTER 2

It had been a week since their last race. Bucky could hear a commotion coming from the stable. When he walked in, he saw Roundaboutway kicking the back of his stall, and Voltrain beside him neighing away incessantly. In the middle of the barn was Summer Rose, waiting patiently in the crossties to be tacked up and taken out for a jog. If there was one face Bucky liked to see first thing every morning, it was hers. He went over and whispered a greeting to her, combing her mane with his fingers and rubbing her velvety muzzle. Summer Rose had always been one of his favorite horses. A light chestnut, she had a flaxen mane and a tail that flowed behind her like a banner when she ran. Her eyes were wide set and humanlike, the lashes darker than her coat. Her body had developed the muscle they had hoped for, and although she wasn't the fastest, she knew how to squeak out a win when she was leading down the stretch. The running joke was that she usually won whenever there was a job that needed to be done around the farm. The first time that had happened, money had been needed for a tractor repair, and she'd come first in a photo finish. The next time, a section of the barn roof had caved in and she'd won by a length.

When Clarence noticed Bucky, he immediately set him to work gathering everything they'd need to tack up the mare, calling for each piece of equipment like a surgeon requesting instruments at the operating table. The early mornings and hard work weren't a problem for Clarence. Although the pay was paltry and his living conditions in the stable were meager, what got him up every morning was the opportunity to work with the horses.

When Summer Rose was ready, Clarence led her out of the stable. The limp that the horse had shown just days before was gone, and she seemed ready to race.

While Bucky milled around the stable, Clarence jogged the mare in a long straight line in front of the stable, and then shouted at Bucky to run to the house and get his uncle.

Max wanted to exercise the trotter this morning to see if they could race her in the next week or so. But, as usual, Max was late, having been deep into a card game and his whisky the night before. Just as Bucky was about to enter the farmhouse, Max came out yawning and holding a cup of coffee. His shirt was half-tucked into his unzipped pants, and his suspenders were secured over only one shoulder. Bucky wondered if his uncle had started getting ready in the wrong order again. He had seen him pour orange juice into his cereal before, and he recognized the lazy shamble that indicated that Max had started the long, slow procedure of getting his engine started in the morning.

Max had plateaued as a driver years ago, and no longer brought in the purses like he had when he was on the Grand Circuit. It wasn't that he was a poor reinsman or didn't have the talent; it was that he had lost the drive, the willingness to race one track in the morning and another track in the afternoon and then keep on going—day after day, month after month, year after year. Any great driver would tell you that a thousand wins came as a result of five times the losses, but Max had become lazy. He had fallen prey to the easy money. When it stopped rolling in, he stopped trying to chase it so hard. Then there was his ex-wife, who had contributed just as much to Max's ruin. Her name was Marge Tate, and she was a wiry blonde who spit and swore. They'd met at the track. Max had been coming off a race at Batavia when he heard an angry voice off the rail.

"You fuckin' asshole. You just cost me twenty-five bucks, you useless son of a bitch!" When Max looked over to see who'd laced together such obscenities, he was shocked to see a petite blonde lady barely five feet tall standing there in a white dress that clung to her body, revealing small breasts and bony hips. He then got off the sulky, took a wad of cash out of his pocket, and put it in her hand. She looked down at the money and then back up at Max.

"You went off at ten to one, superstar," Marge said, still holding out her hand.

Max knew right then he was in love, so he asked the woman out to dinner. The rest of their courtship and marriage could best be likened to a tornado that left no structures standing—a complete obliteration consisting of booze-fueled fights that would last all night, where regular household items turned into deadly ordnance. Just as Max was hard to contain, so was Marge. In fact, they were just about the mirror image of each other but opposite in gender, which made it like a confluence of waves ceaselessly smashing into each other. Just the bare foundations were left on a scorched earth once Marge Tate was through with Max. For her part, she couldn't help it. She was a shack-up queen who would go town to town, maybe work in a diner, and in worst cases turn tricks until she found a man. Then one day she'd just left. The fact that she'd stayed with Max so long was testament of her genuine love for him. Chances were that just as Max drank to forget, so did she—wherever she was.

Max splashed his unfinished coffee on the ground and walked past Bucky to talk to Clarence, who'd hopped off the sulky.

"How's she doing?" he asked, as he stroked Summer Rose's muzzle, trying to hold her head while she pulled away.

"Still seems to be favorin' that knee a bit," Clarence said. "I wouldn't work her too hard today, but see how she goes."

Max thrust his empty coffee mug into Clarence's chest and mounted the sulky. He drove it through the paddock and out to the practice track, which was bare but surrounded by a thin layer of snow and bordered by the tree line.

Bucky followed Max and Rose out to the track and perched himself on the paddock gate, watching Max jog Summer Rose around the track. Seeing Max in the sulky was a sight to behold. Although weight wasn't the issue for Max that it was for thoroughbred jockeys, most harness drivers made at least a minimal effort to keep fit. When Max was sitting in a sulky, his belly hung low over his thighs and his helmet strap could barely contain his overflowing chin.

While Bucky sat there, entranced by the driver and mare, Clarence surprised him by pulling up to the paddock gate with Voltrain.

Bucky got down off the fence to unlatch the gate. "Just out for a jog, Clarence?"

"You got it, boy. Still lots of work to do on this one," Clarence said, steering Voltrain onto the track.

If Max was a sight to behold in the racing cart, so was Clarence. He looked too big and too tall for the racing chariot, almost as if he were an adult hunched into a children's ride.

Once the horse started to pick up speed, Bucky thought the horse looked okay, but he could see Clarence still trying to hold him straight.

After a couple of minutes, Clarence and Voltrain came around. When they passed Bucky, Clarence was leaning back to feel the warmth of the sunshine through the cold. On his next lap around, Max caught up to him. Over the clamber of hooves and the smooth, steady sound of the wheel discs, he hollered, "Out of the way!" as he passed him in the practice oval. Clarence immediately let his horse out for more speed. There was a noticeable difference between the gaits of the pacing colt and the trotting mare. Voltrain had power and speed. He wore hobbles to keep his legs in stride and was covered in crisscrossing black leather straps. Summer Rose, on the other hand, had a natural trotter's gait that wasn't as fast but that was elegant and smoother to watch. She wasn't covered in as much gear as the pacer and didn't fight the bit as much.

When Clarence drove by, he let out a *whewee!* as he came around first. Max passed in front soon after, and acknowledged Bucky with a nod. Bucky could watch for hours as the horses came around and then sank away on the backstretch.

Clarence and Voltrain were first to pull up and stop in front of Bucky. Bucky went right up to the horse and pet his forehead.

"Looks like we finally got our racehorse," Bucky said to Clarence, who hopped down from the cart.

"He's still a little bit jumpy, but another week or so and he'll be ready again," Clarence said.

After another lap, Max and Summer Rose jogged leisurely around and stopped in front of Bucky and Clarence. After a brief discussion concerning Summer Rose's chances of returning to competitive racing sooner rather than later, the men agreed she was also about ready to race. Bucky went back to the farmhouse to tell his father.

He entered through the back door and walked through the hallway to his father's office. It was an extension that had been built when things had been more prosperous for the farm and there'd been plans to expand the operation to stable as many as ten horses. The office was cluttered with boxes and filled with cigar smoke. Carl was seldom without a stogie in his mouth. Even if it wasn't lit, he'd chew the saliva-soaked nub until it finally began to break up in his mouth. For a widower who had already endured so much, this was a minor vice. Fortunately, he'd never developed the same taste for booze that his younger brother had. Rather than taxing his liver, the side effects of Carl's cigar smoking showed up in his sad-looking, baggy eyes.

When Bucky opened the door to his father's office, Carl raised his head from deep inside "the books," as he called the accounting ledger, and began massaging what seemed to be an invincible vice grip pressing against both his temples. Bucky sat down across from Carl.

"Rose looks good. She'll be ready next week," he said to Carl, who looked at him blankly.

Bucky knew he always reminded Carl of Delores. According to Carl, it was not only his thick brown hair and dark eyes but also his mannerisms that were similar. Sometimes Carl would tell Bucky that he was just like his mother. When Bucky would ask how or why, Carl would delight in telling some oft-repeated story about Delores, one that never had any significance until after she was gone. And while

Carl rambled on, relishing every detail, he seemed to forget where he was. Then when the story lost its legs and he finally ran out of the long trailing breath that had fueled it, he'd sit back and for a moment realize the magnitude of his loss, before quietly resuming whatever he'd been doing.

By the way that Carl was looking at him, Bucky sensed that one of those nostalgic moments was just about upon them, so he jarred his father from his introspection.

"So, Pops, sound good? Rose will be ready to go. You can put Max on her, and I'll drive the colt."

"Just made a note of it," Carl said, after scribbling into his ledger.

"Good then," Bucky said, getting up to leave.

"You know, I'm proud of you, Son," Carl said. Bucky smiled sadly at his dad.

"I know, Dad. Thanks," Bucky said. Then he sat back down on the edge of his chair. "Is everything good?" Bucky asked, fearing what the answer might be.

"We're just about broke," Carl said. "With the cost of feed, vet bills, and everything else, I don't know what to do."

Bucky leaned back in his chair, looking hard at his father.

"That's why," Carl went on, "the first thing we're going to have to do is sell the mare."

"What? You're not serious?"

"I know, Son, I know," Carl said. Then he quickly moved on to the next item, as this was just the beginning of his budget cuts. "Next, we cut the feed. No more steaks or meals out. And we need to cut the electricity by half, sell some of the old farm equipment ..."

Carl's list went on for about five minutes. Bucky wondered what else could possibly be taken away from them before they would have nothing left.

"Finally," Carl said, turning over the soggy unlit cigar butt in his mouth, "I need you to go over to your buddy Cole's place and collect something his old man left there for me."

Carl and Roy Callaghan had been betting on horses together for years; both had won and lost many times. The difference, however, was that Roy could afford the high stakes, whereas every loss Carl took cut severely into the farm. Bucky suspected that the "something" was most likely a loan, as Roy had been known to bail Carl out on occasion. If it were a bet Carl was collecting on, he certainly would have mentioned it at the top of the order, and wouldn't have had to introduce such drastic measures. Instead of cutting booze, there would have been more of it; and perhaps a new horse or a piece of equipment would turn up. Surely they wouldn't need to sit in roving blackouts to save electricity, or not eat steaks, if Carl were flush with cash.

The next morning, the temperature had warmed considerably; the snowbanks on each side of the lane glistened in the sun. When Bucky walked out, he felt the spring sensation but knew that the change in season was still very far away.

After a few sputters, his red Datsun pickup truck finally sprang to life. He drove down the country roads. He passed the Murphy farm and the Robinsons' silo, made a left, and drove for a few miles along the outer perimeter of Cole's fenced-in property, which had been a wedding gift from his father. If it wasn't the miles of perfect white paddock fence and the championship horses that reminded Bucky of the disparity between the two farms, then it was the fact that Cole, his oldest friend, was married to Anna Miller, Bucky's *second* oldest friend—and his first and only love. The three of them had grown up together, and throughout the years, it had become not just uncomfortable for Bucky to watch as their relationship flourished, but also at times damn near unbearable.

Before turning into the iron-gated stone entrance, he pulled over, reached into his glove box, and pulled out a cigarette. The first inhale was sweet and smooth. He exhaled with relief as the smoke filled up the car. He waved away the smoke, sat back, and closed his eyes.

He remembered the day he'd met Cole before their first year of middle school. It was in the paddocks at the Delaware State Fair, prior to his first amateur race. It was a screaming-hot and dusty afternoon. Bucky was trying to settle down his fussy horse in the stall, and Cole was beside him, gently stroking the mane of his own horse, which stood calm and still. They got to talking. Bucky learned that not only had Cole's immediate family moved to Harrington, but also his uncles and all their families. The Callaghan clan had left Chicago and firmly implanted themselves into the Delaware racing scene. Seeing that Cole was already accomplished on the amateur circuit and was driving top horses, Bucky couldn't help but be impressed. Everything about Cole seemed effortless, from his hair that hung down in curly blond locks to his muscular farm-boy body that already was big for his age. Cole had an unwavering confidence, and at that time Bucky was fragile at best. Only three years removed from his mother's death, he would barely look anyone in the eye.

For the record, Bucky would always remind Cole that it was he who had won that first amateur race. But it was what happened afterward that night that really mattered: they'd both met Anna.

Bucky took a couple of quick pulls from his cigarette. Anna, Anna. Fucking Anna. He'd been eating a popcorn ball in the midway when she'd walked right over and looked directly at him with her big almond eyes.

"Good race today. Almost got away from you there, but you pulled it off."

Bucky stood gobsmacked by his sudden change in fortune. Who was this girl who stood before him, acting like she'd known him her whole life? He took a moment to really look at her as if his eyes were out of focus. She had knobby joints and long gangling arms. She had only the slightest dollop of a chest, and her long brown hair was tied back in a ponytail. Before Bucky could say anything, Cole appeared amid the throngs of people. Bucky's heart sank, and he felt doomed. Sure, he could compete with Cole on the racetrack, but when it came to girls, no way.

"Thanks," Bucky said, trying to get a quick word in before Cole surely took over the conversation. "It was really—well, I ..."

"Who's your friend?" Cole asked, before Bucky could finish. In a way, Bucky was relieved that Cole had interjected because he didn't know what to say.

"I'm Anna," she said, brushing away a strand of hair and tucking it behind her honeycup ear.

"Nice to meet you, Anna. I'm Cole."

"I know who you are," Anna said. "Our dads know each other ... and our moms. They belong to the same golf club." When Anna mentioned the golf club, Bucky shivered. He tried to pretend he hadn't heard that Anna's parents and Cole's parents were members of the club—maybe even the ones responsible for his mother's death. He wondered if they even had the courtesy to yell "*Fore!*" as the ball sliced across the fairway and sailed over the safety net.

"That horse you were driving?" Anna continued, not noticing Bucky's discomfort at those dirty words. "He came from our farm. I was actually surprised you weren't able to win with him. We had to sell him off to make room for another horse we have coming up."

"Oh well," Cole said. "He's a good horse, but Bucky here drove a great race. Can't win 'em all, I suppose."

Both Bucky and Anna seemed surprised by Cole's response. Perhaps they'd been expecting a little more bravado from him, but when they saw that he was just a normal kid, they loosened up.

The three of them drifted through the rows of vendors, eating minidoughnuts, cotton candy, and ice cream until they were too stuffed to eat another bite.

Anna then bought some ride tickets, and they cut the line for the House of Horrors and squeezed into the tiny carts. When the steel bar came down over their waists, Cole mocked the old ride operator, saying, "Ooh, how very scary," before their cart clanked along the first few feet of rusty track, jerked quickly around the first corner, and entered the portable trailer done up as a haunted house. They had all been on this kind of ride before, so they weren't too surprised by the ghostly apparitions that popped up from nowhere, or the flashing green eyes of the mannequin dressed up as Frankenstein.

There was, however, one thing that did scare them. Just after they'd gone past the vampire emporium where fake plastic bats swooped down just above their heads, their cart derailed. They could tell it wasn't part of the effect because of the sudden jolting halt and the terrible sound of twisting metal.

Anna was in the middle of the cart. Her immediate reaction was to grab Bucky's knee and press her head into his shoulder. Bucky's heart pounded in his chest as he inhaled the smell of Anna's cherry shampoo. He was sure in that moment that whatever jealousy he had toward Cole had been unwarranted. It was clear that Anna was in love with him. Why else would she have introduced herself to him in the midway and then thrown herself upon him in the ride?

Suddenly the lights went on in the haunted house. In normal light, the House of Horrors was nothing more than an empty room with movie props, and popcorn and soda cans scattered on the floor. When the old ride operator appeared before them to help them out of the ride, a part of him seemed beaten. His visitors could now plainly see they weren't anywhere near Transylvania, and could tell that he wasn't an innkeeper but a fraud.

But the real highlight of the night that would leave an indelible mark on Bucky had come at the end of the evening.

Now, sitting in his truck, confined to the prison of his memories, Bucky could only imagine what his life might have been like if he'd been the one to marry Anna.

It was funny how things had turned out, Bucky gathered. Both Anna and Cole had grown up privileged, so of course it made perfect sense that they would share such a storied life together. No one wants to marry the poor kid with no mother. *Such a tragic case,* Bucky thought to himself, before taking one last deep inhale from his cigarette and then flicking it out the window. He put his truck in gear and rolled slowly through the front gate.

There were sycamore trees and paddocks on both sides of the

lane. On one side, two horses were running along the fence, and on the other side there was a group of horses huddled together in the distance.

Bucky passed the small man-made pond covered in a thin layer of black ice, and the indoor training facility, and then finally came to a stop in front of the farmhouse that was worthy of a full spread in *Town & Country*. His mind was racing as he walked up the flagstone path. *How could Anna not love me?* he thought. *Are we not bound by the same sense of loss? How come our lives are not connected by something more than this mere acquaintance; our history glossed over as a casual memory; my kiss long forgotten; my touch long faded away? It is true: I was there the day Bobby died. I was a part of it, maybe even to blame, but it doesn't matter. We've been through all of that. I would have never been good enough for you, Anna. That is the truth. That is the plain truth, and we both know it. I'm glad you are happy and living in this massive home, this massive behemoth of a home, this structurally unsound, ostentatious, I-would-rather-squat-than-live-in-this home.*

How humiliating to have to pick up money for my father, Bucky's internal ramblings continued, as he stood outside the door, taking a moment to gather up his nerve. It was bad enough that Cole had already had the main prize, Anna. But now that Bucky had to show up with his hands outstretched was almost more than he could be bear. For a moment he thought about turning around and going back to his truck. Instead, he took a deep breath, looked up at the restored manor with imported stone and oak finish, and rang the doorbell. He heard the loud chime and thought the house had to be empty because the melodic sound seemed to reverberate off every wall inside. He waited for what seemed like an eternity. Finally one side of the double oak doors opened.

"Well, looky here," Anna said, smiling. She was wearing a plaid shirt with pearl snaps and tight blue jeans. Her long brown hair was tied back in a ponytail, and her face was flush from preparing whatever it was that Bucky could smell cooking. "Bucky Whalen!" She opened up her arms to receive him for a hug, and welcomed him into their home. It had been a few weeks since he'd seen her. Anna was just as roll-out-of-bed beautiful as ever. In Bucky's mind, there could be no more perfect woman. He loved her olive skin and full lips. She had a dimple on her chin that Bucky used to pinch, and in her left eye, there was a sliver of black that seemed to be cut from her pupil, set free to drift around her hazel pond of iris. You could only see it in a certain light, and when you noticed it, it shimmered, like you were panning for gold or trying to spot a desert island through the clouds.

Even approaching thirty, Anna showed no signs of losing her figure. She'd always had the perfect contours, Bucky thought. Her hips were just the right size; her breasts, darn well a national treasure; and her ass ... no one could wear a pair of jean shorts like Anna. Sometimes Bucky wondered if Anna was unaware of her own beauty, because she didn't carry on like most of the women he knew from school. She was confident yet demure. She preferred simple clothes and didn't slather herself with makeup. She looked great and smelled great. The only real problem that Bucky could find with her was that she was married to Cole.

"Been a while, huh?" Bucky said, looking around to see if Cole was nearby.

"Why do you stay such a stranger?" Anna asked, removing the elastic from her ponytail and shaking out her hair. "You know how happy it makes Cole when you come over."

"No excuse for it, Anna. You look great," Bucky said, as if it would help erase his spotty record of staying in touch. He did an up-and-down of Anna. Even in her socks, she was taller than Bucky. He wondered how "Shortie," which he'd sometimes called her near the end of that marvelous summer in the sun, could have actually outgrown him by a good three inches.

"Thanks," Anna said, turning around and leading him into the kitchen. "What brings you over?"

"Oh, just some business to discuss with Cole," Bucky said, fidgeting with the keys in his pocket.

"Care to stick around for lunch?" she asked. She took two jars from the cupboard and squinted at both their labels before putting one back. "I'm just making a salad, and I have a shepherd's pie cooking up in the oven. Cole is out in the barn and will be up soon."

Originally Bucky had just wanted to get in and out as fast as possible, but the smell was making his stomach rumble, and he did relish those rare moments when he was alone with Anna.

"That would be great."

"Good. Well, don't mind me," she said, as she continued getting things ready for lunch.

"Oh, I won't." Bucky smiled, watching her as she opened a jar of pickled radishes and dumped them into a bowl.

"You guys usually eat like this at lunch? Over at my place usually it's PB&J."

"No. I have to go into town later, so I thought this would pass as dinner as well. Don't worry; Cole gets his shares of leftovers."

Really? Bucky thought to himself. *Leftovers for Prince Cole? How common of him.*

After the initial moment of seeing Anna had worn off, that is, after Bucky's synapses had stopped firing and his heart palpitations had ceased, he calmed down a little and wandered out of the open kitchen area to give Anna her space.

The interior of the farmhouse was decorated better than any house Bucky had ever been in. It was big and warm. There was a sunken living room with leather sofas and a brick fireplace. There were touches of décor that Bucky was pretty sure only a woman could have added—like the vases stuffed with fresh-cut flowers, and the porcelain horse collection in the glass case. He realized that things such as these were conspicuously absent from his own home.

Bucky sat at the table in the large open dining area, where he was sure that many loving, romantic meals had been shared. While Anna's back was turned to Bucky, he could see her face in the reflection off the window behind the sink.

"So how's it going with Cole?" Bucky asked. He could see her expression change. She abruptly stopped slicing the cucumber she was working on for the salad.

"What do you mean?"

"You know what I mean."

"Bucky, c'mon. That's not fair," she said, turning around to face him and putting her hands on her hips.

"What's not fair?"

"When you come around here feeling sorry for yourself, and blame everything on me and Cole."

"Is that what's happening here? I didn't think that's what's happening here. Just a simple question."

"Nothing's changed with us. Nothing *will* change with us. How many times have we been through this?" Anna said, making a show of exhaustion on her face.

"You say the three of us are still friends, but I can't ask you a personal question? It's impossible to stay friends with you if that's the case. If I was a girlfriend of yours, couldn't I ask how it's going? Then you would probably give me something like, 'Oh, Cole is such a bore. He did this thing or that thing. I'm thinking about divorcing him.'"

"I would never say that."

"You know what I mean."

Anna sighed, turned back around, and resumed slicing. "Cole is out in the barn. Why don't you go say hello while I finish up in here?"

"So we're done talking about this?"

"We were never talking about this, whatever *this* is."

"Anna."

"We made a mistake when I was home from college. That was a long time ago. You need to move on with your life. Believe me, I wouldn't be a friend if I didn't say it."

"Thanks, friend," Bucky said. He got up from the table and approached Anna. "You know, in another life, it's us that are married." He inched closer and reached up to brush a strand of hair off her shoulder. She took his hand, placed it harmlessly back by his side, cupped the back of his neck, and kissed him tenderly on the forehead.

"But we're in this life, aren't we?"

"I suppose we are," Bucky said. Then he backed up a few feet. "If Bobby had never died ..."

"This has nothing to do with Bobby."

"It has everything to do with Bobby," Bucky said, backing his way up to the door. "I'll go find Cole."

When Bucky reached for the door, he could see that Anna had both hands on the countertop as if to support herself. She stood completely still, staring out the window in silence. He was about to say something, but instead he turned and walked out the door. As he walked toward the barn, he couldn't help but think he'd gone too far. Sure, once in a while it was okay to let Anna know he was still—and would always be—in love with her, but bringing up her brother might have been a touch unfair and insensitive.

It was a long stretch from the farmhouse to the barn. While Bucky walked on top of the crunching snow, he couldn't help but remember the day Anna's little brother, Bobby, died. They had been at Anna's parents' stately compound, which certainly could give Cole's estate a run for its money, although it was much tackier. The farmhouse was a large boxy mansion with marble columns, ornate trim, and a lion sculpture guarding the front gate. Inside there were rooms and anterooms, but the most impressive thing to Bucky had always been the outdoor track. It was the same orange clay as Churchill Downs, and had white bleachers installed like a miniature grandstand to host family parties and charity events.

It was the beginning of August. Bucky was looking out at the heat that hovered over the track like a highway mirage, when Anna came up behind him and knocked the insides of his knees with her knees. After stumbling forward, he turned around and grabbed her from the waist.

"You are an evil, evil person," he said. She laughed and ran away into the barn. Bucky chased her, going from stall to stall looking for her, when she suddenly popped out and pulled him into an empty one. After a playful struggle, Bucky managed to wrestle her down. He gave her one long kiss on the lips, and then three smaller ones. He then took a breath and leaned up, and in a ray of sunlight shining through the barn, he could see the splinter in her left eye perfectly—almost as if it were glowing—and pinched her chin.

"What are you thinking?" Anna said, looking up at Bucky, who was frozen in his admiration of her beauty and youth.

"That we're going to be together forever."

"What are the chances of that?" Anna said casually, which caused Bucky to pause.

"What are *not* the chances? Duh," he said, "very slim. We're meant to be. You would have to get kidnapped or die in some kind of fiery blaze, or a natural disaster, maybe a tornado. How would you like to go? Tell me; it's got to be something cool."

"Bucky, be serious."

"Okay, well, Anna Miller, I would say, conservatively, that the chances of us being together are 100 percent. Is that what you want to hear?"

"Yes," Anna said. She reached up and cupped his face in her hand. "That's what I want," she said, continuing to touch his face, and stroking his hair almost as if it were something she'd seen done in the movies.

"Good," Bucky said. He wasted no more time and began trying to devour Anna, starting by kissing the freckle on her neck while she laughed, and moving up to kiss her chin and her cheek, and then her nose. Suddenly Anna shrieked and threw Bucky off.

"What are you doing here, loser?" she said to her twelve-year-old brother, Bobby, who stood gawking just outside the stall. He was standing there with his big ears and soft brown eyes, looking somewhat self-satisfied to have caught his older sister in this predicament. He wore a Yankees baseball cap that Bucky had always ribbed him about, a white tank top covered in sweat and dirt, and a pair of blue shorts.

"Bucky said he was going to teach me to drive," Bobby said. He looked to Bucky for an acknowledgment. Bucky managed a wink from where he was still lying in the hay.

"That's not the point. What the hell are you doing, spying on us?"

"I wasn't. I was looking for you guys. Here you are, and now I wanna learn how to drive, or else I might have to consider telling Mom and Dad about this."

"So you're blackmailing me?"

"If that's how you want to put it."

"All the horses are in. Mom and Dad are out. There's nothing going on. If not now, when? Bucky, you started driving at twelve, didn't you?"

"Well, I, uh—"

"Don't bring Bucky into this." Anna had jumped in before he could answer. "It's not up to him. Did Dad say it was okay?"

It was a long moment before Bobby muttered a "yea-eah," which even then seemed uncertain, but it was enough to make Anna cave, if not simply to get him off her nerves.

"Fine then. You tack up Stormy Normy and then bring him out to the track."

"Great! Thank you. You won't regret this," he said. Then he sauntered off to get the horse ready.

Since Bobby was already a competent stableboy who had done just about everything else with the horses but drive them, he wasted no time getting the horse ready.

Bucky and Anna made their way to the center of the track, and soon Bobby appeared in the thick summer haze, walking the horse out on the lead.

This was the part of the waking dream that always stood out for Bucky. He wished that he'd yelled at Bobby to go back. *Not today! It's too late! It's too hot! We'll do it again another time!* But Bobby kept coming forward, and for a moment his silhouette was stretched out, taller than he was, taller than he will ever be. He seemed like a ghost in between two worlds, his fate in this universe already decided.

"Now, this is what we're going to do. We'll drive around once, and you can sit in my lap and hold the lines. And then if Anna's okay with it, you go solo. Sound good, champ?"

"Got it!" Bobby said, grinning from ear to ear, almost drooling in fact, overwrought with excitement at his very first drive. First Bucky got on the sulky, and then Anna helped boost Bobby into his lap. All these years later, Bucky could still remember the boy's smell of dirty hair, Kool-Aid, and peanut butter.

"The first thing you need to do is feel the bit through the lines. That's where the horse's power and direction comes from. You let him out, he goes faster; you pull him in, he goes slower," Bucky said. He handed the lines to Bobby.

"When you're in the seat, just lean back and get as comfortable as you can. Let the horse do all the rest."

"It's not as hard as it looks," Bobby said, holding the lines tightly in his hands as the horse started jogging.

"Just ease up a little," Bucky said. "Feel that surge of power there? Think of the lines as a gas pedal. But one thing, and you must always, always remember this," Bucky said, looking down at the boy in his lap like he was about to impart the most important lesson he would ever learn.

"Yeah, what is it?" Bobby asked, completely focused ahead.

"Never, ever bail from the sulky. When you're in a race, there are ten other drivers behind you. You bail, you can get trampled and hurt real bad, maybe even die."

For the first half of the track, the horse was a bit shaky as Bobby got a feel for the lines. He veered right and then left. He picked up his pace and then slowed it down. By the time they'd started making their way around the final turn, both horse and driver had finally settled down. Anna was waiting for them at the starting point. She clapped when they pulled up and stopped in front of her.

"Looking good out there," Anna said.

"He's a natural," Bucky said, lifting Bobby off him by his armpits and handing him to Anna to help him get down.

"I wanna try on my own," Bobby said, once back on terra firma.

"I don't know," Anna said, looking to Bucky for reassurance.

"There's nothing to it," Bucky said. "That's how I started."

"You promised," Bobby said.

"I didn't *promise* anything, squirt. I said you could if your sister was okay with it. Anna?"

Anna stood in quiet deliberation for a moment. Bucky could tell she felt pressure from both of them. Not wanting to dampen the mood, she finally agreed.

"Fine, get him up there," she said, rolling her eyes when Bobby started jumping up and down to celebrate. They boosted Bobby back into the sulky. He positioned himself in the chair just like Bucky had instructed.

"Okay, kid, remember what I told you. When you're ready, just give a *hyop* and he'll know what to do."

"You ready?" Anna said, looking nervously on at her brother.

"*Hyop!*" Bobby commanded the horse. Then he balanced himself out after the first initial tug on the line.

Bucky and Anna stood there watching as Bobby took off. For the first quarter, everything looked okay. Stormy Normy was performing as he should, but as they were approaching the first turn, Bucky and Anna heard Bobby yell out something. Maybe it was to them, maybe it was to the horse, but in that moment there was a surge of power from the gelding. Maybe Bobby hadn't understood what *bail* meant when Bucky explained it to him, or maybe he just had to try it because it was forbidden. Either way, from a distance Bucky and Anna watched as Bobby slid off the back of his seat, his head and body landing at a ninety-degree angle upon impact, and then crumpling where he lay faceup, eerily still and lifeless in the dirt.

When recalling it, Bucky always remembered that there was a breeze, the strongest breeze of the day that broke up the excruciating heat; next there was a long moment of silence, of disbelief; and then there was a piercing cry from Anna. It was a cry that echoed through Bucky's head almost every day and brought him right back to the aftermath of the accident, to the days and weeks following Bobby's death, which would change all of their lives forever.

Before going into the barn, Bucky put his arms over the paddock fence, resting on his armpits, wondering what—if anything—he had to say to Cole, and how to go about asking him for the package for his father.

Might as well just get it over with, Bucky thought to himself, and finally walked into the barn. Cole was mucking out a stall and had his back turned to him. Bucky stood there for a moment, watching him labor. He was wearing a jumpsuit that accented his tall muscular body, and rubber boots that went up to his knees. His ringlets of blond hair fell out of his wool toque.

When Cole turned around, Bucky could tell by his expression that he was genuinely happy to see him.

"Son of a—" Cole said. With his eyes brimming, he dropped the shovel, and reached over to pull Bucky in for a hug. "How are you, Bucky?"

"Not so bad. Yourself?"

"Doing pretty good, pretty good. Look at you, Bucky," he said, holding his oldest friend by both shoulders and taking a deep stare. "You look like shit," he said, and then he backed away laughing.

"Ha, fuck you too." Bucky smiled. For a moment it seemed like things were normal again, like they were still just the two boys who rode each other's horses and went fishing and trail riding together, the same two boys who threw fastballs into a painted strike zone on the barn, and who once discovered Max's treasure trove of hidden *Hustler* magazines.

So much has changed, but really nothing has changed at all, Bucky thought to himself. *They have everything; I have nothing. I am pitiable and envious; they are generous and kind.*

"How about a smoke?" Bucky offered.

Cole raised his hand to refuse. "Anna will kill me."

"She'll never know," Bucky said, walking the few feet back out of the barn door. "It'll be just between you me, and this gelding you got up here," he said, pointing to the curious aged horse that was poking his head over the paddock fence.

"I'll pass, thanks. Anna will smell it all over me," Cole said, following him out. "You might want to think about quitting too."

"I don't know about that. You know how those long stretches of road can be."

"The life of a driver, burning up the Northeast circuit, huh?"

"Yeah, right," Bucky said, exhaling, almost tempted to disclose his list of financial woes, but he knew it wasn't necessary given the task at hand, one that Cole must have certainly been aware of.

"So what have you been up to?" Bucky said, trying to delay the inevitable exchange or, in Bucky's opinion, groveling. He looked his friend over, knowing all too well that whatever Cole was about to say was guaranteed to be better than his own current situation.

"I've been racing at the Mega Mile," Cole replied, "and I've got some good entries coming up at the Downs, so I'm looking forward to that. Also got an impressive two-year-old nominated for the Breeders, so we'll see how that goes."

For the twenty-plus years both of them had been friends, their entire well-being had been based on horse terms and drives. If they were doing well, it meant they were winning; if not so well, then they were losing. It was that personal component to their lives—the deeper aspect that could potentially affect them more profoundly—that they had more difficulty getting to.

After they were caught up, their conversation came to an abrupt halt. They both stood for a while, watching the horses in the paddock. After a few awkward moments, Cole finally broke the silence.

"So I got that thing for your dad. It's inside."

A cloud covered the sun, and a screech of wind blew between them. "Not sure why the old buggers make us do their dirty work, but I guess it's convenient."

Count on Cole to be such a gentleman about it, Bucky thought to himself, before the wind blew the top layer of snow off the fence and into his face. He didn't know what to say, or if he should show gratitude or false pride, so instead he just nodded and wiped his eyes, which was probably the worst thing, he quickly realized. Neither of them said anything else about it. After the moment passed, Cole said, "Well, why don't we go grab it then? Anna's up there making lunch. Why don't you stay?"

"I gotta get back to the farm, but guess I can stay for a bit," Bucky said, not revealing that he had already accepted Anna's invitation.

As they walked back to the farmhouse, Bucky felt shame not only in accepting the money but also for his having said those things to Anna. Sure, she was used to it by now, but Anna and Cole had only ever shown Bucky kindness, and how did he repay it? By trying to create a rift in their relationship; by reminding Anna about her brother; by trying to pry his best and only friend's girl away from him. *Perhaps it would be better for everyone if I just went away,* he thought.

When Cole and Bucky walked in, Anna was washing her hands under the kitchen tap.

"Look who I found wandering around the barn," Cole said.

"He was up here snooping around before," Anna said, drying her hands on a dish towel. "Are you still joining us for lunch?"

"Yes, thank you," Bucky said, knowing that now it was too late. Facing them both was more than he could handle. At this point he just wanted to get the money and leave, but there was no way to do that without being rude.

"Good then—have a seat," Anna said. She brought over the bowl of salad and a crystal jug of water and put them both on the table. Cole took two beers from the fridge, straddled the dining room bench, sat down across from Bucky, and gave him a beer. Anna came back with the casserole dish containing the shepherd's pie and put it in the middle of the table. She took off the oven mitts and served Bucky, and then Cole, running her hand along Cole's shoulder before she sat next to him. Cole finally took off his hat, revealing his full mess of hair. He reached into the bread basket, pulled out a bun, and took a savage bite out of it.

"So who you been seeing?" Cole said with his mouth open. Then he washed his bread down with a gulp of beer.

"No one."

"C'mon, who you been seeing?" Anna chimed in, as if their previous conversation hadn't taken place.

Bucky hated when they both took this interest in his life given the circumstances. It was one of the reasons he avoided them, and always did his best to change the conversation as if he were staunching the flow of blood from his carotid artery.

"Nobody, not after you were snatched up off the market," Bucky said. They all laughed uncomfortably for a moment. "Seriously," Bucky added quickly, before it got even more awkward, "I've been keeping it straight. There's lots of work to be done on the farm. Need to start earning. Pops says we're just about bust." As much as Bucky hated to admit it, he knew at this point it was probably no secret. And if it helped change the subject from his dating life, then it was a welcome reprieve.

"Oh no, that's awful," Anna said, her hand in front of her mouth.

Cole shook his head. "What are you going to do?" he asked, taking a deep mouthful of the shepherd's pie with the sterling-silver fork.

"Well, drive. I gotta get some drives, I suppose. That's what we do, isn't it?"

"Right!" Cole said. He banged the table with his fist. "I know you can pull it out. You *will* pull it out."

"We got a couple good horses in our barn, and Clarence insists Voltrain's a winner."

"Well, let's hope he's right," Anna said. "And if you need anything, anything at all, you know we're here to help."

Bucky knew by her offer that she meant it. He was confident that if he'd asked her for a million dollars at that moment, she would have said yes.

"We'll be fine, thanks," Bucky said, thinking about how he could best bolt for the door, how to dig up his last scraps of dignity to ask Cole for the money so he could be on his way.

For the rest of the meal, Bucky did his best to avoid small talk, and made sure to gobble up the shepherd's pie as fast he could. Anna did her best to carry on the conversation while Cole sat there, oblivious to it all. When Bucky passed Anna the salad, he did so with a smile that was wider than necessary, as if in that exchange something was concealed, a subterfuge for what remained just beneath the surface. While Anna rambled on, saying something about a rabbit patch and a place in town where they had cheap picture framing, Bucky realized that this talk was just as insufferable to her, but still she kept it going. Bucky wasn't sure if Anna knew about the money, adding further to his disgrace, and how to go about making the exchange with Cole, so he sat still like a pupil who refuses to lift up his hand in the dying seconds before recess.

When Anna and Cole were finally scraping their plates, and it was clear the conversation between them could not go anywhere else, Bucky announced, "Well, I better be going."

"Already?" Anna protested.

"Sure you don't want to stick around for another beer, pal?" Cole said.

"I really do have to go," Bucky insisted. "I'm sorry it was such a quick visit, but like I said, they need me at the farm."

"Okay, then," Anna said. "Just this time. But next time, we get you till at least dessert. Deal?"

"Deal," Bucky said, grateful that their objections didn't last any longer. He got up to leave.

"Let me show you out," Cole said. He stood up. Walking toward the door, he detoured to a side room, where he pulled the thick orange envelope from a drawer. Then he went to meet Bucky at the front door. Before Bucky left, Anna gave him a hug, which he wished could have lasted much longer.

"Take care of yourself, Bucky," Anna said.

"You know I will," Bucky replied, barely able to look at her.

When they were outside and Bucky could see that Cole had the envelope, he put his hand out. It seemed to hang there forever.

"Here you go, Bucky. Good luck. Let us know how it goes," Cole said. He gave him the package with one hand and patted him on the shoulder with the other. Bucky was glad that it wasn't a more drawn-out affair. He now felt like a prisoner trying to make a break for the outer walls.

"Thanks. It was nice to see you both," Bucky said, all too aware that he sometimes addressed them as a unit. "Tell your old man I say hi," Bucky said, and then he turned away.

"Will do," Cole said, waving and going back in through the oak doors.

While Bucky walked back to his truck, he noticed that the once partly cloudy sky had become totally overcast. He knew that by evening the temperature would plunge back below zero.

After a few false starts, his engine finally turned over. He drove back out along the paddocks and bare sycamore trees, and got back on the road. He looked beside him at the fat envelope in the passenger seat. If it were a gift that had fallen from the heavens, then the sight of that package would be a sheer joy, but it wasn't any such gift. Bucky knew that the money was to alleviate a dire situation, and if used incorrectly—or in Bucky's experience with his father's dealings, on a bad horse—then they would be in even deeper. As Bucky drove that old, familiar stretch of road, he felt like the last ten years of his life were an empty shell, wasted on something that had never even been a remote possibility. And as much as he liked to blame his intransigence on Carl, it was in fact his own creation. He had waited to see what would happen with Anna and Cole. After all, he and Anna weren't *that* far removed from their last indiscretion, which had given Bucky hope well into his adult years.

He went back to the day when the three of them had met at the Delaware State Fair. It had been a cacophony of sounds and smells: the aroma of corn dogs, funnel cakes, and french fries; the sound of bells from the shooting gallery and the carnival barkers; the groaning of the old hydraulic rides and the screams from the people on them who prayed they wouldn't malfunction. The day had turned into night, and Bucky and Anna had gotten separated from Cole. Anna took Bucky's hand in hers and led him across the grounds, and then in front of the stage where families picnicked on blankets and in lawn chairs, and where children wore glowing antennae and flashed their sparklers.

Her skin felt cool and soft, and her eyes glimmered in the dim light. "Come on," she'd whispered in his ear, her breath sweet from the candy apple she'd just eaten.

"Come with me," she said, tugging at him as they zigzagged through the crowd.

"Where are we going?" Bucky asked, feeling more aroused than he'd ever felt before.

"We're going to a secret place," Anna said, smiling mysteriously at him.

"Oh," Bucky said, swallowing hard, realizing that Anna was leading him into the shadows behind the stage. When Anna had finally reached her point, she turned abruptly to face him, stood on her toes, and kissed him deeply on the lips. After what seemed a lifetime, Anna finally pulled away. Bucky stood there with his fingers to his lips, feeling thrilled and breathless, as if he'd just ridden a gravity-defying ride at the midway. Then, almost like it had been perfectly scripted, like the pyrotechnic team had been watching Bucky all along and knew just how he was feeling at that moment, fireworks went off in the sky. There were purple spiders and silver willows exploding all around them. With every burst of color that lit up the night, there were gasps of awe. Bucky wondered, with every stream of color that fell from the sky, if that was how long Anna had kissed him for. He counted each one to himself—*one one thousand, two one thousand*—and then Anna was gone.

CHAPTER 3

Three weeks had passed since Bucky had visited his friends' farm. He told himself that the past was the past, and that now he really needed to move on. But how? A clean break from Harrington had been what he'd always wanted, but in that fantasy he imagined it would be with Anna. Maybe they would move down to Florida and get races at Sunshine Raceway; maybe Pennsylvania. *Anywhere but here,* Bucky thought, as he lay on his back beneath the kitchen sink, hitting pipes as hard as he could in the tight space, and swearing every time his elbow crashed against the stack of pots and pans, which he hadn't bothered to fully clear. After his last whack, the pipe finally came loose, and the dirty sink water that had collected in the drain splashed all over his face. He struggled to get out as fast as he could. Once on his feet, he kicked the green cabinet doors, breaking one of them so that it hung splintered on one hinge. Bucky spit out some sludge, wiped his face with a dishrag, and then threw himself onto the sofa in the next room. In the silence he heard a whistle of wind blow through a crack in the wall, and the shutters rattled against the farmhouse. The fire had died out long ago; the once smoldering embers turned to soot.

After a short rest, Bucky finally got the fire restarted, throwing enough wood in the iron stove so it would be nice and warm when he got back from checking on the horses. Then he bundled up and trudged down to the barn, somewhat expecting to see Clarence there with the horses, but he wasn't around. Bucky took a look into Clarence's small quarters and private sanctuary. There was a small desk in the corner that was cluttered with tools that Clarence used to make custom bridles and other equipment for the horses. It was a skill passed on from his father, a legendary trainer in his own right, who disappeared one night under suspicious circumstances after a late-night card game on shed row. It was something that Clarence never talked about, but you could tell it was often on his mind. There was also a single bed, neatly made, and a picture of Clarence and his three brothers and three sisters back home in Harrisburg, but still no sign of Clarence.

Bucky didn't make much more of it, but then when he went back out to check on the horses, he noticed that Summer Rose's stall was empty. All her stall contained was hay, dented in what was once her favorite corner, and a training harness inscribed with her name on a bronze plate hanging from a nail.

Bucky paced around all afternoon until Carl and Clarence finally returned to the farm after dinner. When Bucky asked his father what had happened to Summer Rose, Carl handed him an envelope containing five hundred dollars and a letter that was barely legible. In Max's handwriting, the letter said that he'd traded in that old bitch for butter, and that she ran like a cow and was much better served in a glass. Eventually the scribble became indecipherable.

"How the hell can you do that?" Bucky yelled at Carl.

"Now, Son, just relax," Carl said, raising his hands as if to calm Bucky.

"I thought you would at least tell me. I thought we were going to try and keep her."

"It was Max. He took her to Freedom Downs and put her up in a claimer. She got sold to some stable in Kentucky. I got a call from Joey Reynolds because I didn't do the entry. By the time I got there, it was too late. I let Max have it, all right, but what else can I do? I couldn't have done anything else."

"Where is he?" Bucky said through his gritted teeth.

"After I let him have it, he wrote that letter and stuffed the money inside. He thought it would make you feel better."

"Make me feel better?" Bucky said. "You know what would make me feel better? If he disappeared—for good. That would make me feel better," he said and then stormed up to his room and lay down on his bed. His room was just as sparse as the rest of the farm. He had a baseball bat leaning in the corner, a dresser with a mountain of clothes on top of it, and peeling white wallpaper designed with a forest of black and gray trees.

On the nightstand beside the bed was a framed picture of *The Kiss*, which he and Carl had come to call it. It had been taken in the winner's circle after a big race, when he was a boy. Bucky told anyone who asked that he remembered the night perfectly, as if it had been written in the stars. His grandfather had on saggy pants, and his grandmother's strong perfume had made the horse sneeze. His mother was in a red dress with a white sun hat and a thick beige belt. When Carl held Bucky up by his armpits, the winning horse, Silent Rider, gave him a surprise kiss right on the lips. Maybe Bucky had assigned the picture somewhat of a boosted sentimentality, but the older he got, the more he realized its true importance. With his grandparents and mother long gone, it was the last photo taken where they appeared as a family. And it wasn't like the coldness had crept in all at once, because Carl tried—Lord knows he tried—but after a while it became obvious that there was no getting back what they'd had. Sometimes at night Bucky would stare at the picture, and when the moon trickled in just right, he could make out the faces from his bed. His mother looked like an old daguerreotyped image, and his father's eyes looked like tiny black beads. Although he knew the picture well by now—every look, every expression—he would always find some new detail. As he looked at his mother's image, he wondered if her passing had always been foretold. He wondered if there was a feeling you get on the day of your own death, or a foreboding sign like an ominous cloud or a raven, but that didn't seem to be the case when his mother died. She had cooked breakfast. Then, after cleaning up, she drove to Dover to browse through shops and buy groceries. The reason Bucky doubted she'd experienced any deadly harbinger was that he'd overheard Miss

Twittle, who ran the local bakery, tell Carl at the funeral that Delores "seemed just fine, her normal self. She bought a dozen scones and was happy and relaxed. We talked about the usual things, the weather, your son, the horses, and then she was off. Had I known … oh, how was I supposed to know?" Her voice had cracked as she'd wiped away a tear.

As Bucky began to nod off, he was looking at his mother. A new detail emerged—the way her eyes were looking at something out of the frame. What could it have been? What was his mother looking at or thinking of? Was she happy? *What would you think, Mom, if you could see me now?*

Having been up all night thinking about what he intended to say to Bucky, Carl was going over the details while frying bacon and eggs on the stove for breakfast. He wondered if the solution he had come up with would be better for all of them, or perhaps kick off the final stage of their financial ruin. He had to do something with that money from Roy Callaghan, and the only solution seemed to be to raise the stakes and double down. Given the nature of his plan, and how it would affect all of them, Carl couldn't help but think about Bucky and how he would react to the news. It was a decision that would put some distance between him and his lone progeny. For a moment, as the faint shadows of dawn dissolved into daybreak, Carl was taken back to those earlier days when Delores was still alive and Bucky would sit in between them on the sofa. Together they'd watched *M*A*S*H* and *Bonanza* reruns. Carl remembered all the questions Bucky asked, and how patient and loving Delores was with every answer. How could Bucky have gone from a child who had so much love to such a thorny teen and adult? *Perhaps I waited too long,* Carl thought. *Perhaps I have been a bad father.* Carl shook his head as if to erase the tragedy from his mind, like the powder words from an Etch A Sketch, but he knew it wouldn't be that easy. The best he could do was live with it, try to compartmentalize that part of his soul where love once flourished but that now lay barren like a dried-up riverbed.

He looked up when Bucky walked into the kitchen.

"Morning, Son," Carl said, smiling at Bucky.

"What's with you?" Bucky asked, still reeking of melancholy from the day before.

"I've been doing a lot of thinking lately," Carl said. He scraped the eggs from the frying pan, scooped up some bacon with the tongs, and in a quick motion had the plate of bacon and eggs in front of Bucky. He paused in his story so he could get ketchup from the fridge, pull toast from the toaster, and pour orange juice and fresh coffee.

"I know it's a tough life for you here," Carl began. "A lot of ghosts around here for you … and me. And I know that after a while it can weigh real heavy. Hasn't been right of me to hold you back, so that's why I've decided … Well, me and Clarence had a chat about it, and believe it or not, your uncle Max was a contributing factor. But, well, I guess I might as well get to it … What would you think about stabling at Speedway and getting regular drives there?"

It was the hardest thing that Carl ever could have proposed to his son, knowing it meant that Bucky would leave Harrington and begin a life in New York.

Bucky still had not said anything, so Carl continued. "I spoke to Bernie and they got space; they're willing to give you a shot."

It took a while for Bucky to show the excitement he was feeling. After he'd fully digested the news, a smile crept over his face, as if in that moment all his doubts and uncertainties about the future had finally been lifted.

"We'll talk about all the details later, and in the meantime you might want to start thinking about finding a place down there and make sure you got everything tied up before you leave."

"Dad?"

"You don't have to say anything."

"Thank you."

"Just make us proud out there," Carl said, stifling the emotion that seemed to jump out at him from nowhere.

"Of course I will," Bucky said. He got up from the table, hugged Carl from behind, and kissed the smoky strands of thinning hair on the top of his head. Carl couldn't remember the last time Bucky had kissed him, or anyone else for that matter. He held his breath until finally it was safe to blink. Letting one lone tear run down his cheek, he tried to keep his hands from shaking while he finished his breakfast.

CHAPTER 4

Near the end of March, Bucky got a place in Yonkers through a connection of Bernie Katz. It was in a brick fourplex with no siding or shutters, beside an empty lot across from a church. Inside, it had a big bay window in the front living room, a galley kitchen, and a good-sized bedroom and bathroom. Best of all for Bucky, it was a fifteen-minute drive to the racetrack. He was on his way out one morning when he heard rustling from the apartment directly across the hall. Not wanting to have idle chitchat before he was fully awake, he tried to lock his door as quickly as he could, but he fumbled with his keys, swearing at himself beneath his breath.

"There he is!" Easy Money Eddy said, emerging sprightly from the apartment, his receding blond hair still wet from his morning shower.

"Morning, Eddy."

"How goes?"

"Oh, not bad. Just getting an early start so I can get some work in with the horses," Bucky said.

"Bernie told me you were a go-getter." Eddy smiled, revealing the gap between his two front teeth.

Since his original plan of expediting his departure had failed, Bucky now reversed his strategy and tried to delay the locking of his door, making faces as if the bolt were jammed. When it was clear that Eddy was waiting for him, Bucky gave up his ruse and walked with him down the hall. It wasn't that Bucky didn't like Eddy; he did. It was just that Eddy was a known loser. And given that Bucky was a newcomer to the track, he was just superstitious enough not to want Eddy's bad juju to rub off on him.

"So how you liking it out here so far? I know lots of people around the track been talking about you—they say you're nothing like your uncle."

"Well, that's good, Eddy. And they're right."

"He's definitely earned his reputation," Eddy said, cupping his hands around the curves of his belly. "But I've the seen the way you race. You don't seem to have the same help Max does coming down the backstretch, if you know what I mean."

"I'm starting to understand, Eddy," Bucky said, opening the door to the front vestibule, where the mailboxes were built into the wall.

"That's good. Keep it like that. You know, some people have said I'm an honest driver—too honest. I think of that as a good thing. Don't fall in with those guys—trust me."

"Got it. Thanks, Eddy. See you over there," Bucky said. And with that they separated, getting into their own vehicles and heading to the track.

When he arrived, Bucky could see Voltrain hanging his head over the stall, somehow knowing it was race day. After feeding him, Bucky hitched him up to his cart and took him for a jog while the amber sun began to rise, eclipsed only by the concrete edges of the grandstand. Bucky liked being out early so he could be the first to carve his tracks into the gravel.

After he did a couple of laps, a few other drivers came out. The morning silence was broken by the sounds of the other horses, their hooves coming on at first like the slow patter of rain, then sounding like a deluge as they got closer.

Because Bucky was the nephew of Max Whalen, some of the drivers didn't take to him. When the New Zealander, Jack Danby, drove by in his blue-and-red racing colors, he yelled out, "This ain't the amateurs anymore. Go back to Delaware, kid." Bucky didn't say anything. He just gave his horse a few *hyops*, and then drove right by

Jack and looked back when he passed. He had become used to being taunted. Being the youngest driver stabled at Speedway, he had to prove himself every night. When he made an error—say, cut someone off, or his horse broke and he didn't get out of the way fast enough—he was mercilessly abused during and after the race.

Pleased with the way his horse was running, Bucky took Voltrain back to his stall. During the afternoon he did some work with Roundaboutway, whom Clarence had sent up after a break. Later in the afternoon, Bucky was taking a nap in an empty stall when he heard someone calling his name. "Bucky! Bucky!" Eddy was yelling as he walked up and down the stable, like he was looking for a lost child in a mall. Surprised by the depth of his half-hour snooze, Bucky slowly got up, brushed the hay off his shirt, and patted down his hair.

"Over here, Eddy. What is it?"

Eddy looked over and saw Bucky emerge from the stall.

"What the hell you doing in there? You duck in for a quick wank or something?"

"No, Eddy."

"Well, I just wanted to tell you, I overheard Bernie talking to some of the guys. He said he made a deal with Max to let you stable here if you started turning some races."

"I never agreed to that, Eddy. If they made an arrangement, that's between them. I came here to win, and that's it."

"Just thought you should know," Eddy said, standing proudly as if he had just made some great demonstration of his loyalty.

"I appreciate that, Eddy. I really do. I won't be doing anything to influence the racing outcomes, so don't worry about me."

"Never was," Eddy said, and then he looked down at his watch. "Two hours till post time. See you at the finish line, sport."

"Thanks, Eddy. I'm off in the eighth race, so I'll see you after," Bucky said, really starting to like Eddy, the perennial loser, and wondering how or when Max or Bernie would approach him about the fix.

At post time it was cold and windy. The stadium flags flapped violently in the wind, and there were barely any fans in the track apron. After a few warm-up scores, the horses were called to the gate. Bucky didn't know all the drivers in tonight's race, but he did know Jo Jo, Guy Boucher, and of course the Kiwi, Jack Danby, who seemed to have it out for him.

Once the starting car was moving and the gates opened, all of the horses were in full stride. Bucky stayed back from the pack jostling in front, and settled into fourth position as the horses raced single file down the backstretch. He debated making his move when they came back around in front of the grandstand, but he was waiting patiently for his opening. The horses traded lengths on their second trip down the backstretch, and when they came around the clubhouse turn, Bucky knew it was time. When finally he started moving off the rail, Jo Jo came up from behind, trying to block him in.

"Get off me, Jo Jo. I'm coming out," Bucky said.

"Okay, have it your way." Jo Jo smiled and pulled away.

Once Bucky was almost loose, Danby came up beside him and tried to hook wheels.

"That's an infraction, Danby," Bucky yelled. "You won't get away with it, so bugger off and let me go."

Spotting some daylight, Bucky gave Voltrain all the encouragement he needed to break loose. Soon he was up on Guy Boucher's horse as they raced for home, and Bucky won by a hair.

After the race, the harness beat reporter, Ronnie Vincent, came down to the paddock to interview the drivers. He was wearing a brown corduroy blazer with elbow patches, his mustache perfectly trimmed, and his black coiffure immovable even in the fiercest of winds. Bucky stood next to him for the interview. Ronnie gave him a few pointers before they went live.

"I'm here with Bucky Whalen," Ronnie began, "celebrating his first win here at Speedway, driving the fine bay colt Voltrain. You finished with a time of 1:57 and four. Bucky, tell us how it went out there."

"Well, Ronnie, as we were heading for home, I saw Boucher's horse starting to get a little tired from racing outside. I knew my colt was ready to move on him, so I just let him go. Really, Voltrain did all the work. I was just a passenger for this one, Ronnie."

"Just a passenger. Kinda like riding on the wings of a fighter jet with the speed your horse showed tonight. What was the difference from your last race, when you placed third in a field that didn't look so different from tonight's?"

"Well, a few weeks ago he wasn't himself, so I put a Murphy blind on him to keep him seeing straight, which made him a lot less distracted by the other horses."

"I guess that really worked out for you," Ronnie said and then paused to receive a message from his earpiece.

"Thanks for talking to us, Bucky. Looks like you got some cleaning up to do, so I'll let you hit the showers. Sheila, back over to you," Ronnie said, delivering his throw on cue, and then standing there proudly like he had really achieved something in that bit, until they cut away.

After taking a shower and changing his clothes, Bucky went back to the drivers' lounge to watch the last three races. It was no surprise to him to find Bernie Katz and Charlie Baker there in the middle of a card game. Bucky's suspicions were now confirmed that Max had cut a deal with Bernie, who'd used his influence as racing secretary to allow Bucky to stable there, and that Charlie Baker, being the horseman's bookkeeper, was probably getting paid off too.

"Get over here, kid," Bernie said, waving Bucky over.

"Howdy, gents." Bucky smiled and took a seat.

"Congratulations on your first win out here. How's your uncle?"

Bernie asked, without looking up from his cards. "That son of a bitch owes me money."

"Thanks. Max is good, I guess. I hear he's been getting drives at Monticello. Sure we'll be seeing him, sooner rather than later."

"How about we cut you in on a hand?" Charlie said. He looked over at Bernie, who acknowledged their chance at easy money.

"Well, I don't know, guys," Bucky said. "I just want to take in the last few races and go home, do it all again tomorrow."

"Christ, don't be a pussy," Bernie said. Charlie dealt Bucky a hand. "Hey, Patty, pour this kid a drink. What do you take, Bucky? Ginger ale?"

"Make it a beer, Patty." Bucky smiled politely at the hardened lounge server, who had a swirl of gray hair that looked like a scouring pad, a lean jaw, and thin gritted teeth. Bucky looked at his hand.

They were playing five-card draw. Bucky discarded all but one of his cards after the first round, and then he stayed when the second came around. When Bernie noticed that Bucky didn't want to exchange any other cards, he asked him if he was sure.

"Now, I know the way your uncle plays cards, kid, and I seen every other two-bit driver that thinks he can play poker come and go, so that's why I'm gonna give you one more chance to get some new cards. What's it gonna be?"

"I think I'll stay. Thanks, though," Bucky said, leaning his elbows on the table with his cards facedown beside him. Then he took a sip of his beer. Charlie was looking intently at Bucky, seemingly trying to find any trace of doubt or fear on his face. Bucky had played enough cards in enough paddocks over the years. Also, what better mentor than his crooked uncle to teach him how to play cards? After Bernie and Charlie both folded, Bucky opened up just to taunt them a little, to let them know he was no patsy.

"Pair of threes. Sorry, fellas." Bucky collected the pot in the middle. He really just wanted to go at that point, but the men insisted he stay so they could recoup their losses.

After the next few hands, another driver joined. As the cigarette butts mounted in the ashtray, Bucky's pile of winnings grew.

They continued playing, even after the last race had ended and the stadium cleared out. There were a few people left in the drivers' lounge who sat around drinking, telling stories, and occasionally tuning to the card game, which at moments ran at a fever pitch as both Bernie and Charlie continued losing. Bucky wasn't yet consumed by money and greed the way those two were. If anything, he was a little naïve about it. Perhaps it was the way he'd grown up. Whenever there was a little extra money it was reinvested in the farm.

When Bernie and Charlie finally gave up on the cards, it was announced that Bucky would be buying the drinks at Bert's Bar, which was just a few minutes' walk from the track. It was already past two in the morning and Bucky wasn't in the mood for going out, but he knew he'd better buy Bernie and Charlie drinks since he'd taken all their money, especially when raucous cries of "Drinks on Bucky!" and "All right, Bucky!" and "What a sport!" rang out in the drivers' lounge.

Bert's Bar was a favorite of the drivers. It stayed open as long as it had customers, and Bert would allow the drivers to sign over their purse checks to settle up their tabs. When the group walked in, the house performer was playing "Ring of Fire" on the dimly lit stage in the back. The small group from the track brought a little more life to the place, but not much. Bucky paid for their drinks. Some stayed at the bar, and others went to listen to the performer. This left Bucky alone, next to Bernie, on a barstool.

The old man threw an arm around Bucky. "You're a special driver, Bucky," he slurred, "and ain't nobody denying that fact, but how long will it last? I've seen 'em come and go, kid. I've seen 'em come and go, and I'll tell ya, it can be a real whore of a business. You ain't no whore, are ya, kid? You're the real deal, ain't ya? Well, God bless ya." He raised his glass, which was promptly met by Bucky's.

"Thank you, Bernie," Bucky said. He was used to dealing with drunks, thanks again to the intensive training his uncle had provided.

"Just tell your uncle to call me, 'cause we're gonna need to talk."

"You got it," Bucky said, slipping off his stool, about to leave the bar. "Take care of yourself." Bucky gave Bernie a friendly slap on the back.

Bernie then swiveled around on his stool and got up, his foul breath close enough to Bucky that he could almost taste it, and whispered in his ear. "Next Sunday, I need you to stiff your horse, okay?"

"What?" Bucky said.

Bernie leaned even closer. "Stiff your horse," he repeated, much louder into Bucky's ear so there was no mistaking it. "Pull up, pull out, force a break. I don't care. That colt you're driving is in top form, and everyone knows it."

Bucky knew what he meant, but he just looked at Bernie blankly while doing up his top button. Then he excused himself before slipping quietly into the night.

Since he'd had a few too many drinks, Bucky decided to walk for a while before taking a taxi. The earlier winds had died down, giving way to light flurries. While Bucky walked, he tilted his head up, trying to catch the snowflakes on his tongue. As the minutes stretched into an hour, Bucky found himself deep in thought. He knew how bad the situation was at the farm, and he wondered if it would make things better or worse if he gave in to Bernie. He thought about home. Although the similarities were a stretch, everything from the wisp of chimney smoke to the empty streets reminded him of Harrington. The road was slick with a dusting of snow, and every ten feet or so Bucky would run and slide, leaving a trail behind him.

He walked (and slid) through the streets, feeling out in the world now, a man free to make his own decisions. But with that freedom, he knew he was faced with his first real test: comply with Bernie and fix next Sunday's race, or ignore his demand and jeopardize his stable in New York, maybe even have to make an early return to Delaware, which he knew he wasn't ready for. As he kept walking, the full moon shone down on the vacant lots.

On one abandoned corner he heard a bottle smash, and in a dirty lane he witnessed a scuffle between two drunks. He knew he was getting closer to his apartment when he saw a greater concentration of flickering neon church marquees. One read, Jesus Loves You; another, Jesus Cares. There was even one with gold ol' JC pinned up to an electric guitar shaped like a cross that read, Rock with Jesus Every Sunday. With all the billboard religion around him, Bucky wondered, *If God exists, why did he take my mom and Bobby so early? If he's up there, all grand and mighty, why doesn't he show me a sign, like an earthquake or flash flood? I'd even settle for a thunderbolt—something, anything, from JC to let me know he's listening.*

When Bucky got home, his feet sore and his head throbbing, the sun was almost up. His TV was still on and playing station identification. When he got to his room and his head hit the pillow, he could hear a fracas in the street as two felines clawed to the death. And then a garbage can tipped over and rats rustled through the trash. Then a car backfired or else someone got shot. Only after the sound of a distant siren did everything finally go silent.

CHAPTER 5

Bucky answered the phone in his apartment. Before even a word had been spoken, he knew it was Max on the other line. He could tell by the wheeze and the coughing fit. It made him immediately regret answering.

"Yes, Max?"

"I hear you're killing it up there in New York," Max said, after another coughing spell.

"I'm doing all right," Bucky said. Usually Carl made the calls from home. For Max to be calling him, Bucky knew something was up. "How's everyone?"

"Who's everyone? Your dad and the help? I guess they're okay. But that's not why I'm calling."

"Why are you calling, Max?"

"Just calling to let you know I'm coming up next Sunday. Not gonna be racing, but the Big Macher convinced me to come up. I hear you guys are tight."

"Tight? Bernie and me? Same as anyone else around here."

Bucky took a calming breath. Since he had been in New York, Max had only been up a handful of times. His uncle liked to keep his contacts fresh, and also so he could go out for a few hard-drinking nights in the city. Bucky resented his visits. It seemed as though every time Max resurfaced, Bucky lost his status around the track and was known only as Max's nephew—and Max was the last person Bucky wanted to be associated with.

"No, boy, he's taken a shine to you. Says you're doing great things."

"Listen, Max, if this is about anything other than—"

Before Bucky could finish, Max abruptly ended the conversation. "Okay, kid, see you next week." He hung up.

The following Sunday, Bucky was up early on race day. It was still dark out, and he could hear the light patter of freezing rain on the window. After a quick bowl of cereal, he made his way to the racetrack. When he got there, he could see the light on in the Airstream trailer where Carl and Clarence stayed overnight to avoid a hotel. A relic from the days when they gypsied around the Grand Circuit, it looked a cross between a fat snail and an aluminum World War Two bomber. It was obvious why they called it the Silver Bullet.

Debris skittered along the ground. The wind and rain whipped against Bucky as he ran to the stable. When he got there, he was shivering from the cold. Inside, the horses were restless and whinnying. Bucky could hear Roundaboutway above all the others. It was his day to race. Bucky worried that the horse might not have slept well enough to get them into the winner's circle. Whatever the case, he still had to go through his morning routine, so he gave Roundaboutway an apple to settle him while he filled one bucket with water and another bucket with grain from the feeding bin.

As Bucky made his way back to the horse's stall, he could see a light at the far end of the barn—the vet's office. Odd. It was unusual for the vet to show up so early. Bucky put the buckets down and went to take a look. When he did, he was surprised to see Max standing beneath the fluorescent light, adjusting a pair of leather pacing hobbles on the long stainless steel operating table.

"What's going on, Max?" Bucky asked, knowing his uncle would slither into New York at one point or another, but not at this particular time or place.

Max gave a start. "Well, I, uh …"

"Not often you make it out of bed before the rooster crows," Bucky said, sensing that Max was up to no good.

"Yeah. I overheard Clarence talking to your father about a loose buckle on the hobbles. I was up, so thought I'd make a quick adjustment and then head out for a morning ride."

"It's brutal out, Max!"

"Yeah, it is, isn't it? Oh well, all done, anyway."

"Whatever," Bucky said. After a quick inspection of the hobbles, he took them and got back to work feeding and getting his horse ready, forgetting about the whole encounter until after the race.

Max left the vet's office. He still hadn't slept—was still drunk, in fact—and hoped Bucky hadn't smelled it on him. He had just come back from an all-night card game in which he hadn't fared well, and now he had to come up with a quick ten grand. And then there was Bernie, who had already been putting pressure on him to get assurance from Bucky that things would go as planned. The solution was simple. Since it was public knowledge that Bucky's horse was the one to beat, Max sabotaged the hobbles so they would interfere with the horse's stride. Later, he would tout the horse's top form, and bet heavy on the other horse that Bernie had been holding back and that was listed at 27–1 on the morning line. If his plan worked, it would be a decent score.

The freezing rain was off and on all day, and by post time it had turned to a mix of sleet and snow, which Bucky could see falling heavily through the track lights. When the race gates opened and Bucky tried to keep up with the cracking pace, he noticed that Roundaboutway didn't feel right. They hadn't even made it past the first marker before he broke his stride. Bucky had to steer him off to the side. While Bucky tried to calm him, the horse fought the equipment, and eventually broke into a gallop. For the next quarter mile, Bucky hung on as best he could. Eventually Bucky managed to calm the horse down, at which point he drove him slowly back to the paddock. When Bucky took off his goggles, the white circles around his eyes were the only part of his body that wasn't caked with mud. You could barely see his Delaware blue racing colors. After getting Roundaboutway settled back in his stall, Bucky walked back to the camper. When he stepped inside, Clarence and Carl were sitting at the small kitchen table awaiting his return.

It was uncommon for that horse to break like that. Bucky was sure they'd want to find out what happened, but he wasn't in the mood to talk. Carl would usually allow Bucky to sulk for a while after he'd lost a race, but Clarence would have none of it.

"Boy," Clarence said. Bucky stepped out of his muddy jumpsuit and kicked it across the floor. "Clean yourself up, and then get your tail back out here." Bucky went into the airplane-sized bathroom and splashed water on his face.

Clarence continued talking to him. "You know that horse that won went off at twenty-seven to one? Twenty-seven to one! You know where we were on the board? Two to one. That horse had no business winning that race."

Bucky leaned against the wall and hung his head.

"You gave that horse too much line right off the gate. It's the only reason I could see for him breaking," Clarence continued.

Bucky turned the tap off. The camper went silent as Clarence and Carl waited for some kind of response from him. He felt like a losing boxer in the last round, no longer able to keep his arms up to block the flurry of punches. Bucky maintained his silence as he came back out. He grabbed a beer from the minifridge built into the kitchenette and slumped down next to Carl to face Clarence.

Before Clarence had the chance to begin what would be, no doubt, a lecture about driving techniques in the slop, Max came stumbling through the front door. He had a big drunken grin, definitely no trace of the beaten look that the others wore. Bucky was actually happy to see his uncle, because it shifted the conversation away from him and onto Max.

"Why *you* so happy?" Clarence demanded.

Max responded by throwing a handful of damp bills on the table.

"We're in the money!" Max sang. "Money, money, money."

He pulled more cash from his pocket and buried his face in it.

"Guess you did all right, Maxi," Carl said. "That's good. We were just sitting here talking about what happened out there."

Carl's sober tone wiped Max's grin off his face.

"Well, it's clear to me what happened," Max said. "The fuckin' dog just broke. No sense in reading too much into it. Maybe he's been thinking too much about them fillies. Might be time to make the colt a gelding, huh, boys?" Max amused himself by making a scissors motion with his index and middle fingers.

"At first I thought it might have been that buckle," Bucky said, "but it didn't snap. I had a look at it afterward."

"Buckle?" Clarence said.

"Yeah. Max was in this morning, said he heard you talking about the buckle on the hobbles. It seemed to hold up fine, so that wasn't the problem. I know that much for sure," Bucky said to Clarence, who slammed both hands on the table and struggled to get up while Carl put an arm bar across him.

"Damn you, Max," Clarence spat. "You're a disgrace."

"C'mon, Clarence," Carl said, urging him to calm down.

"That's what he does. He fixes to lose," Clarence continued. Once he was able to get his arm free from Carl, he pointed at Max. "Watch your fucking step."

"What'd you do to those hobbles, Max?" Bucky asked, still calm, perhaps not having expected that level of brass until now, and kicking himself for not having inspected the equipment more closely after Max had handled it.

Max didn't respond.

"That's it, Max? You just going to stand there and not say anything?"

Several seconds passed. "Sorry, kid," Max muttered. Bucky jumped from the table and clasped his hand around Max's throat.

"You're good for nothing, Max!" Bucky yelled in his face. "You're lucky I don't end your miserable existence right now," Bucky said, tightening his grip on Max's throat. He suddenly released his grip when he realized that he indeed could have killed his uncle at that moment. Max fell back a few steps onto the divan across from the table and held his throat, coughing.

Clarence was still sitting at the table, looking quite satisfied, while Carl stood between Bucky and Max.

"What's the matter, Max? Cat got your tongue?" Bucky said, waiting on anything Max might say and ready to pounce on him again. "That's what I thought," Bucky said. Then he stormed out of the trailer, slamming the door behind him.

CHAPTER 6

It was a Sunday morning. Bucky had to meet Carl and Clarence at the Crossroads bar near Camden, New Jersey. It was just across the Delaware River from Philadelphia, and since it was roughly equidistant between New York and Harrington, they had developed a system whereby Clarence and Carl would bring fresh legs up to the Crossroads, and if Bucky had a horse due for a rest, he'd bring him to the meeting spot so Clarence and Carl could haul him back to the farm.

This time it was Voltrain's turn for a rest, so Bucky drove over to the track to pick him up and begin the two-hour drive to the Crossroads. It was finally beginning to smell like spring. The melting snow along the highway looked like a dirty glacier, slowly receding to reveal dead brown grass that was soggy and smelled like nature seeping through.

There was only one car in the parking lot at the Crossroads. The crowds would usually pick up after the races were out at Freedom Raceway, at which point drivers would be coming and going in one direction or another. Beneath his black vest, Bucky wore his denim button-down with the sleeves rolled up, and jeans he couldn't remember *not* wearing in at least three days. He wore his Texaco baseball hat, and had on a large silver belt buckle with a bucking bronco.

The latest string of races in New York had drained him. The whole goal of the experiment was to see if he could win purses and send money back to the farm, but since his last win with Voltrain, Bucky was in a slump.

Inside, the bar was dark, and you would have no way of knowing if it was noon or three in the morning. It was an open circular bar with a dance floor and a pool table, but now it was empty. And it felt empty, maybe even partly haunted like an amusement park closed for the season. Behind the bar there was a neon Bud Light sign and a mirrored portrait of the Philadelphia Eagles cheerleaders.

Bucky waited silently at the bar, able to smell the cleaning supplies and impermeable beer bilge. He began to grow a little impatient about being completely disregarded.

"*Hello!*" he called out.

After a moment, Scottie the barman came out, wiping down a bus pan. "Be with you in a minute," he said, still not overly concerned that he should rush to serve his only customer.

Impatient for a drink to arrive before Carl and Clarence got there, Bucky lit a smoke. Along with that first exhale went all his worries—his dwindling bankroll, his losses, and that deep, cold crevasse just beneath his chest.

Finally Scottie was back. He was a big, bald man with large hairy forearms and a neck that ran straight from his chest to his chin. Built like a buffalo, he had seen it all, and because of that, the patrons knew not to cross him. He put a whisky and a beer chaser in front of Bucky.

"Thanks. How'd you know?" Bucky said.

"Can see it all over your face, kid; it's in your eyes."

"Well, thanks, I guess."

"No problem," Scottie said. He wiped his bar even though there was nothing on it. He had been doing it so long that it had become habit, like a cat cleaning itself. Right after Bucky shot the whisky, the doors swung open, and for a moment two figures were silhouetted in the bright light that lit up the bar. Bucky turned around on his stool and then got up to greet them. For a moment it was awkward, because after all these years, Bucky and Carl had still not determined if they should hug or shake hands, or shake hands before hug. The result was a dance move, where they both went to the same side and then the other, and then finally they just patted each other on the shoulder and ended in a handshake. Clarence, not one for handshakes or hugs, made immediate eye contact with Scottie and held up two fingers. They all sat down at the bar, and without hesitation began talking about racing.

"I don't know what you been sending me, Clarence," Bucky said.

"You're the driver. I'm doing the best with what I got. We're paying your rent up there and we've still got the farm expenses. Do you think we can just go out and buy the next Rambling Willie? C'mon, boy."

"I know it's not you, Clarence. We've got to get better horses in on some bigger purses. These $10,000 dashes aren't doing shit to our bottom line."

"Well, if it means anything, I bought a stake in a horse with Roy," Carl said, giving Clarence a knowing wink. "His name's Nitro. He'll be running an elimination heat at the Coliseum in June. If he wins, he'll qualify for the Breeders. Clarence gets to work with him, and you'll get to drive."

"That's a million-dollar purse!" Bucky said, almost spitting out his beer.

"I went all in on this one," Carl said, sounding like a nervous gambler who'd just placed his life savings on a craps table.

"What it'd cost?" Bucky asked, bracing for the answer.

"Well, I traded up Voltrain and just have to pay back the nomination fee, sustaining payments, and the entry fee to Roy for our share of the purse."

"That's a big chunk of change ... but not so bad."

"And the deed to the farm," Carl said casually, as if he was just trying to gloss it over.

"The farm?" Bucky said with real concern. He put his head in his hands, leaning his elbows on the bar.

"He's a top horse and has earned his right to be there."

"I know, but—"

"Came from a farm in Lexington. His father won the Jug and came second in the Messenger. He's good stock, Son. Trust me."

"But the farm, Dad?"

"You said it yourself, we needed something ... something bigger."

"If we lose, let's hope they're hiring down at the IHOP, because we're all going to have to get jobs—real jobs," Bucky said.

"Flippin' pancakes is a real job?" Clarence said with a raised eyebrow. "I know your dad isn't exactly known for his horse-pickin' abilities, but this one, oh, he's live all right. You better hang on, because we don't want you embarrassing yourself. You're playing with the big boys now."

"I did my end and got you a horse. The rest is up to you," Carl said, putting his hand on Bucky's shoulder.

"I won't let you down—either of you," Bucky said.

"What about your uncle?" Carl asked. "You heard from him lately?"

"No, not for a while. And that's a good thing. He's got something going on, though, Pops, I tell you."

"That comes as a surprise to you?" Clarence said.

"Well, we haven't seen him the last few days on the farm. He got a drive at Pocono and actually won for a change," Carl said.

"And you haven't seen him since?" Bucky asked. "Max not turning up when he's got a few quick grand in his pocket? There's a shocker."

"Like a pig with two snouts," Clarence added.

"Well, anyway," Bucky said, looking seriously at the two men. "Bernie's trying to get me to fix races. Sometimes he doesn't ask, though. He just looks at me like I should thank him or something. And Max? I don't know, you tell me. I think he's in on it somehow. Even when he isn't around, he's causing trouble."

"Don't worry about him," Clarence said. "We'll have a talk if he shows up at the farm."

"Tell him to stay out of my business, and that I'm not interested in getting involved with him or Bernie."

When they were done with their drinks, the men left the bar and walked together through the parking lot. Clarence led them to where the two horse trailers were parked side by side.

"When we traded up, I got you a throw-in gelding," Carl said. "Just hang in there, get yourself ready."

"Now," Clarence said, as he swung open the horse trailer, "what we have all been waiting for ..."

Bucky and Carl watched as Clarence pulled down the ramp and walked the horse out. "His name's Ace McGee. You be nice to him, hear?"

Bucky looked at the old gray horse with long whiskers and a sunken back, took hold of the lead from Clarence, and patted the horse's forehead and looked deep into his eyes.

"You're with me now, aren't you, fella?"

"He's old, but he'll run a good mile for you," Clarence said. He immediately began unlatching Bucky's trailer to retrieve Voltrain. After Clarence walked him down the ramp, Bucky hugged his neck and gave him one last pat goodbye.

"I'm gonna miss you, boy," Bucky said, knowing the horse was on his way to racing endless buggy nights in a million forsaken towns, to eventually get traded up or traded down, maybe end up with the Amish. This was the most likely the last time he would ever see him.

"I'm sorry, Buck," Carl said. "I wanted to tell you earlier, because I knew how you felt about Rose."

Bucky nodded acceptingly. He knew it was necessary given the situation on the farm. He was close with Voltrain, although not as close as he'd been with Rose. For Bucky, no horse could rival Summer Rose. The thing he was beginning to accept about horses is that they'll break your heart every time.

"All right then," Carl said. Bucky loaded Ace McGee into his trailer, and Clarence loaded Voltrain into the trailer behind Carl's old green pickup truck. "Stay patient; help is on the way. In the meantime, see what you can squeak out with the old-timer."

"A carpenter doesn't blame his tools, right, boy?" Clarence said.

"Okay, I get the point. Adios," Bucky said. Soon both trucks were off, towing their trailers in opposite directions.

CHAPTER 7

In the weeks after Anna had found out Bucky had moved to Yonkers, at first she resisted calling him, but then as time wore on, she creeped around the phone expecting to hear from him. Finally, one night when she could resist no longer, Anna went to the book-lined study, looked out the large bay window at the night that was plastered with stars and a crescent moon, picked up the phone, and called Bucky. She sat down on the leather sofa and waited for him to answer. She had just assumed he would pick up, thinking that maybe he was expecting her call just the same. After all, she was used to Bucky just being there.

Now, Anna had no way of knowing what Bucky was up to, and her usual sources of information had dried up. There would be no more sightings of Bucky at the bar or racetrack. Bucky was off in the world now, the same world that Anna once wondered how she would fare in.

"Hello?" Bucky answered.

"Bucky," Anna said. She could feel the silence on the other end.

"Anna," Bucky said after a pause.

"Everything all right?"

"Everything's fine."

"Cole and I were worried about you after your last visit," Anna said, proffering Cole's name so it would seem she was calling at his behest, or at least that both of them were equally concerned.

"Things are looking up, actually. I moved to New York and got a stable at Speedway. Even got a qualifier coming up for the Breeders."

Bucky said this proudly, not quite boastfully, but with a sense of achievement that he had moved on, that his future was clearly in hand.

"I know you moved, Bucky. I called you. Remember? I got your number from Cole, who had to ask your father for it. You could have called."

"I'm sorry. I thought about it, but I just …"

"Just what?" Anna said, when she noticed Bucky faltering and didn't want to give him time to come up with an excuse.

"It just got away from me, Anna. Everything moved so fast when I got down here, and now, now … it's like I have this whole new life. I'm happy to have made a clean break from Delaware. You were right."

When Bucky said this, Anna eased off, sinking her head back into the sofa. *What did he mean by that?* she wondered. *Has he finally moved on, not just from Delaware, but also from me? Has he closed that part of his heart where there was still a faint glimmer of hope that we could be together?* For a moment Anna thought she had been too harsh. After all, Bucky was a grown man. It wasn't his responsibility to report in, and why would he? Every time they saw each other, it was the same thing; Bucky would proposition her, and Anna would dodge and weave. In fact, it had happened so many times by now that Anna was running out of ways to deliver the message. But now, was this finally it? Was Bucky over Anna? What about the promise that he would love her forever? Ever since that first time in the barn when Bucky had uttered those words, perhaps she had come to believe them in whatever way. Anna berated herself for having such selfish thoughts. After all, wasn't that what she'd always wanted for Bucky, for him to be liberated, to escape his life of perpetual loneliness, of brooding around and fantasizing about his best friend's girl—or was it?

While they continued to talk, Anna thought that Bucky had never seemed so distant. They might as well have been on different planets or talking through two Styrofoam cups tied together by string.

"So what's next for you?" Bucky said to fill the dead air.

"What's next? Let's see, such a short question for a long answer." She sighed. Sitting there pondering the simple question of what was next, she only came up with one thing—nothing. Nothing was next. This was it for her. She thought about her college friends, like Jane Peterson, who'd met a lawyer and moved to New York, and Tracey Carmichael, who'd become an architect and lived in Philadelphia with her husband, twin girls, and Labrador retriever—and now Bucky. *What have I done?* she thought. *I went four hundred miles away to college, only to move back home and live in a house that is fifteen minutes away from where I grew up, with a man I grew up with.*

Why had Bucky's move caused such a tumult in her emotions?

"Whatever you do, I'm sure it will be great," Bucky said.

Is he playing with me now? Anna thought to herself.

"I'm gonna miss you, Anna."

"Don't say that. You know I'm always around."

"I know that. It's just ... things are different now."

"Different how?"

"Different in that there's finality."

"C'mon, Bucky, you knew years ago. You just didn't want to believe it."

"I guess you're right."

"I'm sure it's hard for you. It's hard for all of us. We enjoy having you in our lives; we don't want to lose you. We won't lose you, will we, Bucky?"

"That's just it, Anna. I don't know if I can do it."

"You can."

"I can't, Anna. It was hard enough for me when you went to college. You're all I've ever wanted, and then there was ..."

"Shh," Anna said, cutting him off. "Nothing will change now. You know I love Cole ... *and* I love you."

"The love you give and the love I need are two very different things."

"I can never give you the love you need," Anna said. As the words came out, she realized the harshness in them. She felt empty for a moment, and sad for Bucky for being on the losing apex of their love triangle. Realizing this, she quickly added, "I'm sorry. That didn't come out right."

"I agree," Bucky said.

Anna wasn't sure if he was sad or resolute.

"Some of those things you said last time you came by were true."

"About Bobby?"

"I handled it all wrong."

"We don't need to do this, Anna."

"My mother. She was never the same after that. She blamed you for it. Still does."

"I blame myself."

"Marrying you was never an option."

"Do you love him?"

"Of course I do."

"Do you love me more?"

Anna was used to Bucky's overtures, but this question caught her off guard. The two men were very different, and she had spent the better part of her life flip-flopping between them.

"Parts of you."

"Which ones?"

"You were right, we don't need to do this," Anna said, realizing she was not prepared to access those womanly secrets buried deep inside her, secrets that would most likely accompany her to the grave. But whether she liked it or not, Bucky somehow had finally gotten through, and the parts she loved about Bucky came floating up to the surface like flotsam bobbing around in the ocean. She loved his fight. Bucky had to fight for everything. Nothing was ever given to him. And in those moments when Anna was frustrated by whatever hardship, she thought of Bucky and just how resourceful he was, and it gave her strength. She loved his body, which was pale and lean and small. She could hold Bucky, all of him, unlike Cole, whose lumbering body seemed to leak out everywhere, especially in bed. She loved Bucky's dark brown eyes. She loved his love of horses. She loved his loneliness and his rebellion. She loved the fact that he was everything

Cole wasn't, but she couldn't bring herself to reveal just one of those things to Bucky.

"Is everything all right?" Bucky asked Anna, who had stalled again. Her train of thought and the distance between them caused her to reflect more on what Bucky had meant to her throughout the years.

"I'm fine," Anna said, dabbing away a tear with her shirtsleeve. She could hear Bucky's television on in the background, and pictured him sitting with his feet up on a coffee table, only half listening, and not having any idea as to just how close she was at that moment to opening a door that had been slammed shut so many times.

"Okay, well, if that's it then, I gotta go," Bucky said.

"Wait," Anna said, just about ready to expose the disquiet in her heart.

"Yeah?"

"Nothing. Just being silly. Good luck up there. Those New York drivers don't know what's coming."

"Thanks, Anna. Goodbye," Bucky said. He hung up the phone.

Usually, it took Bucky longer to hang up, Anna thought. They would have more back-and-forth, and he'd make obvious, desperate efforts to try to keep her on the phone. Not this time.

Much like Bucky, Anna's immediate reprieve from any kind of sadness was her ability to ride it out, so she put on her beige riding pants and equestrian boots, went out to the barn and switched on the flood lights. The early chill of spring had finally broken. Anna could tell by the size and voracity of the mosquitoes that it was going to be an itchy season. As she walked through the stalls, she could tell by their randiness that even the horses could sense that better weather was upon them. Even at nighttime they all wanted to get out. Anna decided to take out the roan filly, so she tacked her up and rode her out of the barn. In her black velvet riding helmet, she cantered around the lighted paddock. With every long, graceful stride of the horse, she allowed herself to sink deeper into the numbness. *Why has it all come back now?* she wondered. In her mind she replayed her conversation with Bucky, and his mention of her departure for the University of

Massachusetts. Anna recalled the incident years earlier when she was home for Thanksgiving and had invited Bucky over to visit at her parents' place.

It had been a while since they had seen each other. She'd ushered him up to her room to avoid her mother. When Anna opened the door to her bedroom, right away Bucky jumped on her bed and tucked his hands beneath the pillows and under his neck.

"Get comfortable, why don't you."

"Good idea," Bucky said and sprawled out even more. "Your room is the same as I remember. Same pink carpet, same flowery duvet ..."

Anna looked around, and indeed it was the same, still containing some of the most cherished vestiges of her youth, like her horse jumping and dressage trophies, and the hand-stitched throw pillows made by her grandmother. There were still posters up of her teen idols Jason Priestley and Garth Brooks, which she made a mental note to take down before she went back to school. Tucked away in the bottom left corner of her bookshelf, Anna noticed her family albums. Between those aging cellophane pages and cardboard that had long lost its stick was a veritable treasure trove of family memories. There was one grainy picture of her naked in a tub; and then at age three running around with a Hula-Hoop; and at six, laughing on the back of a horse. Her mother, Judith, beamed in every picture taken, and then, near the end of the second album, she began to show a baby bump. Once Bobby was born, there was a flood of new photographs (Bobby with chocolate pudding all over his face, Bobby on his tricycle, Bobby in his little league outfit—so many more of Bobby that Anna already believed she was the lesser loved), and the albums proliferated and had been catalogued, eventually ending up in Anna's room. Not surprisingly, the last year on record was 1986—the year Bobby died. That's when the memories ended for Anna's family. That's when things changed with her and Bucky. That's when the very core of everything she had ever known and believed in was uprooted forever.

"So?" Bucky said, looking at Anna expectantly.

"So?"

"How's school? Tell me everything."

"I don't even know where to start. I'm learning so much more about horses, from how to apply a poultice, to what medicines to use, to breeding techniques—so many things that I love it. I just love it."

"I gotta learn the old-fashioned way," Bucky said. Anna knew full well that college wasn't an option for him. "After all, it's not so hard to tell the difference between a colt and a gelding, right?"

"There's more to it than that, Bucky."

"I know, I know," Bucky said and then sat up in her bed. "How's Cole, anyway?" he asked, trying not to appear jealous or overly concerned.

It turned out that Cole, unable to be away from Anna any longer, had transferred from his school in Pennsylvania to a similar program at UMass. It was the most upset that Bucky had ever been with Cole, knowing full well that could be the deciding factor for who might end up with Anna. Up until then, they had sparred back and forth for her attention, but when it came down to it, Cole had the means to pursue her across state lines and, more importantly, far away from Bucky.

"Oh, he's good," Anna said calmly, knowing where the conversation could be headed, so she tried not to offer too much.

"See him much around town?"

"Yes, I do see him a fair bit," Anna said.

"I keep saying I'm going to visit—"

"It'd be great if you came to see us sometime, Bucky," Anna said, for a moment her face flushing a bright red.

"You could show me the spots. I hear there are lots of parties. Maybe we can go to a football game."

"Sure, Bucky. Sounds fun," Anna said, humoring him now because she knew he wouldn't come. And if he did, he would be in for a big surprise.

What Anna had failed to mention was that she and Cole had moved in together. And didn't it just make sense to do that anyway? Two close friends from the same hometown. It was practical. But what had started out as a simple living situation had begun to evolve. Cole had always been in love with Anna, but until they left for school, he'd never made the same romantic overtures that Bucky had: no wild declarations of love, no leaning in for kisses. Cole played it straight and let Bucky do all the heavy lifting, waiting for just the right time to choose his moment.

Anna had been somewhat naïve moving in with Cole, not thinking they would be anything more than roommates. After all, it was a two-bedroom apartment. But when Cole started looking at Anna differently, she knew that something was bound to change. At first, it was awkward for her, trying to ignore Cole as he watched her from over his books, and other moments when he was sure she wasn't looking. After a while, she began to enjoy it, and even though Anna had never been a fancy dresser, she did little things like primp her hair, or wear a barely discernible amount of makeup, to gain even more of Cole's attention. Finally, it happened one day for them. Anna was doing the dishes and Cole came up behind her and put his arms around her waist. Anticipating rejection, he was surprised at how easily she'd turned around and, without hesitation, put her arms around his neck. They began kissing. Since that moment, their relationship had changed, and Anna started to fall in love with Cole, just as Cole had intended.

The pendulum of Anna's heart had always swung more in Bucky's direction, but now that she had started to fall for Cole as an adult, it made it harder for her to deal with Bucky. She felt that she was being dishonest with him. She didn't want to deceive Bucky, but since she knew just how hard it would be on him, she decided to keep the news to herself.

"Come sit beside me," Bucky said, pretending to dust off a section of the duvet for Anna.

"Bucky, I—"

"C'mon, Anna. I won't bite," Bucky said. Anna recognized that look in Bucky's eyes. It was the exact same as Cole's whenever he was looking for something more than just conversation. The two might as well have been twins in that respect. Anna got up from where she'd been sitting on the floor and sat next to Bucky.

"Hi," he said to her, now that she was up close.

"Hi," Anna said. It was just what she had feared upon coming home and seeing Bucky. In between their extended absences, Bucky was becoming more bold, knowing that Cole posed a serious threat.

"You know, Anna, I miss you. God, I miss you. I miss you so much it hurts."

"You're sweet, Bucky," she said. *How had it come to this anyway?* she thought. How were the three of them such close friends as kids, and now everything over the years had come to such a head? Why was she in this position where she had to choose between the two most important people in her life? When she looked at Bucky, she saw far past his crooked and shaded front tooth, past his shaggy hair, past his small stature and unrefinement, and saw the person she had always been in love with. She could tell that Bucky was getting restless. Soon, the evening would be over, and then the weekend, and Anna would be back at school with Cole. While Anna began speaking nervously to break the sexual tension that now filled the room, she could tell Bucky was psyching himself up to make a move. He was not listening to anything that Anna was saying and instead was looking at her cheeks, her lips, her neck, her hair, her breasts. Finally he quickly got to his knees, grabbed the back of Anna's neck, and pulled her face to his. At first, Anna resisted just a little, but as she became used to the circles and spirals, the motion of Bucky's familiar kiss, she fell right back into it as if it was something she had been longing for just as bad. They clacked teeth and bumped noses. Anna had to swallow a couple of times so she could come up for air. After a few minutes of passionate kissing, Bucky used his body weight to force Anna to lie back on the bed, and she lay flat, giving into him completely.

"I love you," Bucky said, stopping suddenly, propping himself up on his elbows to look at Anna, into the speckle of her eye, the tiny black diamond adrift in the sea of iris. Then he pinched her chin and gave her another kiss.

"I know you do, Bucky," Anna said, as if by not returning the sentiment she hadn't completely betrayed Cole. He kissed her again and again, one time on her forehead, another time on her cheek, and a whole lot of kisses around her neck. When he kissed her head, Anna could swear the kisses left deep impressions. Each one was sweeter than the last. She fully succumbed to his embrace, melting into him like wax down a candlestick.

Emboldened by Anna's submission, Bucky tugged at her shirt. Eventually she raised her arms to allow him to remove it. And then when he unbuttoned her jeans, she wiggled them around her ass and then down her legs. Bucky helped slide them off with his foot once they were down around her ankles.

Had Anna ever really had a choice in being with Cole? It seemed from a very young age that that was all her mother wanted for her, and in a way she felt she had shortchanged not only Bucky but also herself. True, she did love Cole. She loved Cole as much as she could, and chances were that if things were reversed and Cole was the one on the outside, she would have done the same thing for him. Call it a romantic courtesy, the casual fulfillment of her best friend's fantasy. She had thought about it all the previous night at school while she'd watched Cole snoring in bed. *Is this the man I'm supposed to marry? He's a good man,* she thought, but after thinking about it, she realized he never made her feel quite the same way as Bucky did. Perhaps it was because that sometime after Bobby's death, Bucky's love became forbidden.

It was in this way that Anna justified her actions. She slowly unbuttoned Bucky's shirt and then ran her hands along the trail of hair from his stomach to his chest. Bucky quickly pulled down his jeans and boxer shorts. He continued kissing her, running his fingers through her hair. He fondled her breasts like they were two mounds of Plasticine and sucked on her swollen nipples. It seemed to Anna that he wanted to do everything and all at once.

Just when Bucky was about to enter her, she pushed him away and he fell back on the bed.

"Let me do all the work," she said, looking down at Bucky, flushed from the sexual tension she could feel burning in her loins. She wanted Bucky inside of her already—it had been long enough. After she mounted him, she got into a rhythm of slow pelvic gyrations. Bucky lay there with his eyes closed, seemingly in carnal bliss. They never did get around to losing their virginity together as teenagers—Bobby's death had put a swift end to that—but despite the fact that they'd never made love before, it seemed familiar. She remembered Bucky's touch, and his smell so well that it all came back like cotton candy, like an old familiar song on the radio. With Anna's pleasure came torture, as she tried to erase the thoughts of Cole while enjoying making love to Bucky for the first time. Looking down at him, Anna knew how much he loved her. She fought with the notion of just how much she loved him. As she continued to ride him, clearly the pilot throttling the engine, her hair swept from side to side, and beads of sweat gathered on her upper lip. When Bucky opened his eyes, Anna was running her hands down her stomach. It must have been too much for Bucky, because that's when he exploded deep inside of her. For Anna, it felt like Bucky had not only one orgasm but two and three and four, as he flexed his legs and squirted into her with every last pump, until finally he fell back, completely drained. When Anna lay down beside him, they both looked up at the ceiling with their hearts racing, trying to catch their breaths, while reality and the obvious question set in.

"So," Bucky said, "What now?"

Lost in the moment, Anna was pondering this complicated question, when suddenly the door swung open and there Cole stood before them.

"Cole!" Anna jumped naked from the bed, and quickly scrambled for her bathrobe, which was hanging from the back of the door. "I thought you were staying at school to finish your paper?"

"Well, surprise, surprise," Cole said. "Your mom let me in."

"Hi, Cole," Bucky said, pulling the blanket over him. Anna

wouldn't have been surprised if Bucky had flashed him an indiscreet wave of one-upmanship, but fortunately he didn't. Cole ignored him.

"I can explain, Cole," Anna said.

"Explain?" Bucky asked. "Why should you have to explain anything?"

"Bucky, just—" Anna tried to hush Bucky, as if it would make the whole situation just go away, before Cole cut her off.

"Oh, I guess you didn't tell him?"

"Cole, please. Not like this."

"Okay, well, good pal, best friend, Bucky. Sorry to drop this on you, but Anna and I are living together. We are lovers ... as they say."

If Bucky had originally felt as though he had somehow beaten Cole when he walked into the room, it was clear now that those feelings had changed. All of the color had disappeared from Bucky's face, and tears welled up in his eyes. Anna went back over to the bed, wrapped her arms around him, and kissed him on the cheek.

"I'm so sorry, Bucky. I ... this is so hard for me. You guys ... are so hard for me. I just can't do this. I can't do this," she said, bawling into her hands.

Bucky and Cole remained silent in the awkward vacuum of Anna's hysterics. It would never come to blows for the two men; after all, competing for Anna was nothing new—they had been doing it their whole lives. But there was a sense that something had changed for good.

"So what now?" Cole asked.

"You win," Bucky conceded, without looking back at him.

"Buck—" Cole said, throwing his arms up as if Bucky was refusing to cooperate.

"What do you want me to say?"

"I don't know. Something. I mean, maybe I should be the mad one here. I walked in and found my girlfriend cheating on me."

"Girlfriend?"

"Well ... yeah. We live together. We're ... together."

Bucky winced.

"That's right. I forgot you two are common-law now."

"Don't do this, Bucky. You've had your chances with her. God knows I've been on the sidelines long enough."

"Must be nice to be able to follow her to the edge of the earth. You really went to extremes on this one, Cole. You knew I couldn't go away to college, and really, well, I guess congratulations are in order."

"It's never been a game for me, Bucky. I've always loved her, just as much as you have."

Bucky harrumphed at this last comment. No way Cole loved Anna more than he did.

"You know, I've always seen the way she looks at you, and I've wondered my whole life if she'd ever look at me the same way. I transferred to UMass, and true, the decision was easier knowing that Anna would be there, but I had no idea things were going to happen the way they did."

"And now you've got what you wanted. I'm happy for you, Cole."

"Helloo, I'm right here," Anna said, finally through with her sobbing. "And I'm not a fucking stakes race. You guys are children." The two both looked at Anna for a moment, and then back at each other.

"I guess that's it," Cole said. There was nothing else to say to Bucky. No way Cole would give up what he had gained, although from his expression it was clear he felt bad for his friend.

"Yes, that's it," Bucky said. "Go back to school and have fun playing house."

"Buck—"

"Just go."

With that, Cole got up and left the bedroom. Anna could hear his voice from downstairs as her mom, Judith, made a fuss that he should stay for dinner. She sat alone with Bucky while he looked around the room, still in shock.

"Bucky."

"You don't have to say anything."

"I want to explain."

"Save your breath," Bucky said. Then he got dressed and walked over to the window. He watched Cole spin the tires on his Ford Mustang and peel out of the farmyard.

"I best be going as well."

When they walked down the stairs, there was Judith clutching her wineglass, bejeweled in gaudy bracelets with a pearl necklace and dangling earrings. She was looking hard at Anna as if words couldn't express her disappointment.

"Bucky," she said through tight lips, flipping her wispy brown hair.

"I was just leaving, Mrs. Miller," Bucky said. There would be no offers extended to Bucky to stay for dinner.

CHAPTER 8

Bucky was having a drink in the drivers' lounge watching some of the later races from the glass windows that were level with the track outside. It had been a few days since he'd met Carl and Clarence at the Crossroads. Bernie had asked to meet him for a "career discussion." Word had gotten out that Carl had partnered up on Nitro, and Bucky was certain that Bernie wanted to meet to figure out how to get a piece of the action. What he didn't know was how to handle Bernie without showing his brewing discontent for how things were going in New York. If Bucky agreed to everything that Bernie asked for, then that would make him just as crooked as the old man was. But he couldn't risk throwing away his permanent stable, as that would threaten his whole family's enterprise. Because of that, he began to realize that perhaps he had to start making some small concessions.

Bernie walked in, yanked the chair that Bucky was resting his feet on, and then sat down.

"What's the word, superstar?" Bernie said.

"Oh, not much. Just thinking about the races I have coming up."

"I hear you're in the Stakes qualifier."

"News travels fast."

"Your uncle tells me you got a girl back home."

"My uncle says a lot of things."

"Did he mention I need you to lose with Nitro?"

"No, he didn't say that," Bucky said, shaking his head, "and I won't.

That's bullshit, Bernie. I didn't come down here to lose all the time, especially to you guys who are fixing races."

"I know, kid. I know. But just do me this one favor. My associates at Pistol Farms have a horse going off as a long shot. They say he knocks knees and can't run straight. You'd be surprised by what a bit of rest can do for a horse," Bernie said, unable to contain his chuckle. "Anyway, they got the one and two, and if you show, then they hit big money on the triactor. And, by all means, kid, you can get some action on it too. This could be a good situation ... for everybody."

"Pistol Farms, eh? Can't do it. Sorry, Bernie," Bucky said, getting up to leave.

"About that," Bernie said, as he reached across and put his hand on Bucky's arm.

"Yes?" Bucky said, sitting back down, remembering the reverence that Max and the other drivers had for the Big Macher, and the stern warning he'd been given to ensure he showed the same respect.

"Not so easy," Bernie said. "You see, those guys who own Pistol Farms? They're gangsters."

"Gangsters?" Bucky said with some surprise. He knew the lot from the track were unscrupulous, but gangsters? This was a whole new level Bucky hadn't anticipated.

"Yeah. Ever hear of the Caruso gang? Frankie Fingers, he's their leader, and trust me, you don't want to fuck with him. Just so happens your uncle Max made a deal with him."

"Oh fuck, Bernie. Don't say that."

"I'm telling you, kid: you don't blow that race, they're going to break your legs."

"What if I say I'll think about it?"

"I don't know if that will cut it with these guys," Bernie said. "They're not the type to fuck around. You say you're going to come in third, you come in third. If you don't, it's your ass ... and mine."

"All right, Bernie." Bucky sighed, then looked out the window and watched the horses in the post parade. There was a beauty in the way they pranced with their heads upright, stiff and confined to the headgear and bit. Although they had all been bred to race, he wondered if there were ones who actually detested it. In that moment, he felt like a horse that didn't want to race but knew he had to or else he'd get whipped, or something worse. He thought about his father and Clarence back home. What would they have to say about this? Could he even tell them? If he did what Bernie suggested and made side bets on their racket, how would he explain the sudden cash infusion when they'd lost the race? Would he have to hide the dirty money in his mattress, or come up with some kind of reason to launder the money back to his own farm? Maybe he could secretly pay off Roy Callaghan, and tell him to advise Carl that from the kindness of his heart he'd decided to forgive all the entry payments, and still own his stake in Nitro.

"Thanks, kid," Bernie said, getting up. "You know the harness-racing world ain't big. It's getting a lot smaller, as a matter of fact. Everyone gets greased once in a while—even the good guys."

Bucky just gave him a nod and didn't say anything as he left. He sat alone, fidgeting with the straw in his empty glass, and tore up a napkin on the table. He couldn't believe what he had just agreed to, and for a moment he thought about running after Bernie to tell him he'd changed his mind, that he couldn't go through with it, but he knew that now there was no turning back.

Fifteen minutes passed between races. When the next group of drivers and horses was on the track, he got up and left. Just as he was walking out of the paddock, he ran into his neighbor, Easy Money Eddy. He was cleaned up from his race, and actually looking quite spiffy for him, in khaki Dockers, a brown suede jacket, and matching brogues.

"Hey, Bucky. How goes? Fancy a drink in the Grandstand Lounge?" Eddy asked.

"Thanks, but no, Eddy. Just want to get out of here, watch some junk on the tube. Maybe listen to Marcus and Rita fight it out."

"C'mon, Bucky. When's the last time you've been with a woman? You said so yourself. And shit, tell me one other place where anyone actually knows you're a harness racer? We're celebrities there ... trust me," Eddy said, putting his arm around Bucky and leading him across the parking lot toward the grandstand.

"Okay, you got me, Eddy. What's the worst thing that can happen?"

"You finally rotate your tires?"

"Maybe that wouldn't be so bad." Bucky smiled.

When they walked into the lounge, some fans immediately came over to shake their hands. The lounge manager, Westing Schmidt, also came over and introduced himself. He was a short man, almost as short as Bucky, but plump with spiky dirty-blond hair. By his cocksure attitude and loud voice, it was clear to Bucky that he enjoyed whatever social status that being a lounge manager brought him. He made a point of taking both men aside from the fans for a quick talk.

"Lot's of girls here tonight, boys. Lots of girls," he said, waving his arm across the room at some of women who were around, as if they were on display and all readily available. Eddy gave Westing Schmidt a tip and soon peeled away with a woman half his age. *Is that what's going on here?* Bucky thought to himself. *Is Westing a pimp?* Schmidt soon introduced Bucky to a blonde beauty named Nikki Ivanoff. She wore bright red lipstick, which she was reapplying while talking to Bucky.

"I never knew about harness racing until tonight," she said, peering up at Bucky from her compact mirror, and then stretching her mouth back to check if there was any lipstick on her teeth. "You guys race around in your chariots like Ben-Hur; it's cute."

Cute, Bucky thought to himself. *Puppy dogs are cute.* But he just smiled politely. In the spirit of jocular fraternity, Westing Schmidt whispered into Bucky's ear that she was "good to go." Bucky looked back at Nikki to size her up for a possible "tire rotation," as Eddy had put it. The truth was, Bucky just wasn't into it. In fact, the very smell of Nikki repelled Bucky, as she wore a strong perfume that, mixed with the other aromas of her hair and her deodorant, made her seem cheap and overdone. So far, romantically, things hadn't gone exactly as expected in New York for Bucky. When he left Delaware, he'd pictured finding Anna's equivalent in the city. He had hoped that by now he would be experiencing romantic dinners and Broadway shows; he wanted to drive through the Palisades; he wanted to spoil his girlfriend with trinkets and chocolate; he wanted to make love in the morning, go out for breakfast, and then come back home and do it again. He was beginning to see, however, that the women who made themselves so readily available would never fill the void of his first and only love.

As Westing Schmidt and Nikki did shots at the bar, Bucky discreetly walked out of the lounge and found a seat in the grandstand, which was speckled with fans. He spotted a girl whom he thought looked like Anna—something that happened often during his lower moments—and cursed her boyfriend, because with every caress, he imagined it was Anna's love being doled out onto that stranger and he hated him. He didn't blame Cole for marrying Anna, because, in a way, it could be said they both had an even chance with her, and that he'd even had a second chance. However, something about the randomness of love—of her love, of everybody else's frolicking love—seemed to be a giant conspiracy against him alone at that moment.

It had been a while since he had watched a race from the grandstand; he was usually trackside with the other horsemen. He looked around and saw desperation in the faces of men; the arena of horses and carts seemed at that moment to represent greed, lust, desire, and broken dreams. The whole false world was lit up beneath the dark night. Bucky thought about his elimination race coming up at the Coliseum. He had never thrown a race before, but now it seemed like he didn't have a choice. Maybe after this he would tell Bernie that he was done. He wanted no part in any races where he influenced the outcome. He just wasn't about that, after all. As he sat there, he thought about the innocence of the amateur fair circuit he had raced so long ago, where there were no purses or betting allowed. It really was the last time he had truly been happy. Then, he had the friendship of Anna and Cole, and now, he felt cast adrift, never having been in a serious relationship. There were lovers—yes, there were lovers, most of whom Bucky was not so proud of—but nothing like Anna. Besides her, he had never said "I love you" to anyone, nor ever heard it in return. He thought to himself how sad it would be if he died today, because he would die having never been loved. He wondered if it was normal for him never to have experienced an adult relationship, and what it would be like to hit the three-, six-, and nine-month markers. Heck, even a year! A year seemed like a long time to be in a relationship. He wasn't sure at that stage how it went. Did it fire out of the gate and then fizzle or break, or was there more passion you could induce with grand romantic gestures? He couldn't remember much of his parents' relationship, other than it was loving. Carl always fussed about Delores, doing sweet things like making her snacks, and always touching her and trying to be near. Carl was a man who'd truly believed he was the luckiest man in the world.

Bucky took one more look at the obnoxious, driveling couple—*I mean, what do they want, an award?*—and again saw Cole in the man the woman adored, and fought off those pangs of jealousy that ripped him apart. He thought for a minute that maybe he *should* try on Nikki Ivanov or see what else Westing Schmidt had on offer, but instead he let the moment pass, avoided the lounge rats, and went home to his silent apartment, where even the sound of his neighbors fighting would have been a welcome distraction from his solitude.

On the day of the qualifier, Bucky waited in the paddock for Clarence and Carl to arrive with Nitro, but Bernie Katz got there first. He was wearing a white short-sleeve shirt, a tweed duckbill cap, green pleated pants, and a pair of white orthopedic shoes. He squinted through his milky cataracts before he recognized Bucky.

"Oh, hey, kid," Bernie said, "glad I ran into you. Frankie's guys should be pulling up with Whisky Pete any minute now."

"Well, that's what I wanted to talk to you about, Bernie. I don't know about this."

"Why don't you relax? Tell me about this girl you've been seeing back home."

Bucky bit his lip. There was always an element of control he had to retain with Bernie. It could spell big trouble if he lost his temper. "She must be a real dandy."

"Bernie," Bucky said. Just as he was about to pop, two men who looked like they'd never handled a horse came around the corner trying to contain a fussy colt.

"Welcome to the Big C," Bernie said to Frankie Fingers's men Gino and Tony, who acknowledged Bernie but were still having a hard time managing the horse.

Gino, the shorter of the two, had a low forehead, slicked-back hair, and thick eyebrows. His face, looking almost as if it were mashed together, appeared old and tough. He was wearing a black leather jacket, and was trying to block Whisky Pete while Tony tugged the lead. Tony was tall, and bald on top, with a fringe of black hair around his head and a thin, well-groomed beard. He wore a red tracksuit with white stripes down the sides, and had on a gold watch and a silver chain with a crucifix. He was finally able to control the horse by forcing him still with his brute strength, and ultimately staring him down into submission.

"So this is Whisky Pete," Bucky said, sizing up the horse and walking slowly around him. He was brown with a muscular chest and well-defined shoulders and legs. *Good conformation,* Bucky thought, but he wondered how the horse could pass as a long shot.

"Doesn't look like such a dud to me," Bucky said.

"He was good enough to qualify. Let's just say he's the best of the worst," Bernie said. He sidled up to the horse, who watched him timorously through the corner of his eye.

"Okay, well, doesn't matter, I suppose. He looks like he can win, so it'll look believable. Just don't talk to me about it again, okay, Bernie? I'm out."

"We'll see when you're out, kid,"

"Hey, boys, right here in this stall." Bernie pointed Gino and Tony to a stall across from Nitro.

"Call Frankie and let him know that the horse arrived safely," Bernie said to Gino, who must have been the more responsible one and was certainly the more serious looking, as his eyebrows were permanently locked down like a broken drawbridge.

After they dropped off Whisky Pete, Gino and Tony were off. Bucky pulled up a chair and sat outside his own horse's empty stall.

"What are you doing now, kid? Where's Nitro?"

"I'm waiting."

"All right, well, don't mess this up," Bernie said. "I know you know what's at stake."

"Got it, Bernie. Bye," Bucky said, hoping he wouldn't have to see the old man again until he got back to New York, or ever.

Bucky was beginning to get restless, when Clarence and Carl finally arrived in the paddock with Nitro. He was a pure bay without a mark, and he tugged at the lead, tossing his head in agitation as Clarence led him through the paddock and into his stall.

"I know, I know," Clarence said to Bucky, who was watching with raised eyebrows. "You'll see. Get this one tacked up and he's all business."

"I hope so," Bucky said, petting the horse's neck to settle him down.

Carl joined them in the stall, and they sized up Nitro. Clarence ran his hand along the horse's long muscular neck, and Carl gave a few hard pats on the large barrel torso.

"Yep," Carl said. "What we have here is a racehorse."

As Bucky listened to the men's approval of the horse, he couldn't help but think he was cheating them. He had to lose to Whisky Pete or the gangsters could ruin them all. What choice did he have? *If he couldn't win this purse, there would be others,* he thought to himself, trying to justify his actions. *This might even help. This will get everyone off my back. I've already told Bernie that I'm out. After this, things can go back to normal.* He realized he wasn't certain what normal was anymore. *How did I ever get in so deep?* he wondered. *All I ever wanted to do was shoot straight and race horses. Since when did winning become so unimportant? Is that what I'm all about now? Am I becoming my uncle Max? Christ, please don't let me be like my uncle Max.* Almost right when he finished the thought, who strolled into the paddock with a cigarette dangling from his lips?

"What's he doing here?" Bucky sighed and looked at Carl pleadingly.

"He paid for the gas," Clarence said, looking at Max as if he were pathetic.

"I can't come down and watch the biggest race of my nephew's career?"

"Don't worry about him," Carl said. "He'll be sticking to the lower level of the grandstand. Right, Max?"

Max didn't answer.

"I'll be up in the lounge watching with Snooky and Roy," Carl said.

"Roy's here?" Bucky asked with a sudden interest, which made him realize just how high the stakes were, as if he could forget.

"He wants to see how you handle Nitro."

"Great," Bucky said, all too aware of the pressure building on all sides. Roy naturally wanted to see Nitro advance to the Breeders, and the gangsters wanted Bucky to lose. *Where is the middle ground?* Bucky wondered. He seemingly had no way out of this situation, and hated that this loss would put even more pressure on Carl to sign over the farm. The one shining light that Bucky saw was that with Roy, at least there was no threat of violence. With the gangsters, violence was a given, as Bernie had made abundantly clear.

"You know what that means?" Clarence asked.

"What?" Bucky looked at Clarence starkly, knowing he had no idea how much was *really* at stake. He was ready for anything.

"You gotta win, boy."

"Thanks, Clarence. You always provide such great insight."

While they talked more about their racing strategy and plans for afterward, more drivers, trainers, and horses arrived. Preparations were on. The small village of people behind all the excitement guarded their respective horses' conditions like treasured secrets.

"Okay then, Son," Carl said to Bucky before he left, "I'll be watching you from the eye in the sky, so make me proud."

"I'll do my best," Bucky said. He was about to add a caveat in the event he lost, something like, "Looks like a tough field," or "If we don't win tonight, there's always the next race," but he held off and instead just gave Carl a thumbs-up as he left with Max. Clarence stayed with Bucky in the paddock.

Right after Carl and Max got back to the grandstand, Max slunk away to the sports bar on the ground level, and Carl took the escalator up to the lounge. Max sat alone at the bar, drinking straight Jack, making small adjustments to his sideburns and mustache, and looking into the mirror between bottles of booze on the shelf behind the bar. As he looked at his reflection, it was almost as though he was looking at a stranger. With his thumb and index finger, he felt the prickly flap of his chin like a turkey wattle, and looked into his vacant eyes. He felt hollow. He always felt hollow. Max was an amalgam of his different vices—gambling, booze, women—and they had all brought him to his knees in equal measure. Usually around his tenth drink he would get to thinking about his ex-wife. He seemed now to be warding off those pangs of heartache in a liquor burn as he took a shot and then winced for a moment, but he didn't succumb to the small seam, because for now, Max had bigger worries, like the gangsters. This time he was in to them for twenty-five large. To get out of his mess, he'd promised them that Bucky would choke. He had other helpers in the field to assist with the outcome, but knowing his nephew, there were no guarantees. He ordered one more shot and then made his way to another bar, where he recognized George D'Angelo, who was tall and gaunt, with five-o-clock shadow and saggy jowls, drowning in a cheap suit. D'Angelo owned a small stable close to Freedom Raceway. Max tried to sell him on a business idea he had for a new "cutting edge" feed that was sure to trim seconds off their race times.

"Dan Patch feed ain't got nothing on this stuff, George. All I need is a deposit today, and I'll send you your first batch for next Monday."

"No thanks, Maxi."

"Well, how about the races tonight? Who do you like?"

"Well, I like Snow Queen in the first, Highlander in the—"

"Stop right there. I got a line for you on the fourth: my nephew, Bucky Whalen, on Nitro. Make sure you bet on him. Trust me, okay?"

"Okay, Maxi, whatever you say."

"All right, then just pick up my drinks and we'll call it even for the tip," Max said, not waiting for any kind of resistance from George, who'd just unwittingly paid for two quick drinks.

Right when Max turned around, he saw Bernie Katz walk into the bar, followed by Jo Jo and Charlie Baker. When Bernie noticed Max, he strolled over with his men. "Nice to see you, boys. Nice to see you," Max said, shaking hands with Charlie and Jo Jo. "What brings you out to the Big C?"

"Don't play dumb, Maxi," Bernie said. "I'm out here for the same reason you are—to protect my interests."

"Okay, well," Max said, twirling his greasy mustache, "good thing we're on the same side." When this last comment was met with silence, he asked, "We *are* on the same side, aren't we?"

"Let's talk about your nephew."

"He's been looking good lately."

"I guess you could say that he's out here representing Speedway," Bernie said, looking for some kind of reassurance from Max.

"Well, I don't know, boys," Max said, scratching his elbow. He then put his hand behind his neck for a moment, as if he were massaging out a kink, and looked up at the ceiling. "You know how the kid can be. It was hard to get him on board for anything before, and now ..."

"Now what?" Bernie said, inching closer to Max.

"He'll be fine, he'll be fine," Max said, backing up defensively. "I had a talk with him, just like you asked. He seems okay. If not, well, I guess we're just going to have to have another heart-to-heart, isn't that right, boys?" Max said. He then let out a few strained chuckles. He was just about to excuse himself when Frankie "Fingers" Caruso walked into the bar with Gino and Tony.

"Oh, fuck," Bernie said, "it's the Caruso gang."

"Well, I best be on my way," Max said, punching his fist into his palm.

"Not so fast there, Maxi," Bernie said. Charlie put his hand on Max's shoulder to hold him in place.

Noticing the familiar faces, Frankie walked over. His men followed.

"Oh, hey. It's the Big Macher," Frankie Fingers said, laughing with his men. Frankie himself was the scariest-looking of the gangsters. He had a full head of silver hair, but years ago he'd been stabbed in the left eye with a broken beer bottle. After successive surgeries, the best the doctors could do was fix his working blue eye in such a position that it appeared as if it were in a perpetual stare, surrounded by scars. But more important than his deformity were Frankie's fingers. To divert from the horrors of his face, years ago Frankie took up an active ring collection on every finger and both thumbs, so if by chance you were caught staring at his eye, you would quickly glance down at his gold rings. It was the obvious backstory for his moniker, as opposed to, say, Scarface, Volcano Eye, or Freaky Deaky, and was a welcome diversion from his eye, which could hypnotize you if you stared at it too long.

"Hi, Frankie," Bernie said. He stuck out his hand for a shake, where it hung suspended, before he put it in his pocket.

"Let's cut the bullshit, Bernie. It's no secret that you're the man in New York, but you're in Jersey now," Frankie said, lighting a cigarette and blowing the smoke directly into Bernie's face. "We have our own system out here. If you're going to bring your boy out here to race with the men, we expect an even bigger cut. I can influence the entries just as much as you can at Speedway, so it'd be best if we worked together."

"Of course. That's what we're doing, isn't it? Everything is set up," Bernie said.

"The kid went for it?"

"Everything's good, but ..."

"I don't like hearing buts."

"He doesn't listen to anybody. We can't control him. Go on, Maxi, tell him."

At that point Max was trying to peer out the glass window to get a look at the tote board outside. He hadn't been expecting to be brought into the discussion.

"Bucky, my nephew? He's a good man. I taught him how to drive. You lads know that? Shit, it'd be nice to get an ounce of credit once in a while."

"Max," Bernie said, looking at him imploringly.

Frankie put his hand on Max's shoulder and squeezed tightly. "So you talked to him?"

"He'll come around, Frankie. Don't worry about it," Max said.

"And if he doesn't?" Gino asked, looking at Max as if to say, *I am the muscle.*

"I'll be dipped in shit if he doesn't," Max said.

"Forget about it." Frankie called off Gino when he seemed satisfied with Max's assurance.

Max was relieved that the situation was defused for now, but he worried what would happen if Bucky didn't come through. Looking at Gino, his diminutive stature was apparent, but Max had heard enough stories to know that Gino was one to be feared. Gino was the guy who cut off fingers and removed teeth so the corpses couldn't be identified, but worse than that, he preferred to do it while his victims were still alive. They called it the Italian manicure and root canal.

"So you'll have my money after the race?" Frankie said, with his steely eye trained on Max.

"I should."

"He should. He should," Frankie said, looking at his men and shrugging his shoulders. "Maybe he will. Maybe he won't. Maybe I cut off your balls; maybe I rip your nose off your big fat fuckin' face."

Max didn't say anything.

"C'mon, Frankie. He's going to get you your money. We have a good thing here. Let's all play nice," Bernie said.

"Okay, Big Macher. This jerk-off is your responsibility. He fucks up, you sign his death warrant."

Max breathed a sigh of relief.

"Let's go, boys," Frankie said, motioning to Gino and Tony. "Time to hit the windows."

Max watched Frankie and his men leave.

"He's always so pleasant," Max said, when he was sure they were out of earshot.

"Shut up, Max," Bernie said.

"C'mon, Bernie," Max said. Then he looked at Jo Jo and Charlie Baker for support. "Just trying to lighten things up."

Even though Jo Jo and Charlie were buddies with Max, when they were with Bernie, it was clear where their allegiance was. They made their living off the old man so would always fall in line.

"Don't make me look like an asshole," Bernie said. Then he left abruptly, with Charlie and Jo Jo at his heels.

"I won't!" Max called after him, before sidling up to the bar for one more drink.

Carl and Roy Callaghan were watching the races in the dining room with Snooky Goldman, who was the track manager at the Coliseum. Snooky, in his seventies, had a full head of dyed black hair with gray sideburns, wore a mustard-colored cardigan, and was still fit for his age thanks to the five miles he walked on his treadmill every day, which he usually made a point of mentioning. He had his binoculars trained on the third race. Carl was clutching his mutual ticket, trying to will his horse across the line.

"Aw, fuck," Snooky said.

"No sure things, you know that," Carl reminded him.

"But he went off at two to one."

"Doesn't matter what he went off at. It's where he finishes, old-timer."

Both men tore up their tickets and threw the pieces on the table. Roy had won on a horse called the Sultan, of which he was a part owner, so he sat back satisfied.

"I told you guys, but you didn't listen," Roy said, running his hand through his long, curly white hair. He was wearing a white suit, and if it weren't enough that his suit was white and his hair was white, his teeth were *blistering white*. They were convex and oversize. He could have easily gotten work in a toothpaste commercial. He was broad like Cole; in fact, when the two were side by side, their resemblance was striking. The only differences were that Cole still had his golden locks and baby's-ass skin, whereas Roy's cheeks were rouge and he had tiny blood blisters and dry white lips. He also had more years on him, more years of filet mignon and shrimp cocktails—good living, essentially, which came along with the privilege of his wealth and prosperity. He had once owned an automotive parts business called Roy's Carbs. When he sold it, harness racing became his new passion project. Since he had the money to invest in the best of everything, the results paid off quicker than for most. In his first year, he had a Triple Crown winner, who in subsequent years would breed his own offspring of champions. It seemed to Carl that whatever Roy touched turned to gold.

Carl reengaged his cigar, which was lying limply in the ashtray, and tried to avoid eye contact with Roy. There was always an awkward dynamic when Carl was into Roy for money or horses, because they were friends and it seemed to bring every bet or purchase he made into question.

"Nitro's been looking good," Roy said, looking down at his manicured nails, almost as if he were about to blow them dry. For him it was bottom line, and Carl knew it—heads or tails, he was going to win.

"Clarence's been doing good things with him on the farm. He's ready."

"Let's hope so, old boy. A lot riding on that pony."

"Shit, Roy, you guarantee me a winner and I'll buy you a coffee. He's our best chance. Best in the pack. Not only are we going to qualify, but also we're going to win the Breeders."

"From your mouth to God's ears," Roy said.

"What God?" Carl said, unintentionally exposing his true belief, looking for a moment as if he had been stripped of something.

"The racing gods," Roy said. Then he got up to cash his bet. Carl felt relieved, like he'd been holding his breath under water the whole time. Trading horses and bets with Roy had become exhausting. This time it could be checkmate, and they both knew it. But Roy was a friend, and perhaps he would take small increments, maybe garnish wages. Maybe he would even set up a little tax office with a secretary. Didn't it just seem like Carl was always working for Roy in one way or another? The deal was to begin his payments as soon as the horse started earning. If Nitro was a bust, then how else would he pay Roy back? It had happened once before, when Carl seemed to be on the verge of financial ruin, that Roy invited his lawyer to dine with them in the lounge. The lawyer had slyly brought up the discussion about Carl's assets and how certain items might be "reallocated" or "transferred." In that way, the stain of collecting was not on Roy but on his lawyer, whom Roy wasn't shy to use when anyone got in too deep.

When Roy got back to the table, he had just finished counting a wad of bills that he could barely stuff into his pocket. Roy's winnings were enough to pay Carl's farm expenses for a month, maybe more, Carl thought. He couldn't help shaking his head.

Snooky was the first to spot Max strolling into the lounge. He elbowed Carl to bring it to his attention.

"Well, well, well," Max said, making his way over to their table.

"Max," Carl said, "I thought we had a deal. You said you'd stick to the lower level and track apron."

"Ah, Brother," Max said, putting his hand on Carl's shoulder, "how could I miss an opportunity to sit with the greatest minds in the industry?"

"Take a seat, Max," Snooky said. He kicked over the empty chair across from him.

"Well, thank you, Snooky." Max smiled, looking at Carl as if to say, *There you have it.*

"So, Snooky, it's been a long time, hasn't it?"

"Sure has, Max."

"What do you say to giving me another shot here?"

"I don't think so."

"Okay, okay," Max said, raising his hands. "Let's at least not spoil it for the pride of Delaware then—Bucky Whalen. You've heard of him, haven't you?"

"Who do you think entered him?"

"Of course, of course," Max said, his finger to his lips. "Well, how about getting the kid here more often then, like every night? I can talk to him and work something out if you like. He listens to me."

"He listens to Carl, too, Max. I'll just work through him for the time being ... if you don't mind."

"Sure, sure." Max sat back in his chair, somewhat defeated in his effort to create a quick moneymaking scheme.

"Here comes Bucky," Carl said, watching him on the monitor, larger than life, resplendent in his Delaware blues on the giant screen in the infield. From where they were, Bucky looked like something of a fiction to Carl. When he saw his son on the big screen, racing at the sport's greatest venue, he felt like he was watching some kind of movie. *If only his mother could see him now,* he thought to himself, rubbing his eyes.

"Yup, there he is, all right," Roy said. "Let's see what he can do."

"Let's hope he doesn't pooch it too much. I got some pretty good action on it," Max said. Then he took a sip of Carl's drink when he wasn't looking.

By race time, the grandstand was getting restless. Finally, the overweight bugler, who looked like he'd just stepped out of the Civil War, sounded the horn to announce the post parade. During his warm-up scores, Bucky found out right away just what Clarence had been talking about when he said that this horse was "live." He could feel the power on the bit as the sulky surged forward with minimal encouragement.

Bucky looked up at the stands and couldn't believe the enormity of the Coliseum. Made to house forty thousand, the grandstand had massive glass-enclosed levels from where you could look out onto the oval. It was a stadium built to be big, to be the best. It was a one-miler, and there was a large pond with a flower display in the middle. On the backstretch, Bucky felt far away from the fans and stadium, and from life in general. When he came around front to finish his warm-up, he observed the crowd as they observed him. Some chirped at him, and some let him pass, surely saving their heckling for his next time around.

It was the perfect mid-June night, the air still and buggy. The sun and moon could still be seen together in the sky, moving in opposite directions. The track lights were finally beginning to light up the shadows. As Bucky jogged Nitro up to the starting car, he wondered how he would be able to pull this off and still respect himself.

Once all the horses were lined up, they fought to keep up with the white Cadillac before the emphatic call of "*Go!*" crackled from the megaphone mounted on the roof, the gates were pulled back, and the starting car drove off to the side.

"And they're off!" came the track announcer's voice over the grandstand speaker.

Bucky, off the gate with early speed, moved right ahead of Night

Raider, Whisky Pete, and Devil's Advocate, with Mr. Speedy behind. At the first turn, Bucky was still in the lead. Although his focus was on the race, he thought for a fleeting moment about the bad guys. He knew he was supposed to keep a low profile, yet he was defying them by launching Nitro into the lead.

Bucky dropped back after the first half and raced under cover provided by Devil's Advocate in front. Whisky Pete was right beside him. Bucky knew the driver, Stan "the Whip" Webber, who yelled over the sounds of the stampeding horses, "Hey, kid, what the hell do you think you're doing? You know how this one's supposed to go," and then drove past, becoming neck and neck with Devil's Advocate, whose driver, Bucky figured, must have been the other one who had colluded for the race outcome.

Whisky Pete, pulling further away from Nitro on the backstretch, was still tied in front with Devil's Advocate. Bucky, able to hear the horse behind him breathing in his ear, knew he had to get off the rail or he could get pinned in while everyone passed. Going around the final turn, he made his move and raced to the outside. Then when they came around the corner and headed for home, it was Whisky Pete, Devil's Advocate, and Nitro—one, two, three—with Bucky's horse dropping back.

Recalling it later—and Bucky would have his whole life to re-create the race in his mind, which he did—he'd felt Nitro tugging on the bit, asking for more line. His horse had no idea of how he was supposed to finish. Bucky, in the heat of the battle, not wanting to stiff his horse or kowtow to the Caruso gang, had opened up the reserve of strength and speed, and just like that, not thinking about the consequences, he let his horse pass Whisky Pete and Devil's Advocate. The photo finish camera lit them up, and a fraction of a second later, the second-, third-, and fourth-place finishers crossed the line.

Then the track announcer's voice came over the loudspeaker: "We're going up to the booth for a photo finish. Please hang onto your tickets until race results are final."

Bucky drove around impatiently. Certain he'd won, he'd had a quick exchange with Stan Webber as they jogged alongside each other. "You just fucked yourself, kid," Stan said to him, and then drove away. While Bucky jogged Nitro around to cool him off, the reality sank in: Stan was probably right. Then the loudspeaker came back on. "Final results are in for the fourth race. It's Nitro in first, followed by Whisky Pete, and Devil's Advocate in third. Seventeen minutes to post time for the fifth race, which will be the first half of this evening's daily double."

When Bucky arrived in the winner's circle with Clarence, Carl was already there with Snooky, Roy, and a scrum of other people representing the race's sponsor. Bucky was quickly surrounded by people wanting to ask him about the race and the horse, wanting to know who he was and where he had come from that he should sneak a drive in with these top-notch horses and drivers to take his biggest payout yet, both literally and figuratively, as it was made out on a giant cardboard check for fifty thousand dollars. Bucky held it up for the cameras while the vice president of Pan Am Airlines shook his hand and told him, "Was a fine thing you did today, son. A fine thing." Right after that, his beautiful blonde wife gave Bucky a kiss on the cheek, and everyone dispersed. Then, in the track apron, Bucky saw a man staring at him through a clearing. His arms were crossed and he was wearing a dark suit with a silver tie beneath his open trench coat. His left eye, unblinking, was surrounded by scars. If Bucky had to describe what evil incarnate looked like, this man would certainly be close. His focus was so intense that after a while Bucky had to look away. And then, when he realized who it must be and tried to spot him again, Frankie Fingers, like a ghost, had disappeared.

CHAPTER 9

While Clarence and Carl celebrated the win, Bucky knew that for him, it was the beginning of bad things. No way would he escape Bernie and the gangsters unscathed. And it didn't take long to encounter them. Just a few days, in fact, when Bucky decided to go to the one place he shouldn't—Bert's Bar. It was a rainy night. He pulled in at the far end of the parking lot, where he was lucky to find a space, and made a run for the door. Inside, Tombstone Shadow was blaring on the sound system. There were some bearded bikers dancing with their girlfriends on the dance floor. Bucky sat at the bar. The pretty redheaded barmaid, Josie, soon came over.

"Big race tonight?" she asked, putting a beer in front of him.

"Thanks," Bucky said, grateful not just for the beer but also for a friendly voice. "Not tonight. But every night's a big race." Bucky smiled. He couldn't help but look at her tight jeans and her breasts that heaved over her halter top.

"Big shot like you must win a race or two, I imagine?" It had been a while since Bucky had been flirted with. He wasn't sure if that's what was happening.

"I won my last race," he said, "but I wouldn't call this a celebration."

"Oh no? Sounds pretty good to me, sweetie. Maybe you can take me away with all that purse money?" she said, smiling while leaning over on the bar.

"Where'd you like to go?" Bucky asked, knowing he was just

humoring her now, as that was the single purpose of a barmaid, to make her patrons feel happy and loved.

"Anywhere but this dump."

"I wish it could be like that," Bucky said. He pictured for a moment what it might be like to run away with Josie.

"It's busy here tonight," he quickly added, realizing their conversation would soon be over if he didn't do anything to prolong it.

"Yeah. Usually we get a crowd in here when it's not so nice outside. The natives get restless, as they say."

Just as Bucky was searching for something clever to say, she bounced over to the next customer to take his order. Then, while Bucky was looking deep into his drink as if it were the well of all his misfortune, Bernie sat down next to him.

"There ya are, kid," Bernie said. "Was wondering where you disappeared to the last few days. We've missed you."

"Hi, Bernie," Bucky said, looking around to see if Bernie was alone. "It's nice to be missed."

"Isn't it, though?"

Bucky nodded.

"Do you think you'd be missed if we tied your ankles up, weighed you down with a cinder block, and dropped you in the middle of the fuckin' ocean?"

Bucky, taken aback by Bernie's comment, took a deep breath.

"Whatsa matter? You don't like swimming with the fishies?"

Bucky remained silent, calculating what to say next, knowing he was in a bad spot.

"I'll tell you something: you fucked over some important people. Normally ... well, you know me, I'm not the violent type. But these guys want your ass."

"Bernie ..."

"Wait a minute, kid, I'm not done. You knew you were supposed to stiff your horse, and there you were, riding into the fuckin' sunset like you were on Secretariat."

"I can explain."

"Well, go ahead then, explain."

"He just, he was asking for more line, Bernie. I couldn't stop him. He's a winner."

"Well, I'll tell you who didn't win," Bernie said, pointing to the corner table in the back. "Those guys over there."

Bucky looked over at the men. There was Gino, Tony, and Frankie Fingers. Scanning the rest of the room, Bucky also noticed Bernie's guys, Jo Jo and Charlie Baker, who were sitting at the opposite end. If Bucky only had to answer to Bernie's men, he thought that maybe he could talk his way out of it; after all, he knew Jo Jo and Baker, and figured he could probably just offer them money from his next few wins. Looking at the door, Bucky noticed there was an unobstructed path to it. He could run, but even if they didn't catch him, eventually they would.

"All right, then, Bernie," he said. "What do you want me to do? What are they going do to me? I can't see anything being worse than just waiting for it."

"Oh, it will get worse, kid. Believe me. But I'm not the bad guy here. Remember that. I told your uncle to warn you. Probably should have stayed home and learned how to milk cows or something."

"The only thing I've ever wanted to do was be a driver, Bernie. Then I get mixed up with you guys because of Max. I'm just … well, I'm done. It doesn't matter anyway."

With that, Bucky looked across the room. He saw the Caruso gang watching him from their corner, and Jo Jo and Charlie Baker watching him from the other corner. When Bucky got up, all of them stood up.

"See you around, kid."

"Yeah, you too, Bernie," Bucky said. Instead of running for the door, he walked to it slowly, with his shoulders slumped and his eyes downcast, like a prisoner walking from his cell to the electric chair. When he opened up the door, the rain was still heavy. He watched for a minute as the cars drove by with their windshield wipers on. He wished he were in any one of those passing cars. He thought about Anna and Cole, his father and Clarence, his mother. Having no idea what was going to happen to him, he didn't wish to cause anybody pain if he were to die on this rainy evening.

He wasn't more than ten feet from the bar when he heard a voice call out to him above the rain.

"Remember me? Well, I know you. Saw you that day in the winner's circle when you were supposed to lose. You're that fuckhead that cost me a trip to the Breeders. My name is Frankie Caruso, and right now, I'm your worst nightmare."

Bucky turned around. Sure enough, it was the man with the scar, standing beneath the awning. He recognized him, all right. How could he forget that eye socket that looked like it'd been clawed away by feral cats?

Frankie's men were soon behind him, and then Bernie and his men came out. They were all crammed beneath the awning. Frankie said something in Italian to Gino, who then walked up to Bucky and grabbed him by the collar. He took him around back. The others followed. Frankie's other helper, Tony, got into the black Lincoln, turned on the headlights, and then got back out.

Bucky was past the point of running away or putting up a fight. He knew he was outnumbered, and even if he did manage to get in any punches or kicks, it would probably cause even greater retribution. He was resigned to his fate.

"Okay, guys, do your worst," Bucky said, holding up his hands and spinning around as if to model the body that was about to be seriously abused. "I fucked up. I know that. Do what you have to do. Hopefully, it will be enough and we can call it even, and then just hop along on our merry ways."

Frankie was the first to step onto the stage, which was lit up by the car's headlights. He circled Bucky a few times, rolling up his sleeves.

"You think this is a game or something?"

Bucky didn't say anything; his eyes were closed.

"I've killed shitheads like you before for much less money," Frankie said. He stood directly in front of Bucky. Just as Bucky thought about saying something, he felt the back of Frankie's ringed hand across his face. Bucky stood tall. The next blow was to his stomach. It made Bucky double over. After catching his wind, he came up for air. He looked around for Frankie, expecting more punishment, but he had backed away. *Perhaps it's over,* Bucky thought, knowing that wasn't really possible—they hadn't inflicted nearly enough pain. It wasn't until Frankie lit a cigarette that Bucky noticed he was sitting in the passenger seat of the car, watching as if he were enjoying a play.

Next up was Gino, who stepped away from the men. *So that's how it's going to be,* Bucky thought to himself. *Everyone's going to take a turn.* Gino wasn't as theatrical as Frankie; he went right into it and pounced on Bucky like a wild animal. He swung at him with lefts and rights, uppercuts, and an elbow strike that caught Bucky flush on the chin, knocking him down to the ground. After blacking out for a few moments, Bucky writhed around, struggling to wipe away the rain and blood that blurred his vision.

Gino stopped to catch his breath. Tony walked up to him, and asked politely, "Mind if I take over?"

"Of course you can, Tony, but save some for me. I'm just getting started," Gino said. Both men gave a hearty laugh. Tony pulled out a telescopic truncheon from inside his coat. With a flick of his wrist, it snapped into place. He swung ferociously at Bucky's torso, the cracks clearly distinguishable over the thunder. Bucky rolled into a puddle, and then Tony dragged him out by his leg, lifted him up by his shirt, and delivered a few more blows to his face. After the Italians were done, Jo Jo and Charlie Baker took a few shots as well.

When everyone seemed to be done, Bucky crawled to his knees. By this point, he couldn't tell if the last blow had been delivered minutes or hours ago. He was clinging to his very survival. His instinct told him to get up and try to get help from the bar. Before he could, Bernie walked over to Bucky, who made it up on all fours, and delivered one last kick to his face. Then Bernie looked at Frankie in the car and nodded. It wasn't the strongest kick—after all, Bernie was an old man—but it did make Bucky crumple back down into the muddy parking lot.

Finally, the men got into their cars and left. Looking up from one eye, Bucky was relieved to see that the men were gone; the ordeal was over. He felt his pocket for his cell phone but remembered he'd left it at home. He pictured the device mocking him, safely cradled in the charger on his bedroom dresser.

He heard a loud crash of thunder and tried to feel his body parts to see if anything was broken, but he couldn't move. Seeing a woman leaving and running to her car, he tried to call out, but he couldn't speak. There were a few more people after that who went into or came out of the bar, but the same thing happened, so instead of trying to call out for help again, Bucky let the numbness take over his body and faded away into darkness.

Two men with long hair, wearing cowboy boots and jean jackets, came over. Bucky felt one of them poke him with his boot. He jerked back into consciousness, the pain in his ribs, legs, and arms so intense he almost passed out again. For a moment, he didn't know where he was or what had happened to him. After a bit of compromising, the two men picked Bucky up by the armpits and dragged him over to their pickup truck. Rather than put him in the back of the cab and get blood and mud all over the upholstery, they dropped him in the exposed back, which contained a few pieces of scrap wood, random tools, and bits of trash like empty coffee cups and fast-food wrappers. Bucky rolled around violently as they drove him to the hospital. After dropping him in front of the emergency entrance, they took off.

It was the kind of emergency room that was a revolving door for local drunkards, so the first few people walked right past him, one even stepping right over him. A police officer who was escorting one such derelict finally took notice and sent a paramedic out right away. Eventually, Bucky was admitted and given a private room on the third floor.

In the morning, the sun streamed through the large open window, accentuating the sterile room and the crisp white sheets that had been neatly tucked around Bucky. He was hooked up to an IV. The room was silent, almost heavenly. His dirty clothes were in a neat pile on a chair by the door, and he lay sedately, as clean and dignified as possible.

When Bucky finally started coming to, the first face he saw in his groggy, ethereal state was Max's. Bucky's vision was blurred. He needed to blink a few times before he could make out the face of his uncle. Max's face seemed stretched and gigantic, almost as if Bucky were looking at it through a peephole.

Bucky still had no idea what was going on. Max started speaking at what seemed like just inches in front of his face.

"You got the snot kicked out of you, kid."

Bucky didn't respond. His face was covered in dressings. There were areas where blood and pus had seeped right through and dried.

"Can you hear me?" Max said. Bucky looked on vacantly. "Bernie told me. I got over here as fast as I could. Had to go to three hospitals."

"Ugh." Bucky moaned incoherently.

"So you *can* hear me?" Max said, leaning in closer. "Well, that's good, 'cause ... well, what I wanted to say was ... I wanted to say I'm sorry if you think I brought this upon you in any way. Frankie, Bernie, those guys are animals. And what I also wanted to say"—Max leaned back and looked over his shoulder—"was that I was hoping we could keep this between us. I mean, obviously you're a mess, a complete disaster, but what I think we should keep quiet is *why this happened.* You follow?"

Even though Bucky was out of it, he still understood why Max was there. Any kindness in the gesture of Max's showing up was lost on Bucky.

"Maybe we can say it was over a dolly, or you just got mugged ... or something?" Max said, looking at Bucky as if he expected an answer. "Maybe we just say you don't remember nothin'," Max said. Then he stood up as the pale blonde nurse entered with a young, handsome doctor who had great layered hair, perfect teeth, and an all-American cleft chin.

"Here he is," the nurse said, presenting what was left of Bucky as if he were a stolen automobile recovered in a chop shop.

Max looked at the doctor and was about to light a cigarette.

"You can't smoke in here, Mr. Whalen," the nurse said to Max. Before the doctor introduced himself, he pulled Bucky's chart and stood silent and erect as he observed it. When the doctor finally looked up, Bucky couldn't help but notice that his physician was younger than he—that his life was potentially in the hands of someone his junior. Bucky also thought for a moment that it was strange how he could already be so accomplished, how in the same span of time that he had spent learning how to drive horses and getting his heart broken, other people had gone to medical school, become lawyers, started construction companies, or had families. And now here he was, with his future, and maybe even his life on the line.

"I'm Doctor Green," the doctor finally said, extending his hand to Max.

"I'm his uncle," Max said, stepping forward to shake it.

"Well, your nephew, he got beat up pretty bad. Someone dropped him in front of the emergency entrance, and it's a good thing. He lost a lot of blood and very well could have died last night."

"Is he going to be all right?"

"Let's take a look here," the doctor said, drawing a deep breath as he started reading off the clipboard. "Dislocated left shoulder, broken nose, two cracked ribs, concussion. He's in pretty rough shape. Not to mention the multiple lacerations and contusions."

"What's a contusion?" Max asked. "He's got cancer too?"

"Fancy word for bruise," the doctor said proudly, as if he could really identify with the layman. "All things considered, he got lucky. He'll need a lot of rest, but he'll be all right. What does he do for a living?"

"He's a harness racer."

"What exactly is that?"

"It's like horse racing, but with a cart behind it. Like a chariot."

"Oh yes, of course. Gonna be a while before he can do that again."

Bucky had clearly heard the doctor's last comment; you could see it in his eyes, which looked like two deep pits with no way out. It was no longer as if Bucky had cheated death, but as if he were living dead. If he had been on life support, he surely would have tried to reach over and pull the plug himself.

"We're going to need to keep him here for a while. After that, I'll give you the name of a physiotherapist. I'd suggest a daily regimen until he regains his strength and flexibility."

"Thanks, Doc," Max said.

"See you soon," the doctor said to Bucky, forcing a reassuring smile on his thin lips.

"He's going to be just fine," the nurse said. She smiled and then followed the doctor as he whirled around and rushed out the door.

While Bucky struggled to absorb the news, he wriggled his legs around in the tight blanket and began trying to break free with his arms.

"We gotta talk about that race," Max said, clasping the handrail with his dirty hands.

"Mm-hmm."

"I know it's hard for you kid, but this isn't the end. In fact, it's just the beginning—Frankie's coming after the farm. Your dad, Clarence … no one's safe. That's why—well, I'm going to make myself scarce for a while."

"Tay-tay-take me home," Bucky managed to mutter.

"Smart." Max nodded. "We keep you here, you're a sitting duck. Can you sit up?"

Bucky, letting out a moan, sat up and pulled all the tubes off his body like he was stripping away leeches.

"Attaboy. Good, good," Max encouraged him. Then he walked over to the door and pulled in a wheelchair that had been sitting just outside. "Take a seat and I'll wheel you on out of here. No one will even know."

Max wheeled Bucky out in the hall and past a man lying on a gurney. The nurses buzzed around the nursing station, and two orderlies walked by, casually joking about a recent double date they'd been on. Max and Bucky made it to the elevator without being noticed. When they got outside, Bucky winced when the bright sun hit his face. When he looked around, it seemed so normal that people were dawdling about. Some sat on benches or in their wheelchairs, and the hospital workers were smoking and chitchatting on their breaks. The day itself had turned into a beautiful one. There were rows of geraniums and daffodils planted outside the main door, and there was an ice-cream truck parked across the street.

Max wheeled Bucky around to where his car was parked, cleared away the mess of junk in his back seat, lifted his nephew's limp body, and put him in the car. As they drove along, Bucky leaned his head on the window. He looked out at the tenements and trees as they rushed by while Max continued talking.

"We gotta make this right somehow with Frankie," Max said, his conniving eyes looking at Bucky in the rearview mirror.

"Maybe when you're back racing you can just ... just do what they say for a while, you know. That wouldn't be so bad, would it?"

Bucky didn't say anything.

"Just give them a chance to make back their money, and then move on. Maybe I can help get you more races in Jersey, you know. I'm a friend of Snooky. Christ, you'd think by now he owes me a favor or two."

"Max," Bucky said, barely above a whisper.

"A few more races. That's all it would take."

"Max."

"I don't even know what the hell I'm going to do. They lay the beatdown on you and haven't even gotten to me yet. Fuck, it's going to be worse for me. Much worse. And I already owed them money."

"Max!"

"What is it, kid? Calm down. Don't get excited; no sudden movements. Not in your condition."

"Just shut up, okay? I don't want to hear your voice."

Max took a deep breath. "Fair enough," he said. They drove the rest of the way in silence.

When they got to Bucky's apartment, Max carried him up the

two flights of stairs. Once they were inside, he put him down on the living room sofa.

"You going to be okay here?" Max said, looking around. Then he walked over and closed the curtains.

"Just leave."

"Okay, well, here you go, kid. Here's a few bucks for groceries, and some Tylenols if you need them," Max said, peeling off some bills from his greasy wad and throwing them down on the coffee table. "Call me if you need me," he said. Then he left, most likely believing he had done his best for Bucky and that it was no longer his responsibility.

Bucky closed his eyes. He was relieved to be home, no longer having to rely on Max. But soon the reality of the situation set in. He could barely walk and was in no condition to care for himself. He thought about calling the farm but was worried he'd have to explain the situation. Realizing the danger to Carl and Clarence, he looked around the room for the cordless telephone, and noticed it on the window ledge behind the couch. It was just out of his reach. With his first twist and stretch, he almost had it; was just inches away from the base. On his second attempt, he could feel it with the tip of his finger. And then on the third stretch, he threw his body into it. Just as he was about to grip the receiver, he fell from the couch and let out a mighty wail. The phone ended up on the floor, now completely out of reach. After writhing and wriggling to try to get to it, Bucky finally passed out to the sound of what he was sure could be used as a cruel form of torture for POWs: "This is the operator. The number you have dialed is out of service. Please check your number or try your call again. This is a recording ... *Beep, beep, beep* ... This is the operator. The number you have dialed is out of service. Please check your number or try your call again. This is a recording ... *Beep, beep, beep* ... This is the operator. The number you have dialed is out of service. Please check your number or try your call again. This is a recording ..."

CHAPTER 10

"Hello?" Anna said, pushing Bucky's front door open and looking around the dark apartment. "Anybody home?" she asked, entering with trepidation, feeling like a burglar as she took her first few steps inside. She thought for a moment that the apartment had been deserted. It was musty and smelled of stale cigarettes. There were dishes stacked up in the kitchen sink and empty beer bottles on the counter. She looked in the bedroom. No sign of Bucky. Finally, when she went back into the family room, she saw his legs poking out from one side of the coffee table. Bucky was passed out on the floor.

"Bucky!" Anna said, aghast. Then she hung up the phone just out of Bucky's reach, and kneeled by his side.

"Bucky!" she said again, this time shaking him. Finally stirring, Bucky squinted to block out a beam of light shining directly in his eyes.

"Anna?" Bucky said with a cracked voice, as if he were still in a dream. He licked his dry lips and then leaned over and coughed up some blood.

"Oh my God, Bucky. What's happened to you?"

"Wh-what are you doing here?" Bucky said, still trying to process the situation as he came to. Then he used the coffee table to get up, like a boxer climbing the ropes, and plopped into the armchair. When he landed, a dribble of blood ran down his chin.

Anna opened the drapes and let the afternoon sun pour through. Bucky squinted again as if he were a vampire exposed to light. Anna cranked the small handle to open up the window, allowing a breeze to circulate throughout the room.

"I tried calling, and got worried when I couldn't get through—with good reason, I guess. So I drove up to see you … and to see some friends in the city," Anna said, catching herself, having given Bucky just a little too much.

"What day is it?"

"Thursday."

"Fuuuuck," Bucky said, bracing his ribs.

"How long have you been out for?"

"I don't know, but I have to call the farm," Bucky said, struggling to get up before Anna rushed over.

"Just sit for a minute. What happened?" she said, forcing him back down.

"Let me call first, and then I'll explain everything."

"You look terrible."

"Get me the phone."

"Here," Anna said, handing him the phone.

Anna tossed a pair of Bucky's boxer shorts out of the way and sat on the couch while Bucky dialed the farm. She couldn't believe that he actually lived like this. On the side table next to the recliner was an empty plate with spent ketchup and mustard globs, and in a corner was a small stack of empty pizza boxes.

"No answer," he said.

"Does your dad have a cell phone?"

"No, he's a holdout. Says he's got everything he needs. Doesn't need any hi-tech gadgets."

"One of those. And Clarence?"

"Clarence is even more old-school."

"Can you call Max?"

"Yeah, right. Who do you think's responsible for all this?"

"I guess I'm not surprised."

"What are you doing here, Anna? For real?"

"I just …" Anna hesitated. Should she open up about how she

couldn't stop thinking about him? Should she tell him that lately she'd been wondering how things might be now if she'd never married Cole? Maybe she could move to New York and the two of them could start over—maybe move up to Westchester. She looked at Bucky. He had two black eyes, and all over his face were dressings stuck to his face like giant bits of toilet paper after a horrific shaving accident.

"I was worried," Anna said.

"I'm all right. Look at me. I'm sure I look great,"

"You poor dear. Have you seen yourself?"

"No. Not yet. There's a mirror on my dresser in the bedroom. Would you mind?"

"Are you sure? Might be a good idea just to wait a day or two."

"I'm going to have to face myself eventually," Bucky said, knowing all too well the truth of his words.

When Anna returned, she was holding an antique silver hand mirror, which she gave to Bucky, who cradled it in his lap.

"This was my mother's," he said, running his fingers over the intricate design. It was the only real thing he had of hers besides the infamous photo of *The Kiss*, where she appeared young and beautiful.

Before he looked in the mirror, he braced for how bad his face could be. Would the damage be permanent? Would he have to come up with his own accoutrement like Frankie Fingers to deflect attention from his hideous face? Is this what it would feel like to be a burn victim or a leper? Finally, he flipped the mirror around and held it directly in front of his face. He slowly peeled off his dirty dressings to reveal sewn-up lacerations, the stitches looking like tiny rows of barbed wire fences. There were purples, blues, and reds in different patchworks of colors, marking a boot mark here, a fist there, and road rash for those instances when he'd fallen face-first into the ground. He even noticed something that looked remotely like an *F*, and wondered if it was an impression from one of Frankie's rings.

After he was through with his inspection, Anna took the mirror away. Bucky could tell she was waiting for him to say something, to show some sort of reaction to the carnage that was his face.

"Not as pretty as I used to be," he said, looking back at Anna, who'd never seemed more perfect. *What this must look like to her,* he thought. At first he was making this triumphant move to New York, and now had fallen down hard. And it wasn't only the physical pain Bucky now endured—like the spot on his lower midsection where he recalled an exceptional kick, or his throbbing nose, where he remembered the crack and then the taste of blood as it ran down his throat. He also remembered the emotional pain he'd tried to leave behind in Delaware. For here was Anna, ever present, her hips just as sweet and tight in blue jeans. It seemed that every time he tried to forget Anna, she would reappear—and now this, like God and the angels in heaven had sent this deliverance. Sure, she was here because she cared, because she was a friend, but maybe there was something more. The one way to be sure was to test her, but Bucky was in no shape to do so. He was used to handling the rejections, but not this time. If before Anna thought he had something to offer, that there was at least hope, that it was still not too late for him to miraculously bloom into the man she knew he could become, then now the reality set in. He felt it was so obvious that Anna could see it as well. This wasn't your ordinary, run-of-the-mill broken man; this was Humpty Dumpty who'd fallen off the wall. Every bone in Bucky's body felt like peanut brittle. *That damn truncheon,* he remembered in a flash, able to hear the sound of the small metal appendage snapping into place.

"I got into it with some bad people, Anna," Bucky said. "They wanted me to fix a race to get Max out of trouble, so I did. Well, I didn't. That's the problem. They wanted me to lose, but when I saw daylight ahead, my instinct set in. It's almost like I've turned into my uncle. Oh, fuck, I'm a younger version of Max," Bucky said. He sat there stunned for a moment.

"But you didn't do it, right?"

"Right. I didn't."

"So you didn't do anything wrong."

"Maybe in the eyes of the law, but not in their eyes."

"How much worse can it get?"

"They want to kill me, Anna. First they want money, and then they want to kill me."

"There's gotta be some way out of this."

"You've got to take me to the farm."

"Whatever you want, Bucky," Anna said. She got up to sit on the edge of the recliner, and ran her hand through his hair. When she did this, Bucky's scalp tingled, and goose bumps ran up and down his spine. His whole body shivered, as the tenderness of Anna's touch had awakened a wellspring of sensation. For Bucky, having Anna this close was almost worth having gotten beaten up. As she sat there, slightly elevated on the arm of the chair, he could smell her hair and see the edge of her breast between the buttons on her shirt. Bucky sat there content as a lapdog getting stroked and coddled. When Anna stopped caressing his hair, Bucky looked up as she moved closer. While they stared deep into each other's eyes, Anna's fleck of iris like a sliver of pie for kings or Lilliputians, Bucky could feel her warmth. He was overcome with emotion as she leaned closer still, and then their lips connected for the first time since Anna had come home from college.

At first Bucky thought that Anna had made a mistake, but the kiss soon deepened. She framed his face with her hands and kissed him with even more intent. It was the same kiss that Bucky remembered after all these years: strawberry lip gloss and spearmint breath rushing through his window like a spring shower. At first their tongues just glanced each other's in their mouths, as if they were exploring the same dark caverns of their youths, but then after they'd become reacquainted, they lashed at each other with more ferocity. Bucky tried to wrap his arms around her, but it was too painful. He wanted more—he always wanted more from Anna. Suddenly she pulled away.

"It's nice to see you," Bucky said softly in the awkward silence that followed their kiss.

Anna got up quickly from the recliner.

"I shouldn't have done that."

"*We* shouldn't have done that," Bucky corrected her, as if he'd really had a say in what had just happened.

"We're not kids anymore," Anna said, pacing around with her hand on her mouth.

"I stopped being a kid before I even became one."

"Cole. I'm married to Cole. I love Cole."

"Are you trying to convince yourself, or me?"

Anna didn't answer.

Bucky watched as her guilt swelled. He wondered how to parlay this sudden change of fortune into something greater. Although he did feel guilty betraying Cole, it was nowhere near the same amount of guilt that seemed to envelop Anna. For him, that's just how things were with Cole. After all, he didn't recall seeing any torment on Cole's face at their wedding. In fact, it was unadulterated joy.

While Anna continued pacing around, Bucky couldn't help but revisit the past. He remembered that day at Anna's parents' vacation home in Rehoboth Beach when Cole and Anna had gotten married.

It was a perfect summer day—and why not? Everything else seemed perfect for the couple—Bucky recalled. He pulled up to the large Victorian-style cottage with Carl and Clarence. Bucky hadn't been there for years, but every time he saw it as a kid, he remembered the injustice that the Millers' summerhouse was bigger and nicer than his house back home.

Carl, Clarence, and Bucky walked by the tent that had been set up for dinner and dancing. As they neared the house, Carl looked back at Bucky.

"You ready for this?"

"Ready as I'll ever be," Bucky said, clutching his throat for a moment as if to relieve the noose that was tightening around it.

Clarence opened the screen door for Bucky, and then walked in after him and Carl.

Inside, the house was buzzing with activity. The caterers were all fighting for each other's attention above the clamor, and both sides of the wedding parties could be seen going in and out of the many rooms. The house brought back a flood of memories for Bucky. Not much had changed inside. There were white beadboard walls, and a large papier-mâché starfish above the mantel. There were nautical-themed portraits from the weekend artists' market, and the furniture was made to look worn and old.

Bucky remembered running through the house with Anna and Cole on a sleepover the summer they'd met. Anna's parents had gone out for dinner, and the three of them were playing hide-and-go-seek in the dark. He could still remember the taste of her salty lips when he'd found her hiding beneath the center island in the kitchen and planted one on her before she could object. He then screamed, "Gotcha!" and together they went scouring the house to find Cole.

Carl, Clarence, and Bucky stood just inside the entrance, careful not to get in anyone's way. Suddenly, Anna's mom, Judith, appeared out of nowhere and stood directly in front of them in her white dress with glittery sequins, just as bejeweled as ever.

"How nice that you could make it," she said. She leaned into Carl and kissed the air on both sides of his face, making a *mwah* sound, feigning affection. She looked at Bucky and forced a smile, but she didn't even acknowledge Clarence.

"Wouldn't have missed it for the world," Carl said, smiling politely at Judith, trying to act proper.

"It's going to be quite the reception. As you can see, we hired the best party planners in the Northeast. And the band will be playing as long as you people keep on dancing."

When she said "you people," she looked directly at Bucky and Clarence and then quickly looked away.

"I'd best get back to it," Judith said, standing with her hands on her hips. "Carl, there's a bar set up just in front of the house. You'll find your brother there. And, Bucky, your pal is upstairs. Why don't you go on up and see him?"

With that, she did an about-face and was right back into the fray, pointing fingers and calling out directions to the workers, whom she berated.

"All right, then," Carl said, grabbing Clarence's arm, "let's go to the bar. Bucky, you heard Judith: go catch up with Cole. See you out there; we'll save you a seat."

Bucky made his way down the hall, stopping to look at some of the framed pictures. There was one of him, Cole, and Anna, smiling, arm in arm, taken on the boardwalk. Cole and Bucky both had their shirts off, and Anna was in a pink bathing suit with her braided hair resting like a snake on her shoulder.

Bucky walked up the creaky stairs, somehow remembering the creakiest of the creaky steps when he stepped on it, as it had given him away many a time during those games of hide-and-go-seek. After walking into a couple of wrong rooms where the bridal party was getting ready, he was pointed to the room at the end of the hall that had been designated for the groom. Bucky knocked lightly on the door and walked in before Cole had the chance to answer.

"Bucky!" Cole said. The two men hugged.

When they pulled back, Bucky held Cole by both sides of his lapel and said, "Very sharp, old man, very sharp indeed." It wasn't often that Cole got dressed up. To see him in a tuxedo with a white boutonniere was quite the contrast from his regular farm clothes.

"Thanks, Buck. I'm glad you came."

"Me too," Bucky said, feeling genuinely happy for Cole in that moment, happy as if it was the wedding of his best friend to any other woman in the world, not the only one he believed he could ever truly love.

"Well, I didn't know if you were coming. Otherwise, you would have been my best man, hands down. It's not too late, you know."

"That's okay. I don't deserve it," Bucky said, because after Anna had broken the news about their engagement to him, he'd gone incommunicado for months, trying to accept it.

"Don't be crazy. My dad thought it would be nice to ask my first cousin from Chicago. I'd be happy to yank him; he used to give me wedgies all the time when we were kids."

"No, really, Cole, it's okay. Thanks. I'm happy to sit and watch with my dad and Clarence."

"Your uncle's here too, you know," Cole said, pulling back the curtain to reveal not just the magnificent view of the ocean but also a full view of the front yard, where the bar was set up in front of the wraparound porch, the chairs for the ceremony lined neatly on the lawn. Bucky noticed Max talking with Carl and Clarence, a drink in each hand.

"Oh yes, Max. Where there's free booze, there's good ol' Uncle Max."

"Speaking of which," Cole said, walking over to the glass table where there was a bottle of scotch and six tumblers on a silver platter, "I think it's only tradition to have a drink with the groom before he walks the plank, no?"

"Very well, then," Bucky said, accepting the drink. Then he made a toast. "To my two best friends. Wishing you a lifetime of happiness together."

"Hear, hear!" Cole said. They clinked glasses and shot the scotch.

"So … you're ready to do this?" Bucky said after they'd both recovered from the drink.

"Ready as I'll ever be."

"Sure you're prepared to take on Judith?"

"Oh, Christ. I never even thought about that, Buck," Cole said. They both laughed. "Truth is, she's not so bad. You just gotta stay out of her way when she's on the warpath, which is often."

"She always liked you better," Bucky said.

"I guess I'm just less of a prick than you."

"Yeah, you're probably right."

"Probably?"

"She never got over the time I hawked one of her precious candlesticks. Anna said it'd be okay, and it paid for a whole weekend of beer for us. Remember that?" Bucky said.

"Yes, I remember. I think about it every time I go over to their place and see that one lonely candlestick. I think she puts it out on purpose, as a reminder."

"Well, your problem now ... till death do you part," Bucky said and looked out the window. "Looks like it's starting to fill up out there."

"Any minute now the ushers are going to corral everyone over to be seated and then come up here for one last hoorah."

"You got a dancer hiding in that closet?" Bucky asked, nodding to what had once been one of his many hiding spots in the house.

"No." Cole laughed. "Just a pep talk, I guess ... and another shot. Make sure I don't skip out the back door and get the next flight out."

"Don't see why you would," Bucky said, wanting to keep things light but thinking to himself that he would do anything to be in the same position as Cole right now.

"Just nerves."

"Well, calm down. You're going to be just fine."

"Thanks, Buck. I knew you were going to come, so I got you this," Cole said. He turned around to retrieve something from a bag, and then he handed Bucky a silver hip flask with his name engraved in the middle.

"Bucky Whalen," Bucky said, admiring the engraving.

"Just a little something. You're my best friend—always have been."

"You too," Bucky said, thinking to himself how often he had betrayed Cole just in his thoughts, yet it had only come to the surface on a few occasions—with Anna, of course, at the center of the conflict.

Before the two men had time to say anything else, the door burst open. The groomsmen jostled their way in and surrounded Cole. Bucky was happy with this, as it provided an easy escape. And since Cole had said his piece, and Bucky his—almost—there was nothing left to say.

"Good luck, Cole," Bucky shouted over the scrum of men, giving him a wave. "See you down there."

"Thanks, Buck!" Cole said, too absorbed already with his groomsmen fawning all over him to make a plea for him to stay.

When Bucky walked back down the stairs, he thought to himself how easy it seemed for Cole. True, they were best friends—at least in theory—but Cole never seemed to understand how his and Anna's relationship had affected him. And if he did, he certainly never showed it. Bucky supposed that was Anna's department, while Cole enjoyed the spoils of her love. Even though they'd had a warm exchange not minutes earlier, for Bucky, it never took much to swing from friendship back to disdain for Cole, when it came to Anna.

As Bucky walked back through the kitchen, he noticed the house had emptied, except for the workers who were putting food in the oven and taking things out of the fridge. Since Cole was still upstairs, he knew the ceremony hadn't started, but when he looked outside, he noticed that everyone had taken their seats. He quickly rushed outside and looked around until Carl finally spotted him and raised his hand. They had saved a chair for him on the aisle of the third row. Sitting beside him was Max. When Bucky sat down, Max put his fat hand with dirty fingernails on Bucky's knee. Bucky took one look at it and then placed it back in his uncle's lap.

"Nice to see you, kid," Max whispered in his husky voice.

"Not now, Max," Bucky said, looking him square in the eyes as a clear sign. Before Max could say anything else, the string quartet began playing the Wedding March. As everyone began looking around for signs of the wedding party, the setting couldn't have been any more beautiful. The heat of midday had begun to wane, and the ocean was glinting against the setting sun.

Bucky didn't know the first couple down the aisle. Then came the bridesmaids, paired up with the groomsmen, the latter of whom he recognized from upstairs. Bucky knew they were getting closer to the real show—Anna—when Judith and her husband, Walter, a retired financier, who was spindly, slightly hunchbacked, and a good twenty years older than Judith, walked down the plush red carpet. Then Cole's short and stout mom, Mary-Ellen, walked down the aisle with Roy, who was beaming and waving to the guests. Soon after the wedding music stopped, gasps and whispers could be heard when Anna was spotted at the end of the procession. After the dramatic pause, the music started up again, and Anna began her slow, calculated steps down the aisle. After bobbing his head up and down, Bucky leaned out in the aisle and caught his first glimpse of Anna. She looked beautiful in her white dress with its intricate lace sleeves, and a long train that followed ten feet behind her. Bucky's favorite thing, though—and he'd only noticed it for a split second when she gave her dress a quick lift—were her white cowboy boots. Sure, Judith probably had forced her to wear the magazine cutout dress, but Bucky knew somehow that the cowboy boots were nonnegotiable.

When they were a few feet from the altar, which was covered by an elaborate arch decorated in boughs of white roses and exotic vines, Anna's father took her arm and they walked the last few paces together. Bucky didn't hear the couple's vows or what the priest said, or any other voices at all. There was a ringing in his ears, a tinnitus, like he had been kicked in the head while shoeing a horse. Bucky thought for a moment that he might pass out as he watched Cole lift Anna's veil. Then he lip-read the only real important words, "I do," spoken by both of them as they stood staring deep into each other's eyes, oblivious that there were two hundred people watching. Bucky had to turn away while their first kiss as a married couple seemed to last an eternity.

CHAPTER *11*

"So what are we going to do about these fuckers?" Frankie said to Gino and Tony, who sat around playing cards in their ramshackle clubhouse at Pistol Farms in Secaucus, New Jersey.

It was on a chewed-up piece of land in the armpit of the United States. At one time, pigs were raised there, and then it became a scrap yard, and then a target range, and soon after that it was abandoned. Set back from the road, it was hidden by trees, and behind it there was a rickety barn where Gino and Tony honed their trade. It was the perfect hideout with just the bare minimum to keep a horse or two, set up to be plugged into the New York and New Jersey racing scenes.

"I can put the kid on ice, boss," Gino said.

"Maybe a manicure and a trip to the dentist," Tony added.

"No, no, no. You guys aren't thinking straight. We need to think about our bottom line. If I wanted the kid dead, he'd be dead already—like that," Frankie said, snapping his fingers.

"We gotta find Max," Gino said.

"Fuckin' dirtbag," Tony said, throwing his cards on the table. "I'll find him, and I'll string him up by his gonads. That would be good, right, boss? Send a message that you don't mess with the Caruso gang."

"Tony, would you just shut the fuck up? Everything that comes out of your mouth is pure nonsense. You got no critical-thinking skills. Go on, Gino."

"Well, I have it on good authority that he owns a third of their farm, along with the father and the kid."

"I like where you're going with this," Frankie said, rubbing his hands together.

"We find him. We get him to sign over his deed. Then we make an appointment for him to meet with the Three Wise Men and Mother Mary."

Frankie nodded. Tony pulled out the crucifix pendant from his neckline, kissed it, and then crossed himself.

"What about the old man, Carl?"

"Their farm is in Harrington, Delaware," Gino said.

"Delaware, huh? You don't say. I hear it's a nice drive down there," Frankie said.

"I know a place in Wilmington where they got a great calzone," Tony added.

"Sometimes I don't know about you," Frankie said. Then he looked at Gino. "Can you believe this fucking guy? It's like his mom dropped him on the head when he was a baby."

"I can take the idiot with me, boss. I'll put a call into Charlie Baker to see if he knows where Max is."

"Charlie Baker?" Frankie said, surprised that Gino should have his own connections outside of his sphere of influence.

"I hear they're tight, boss," Gino said.

"Call him then. See what he knows," Frankie ordered.

Gino pushed his chair out with his legs, took his cell phone from his pocket, and flipped it open. Frankie and Tony watched while he dialed. After four rings, Charlie answered. Gino got up from his chair to talk to him.

"Charlie, it's Gino."

Both Frankie and Tony strained to hear, while Gino paced around seeking some modicum of privacy.

"I'm looking for Max," Gino said. "Uh-huh. Uh-huh ... I see ... Okay ... Is that right?"

Frankie was getting impatient, gesturing to Gino to fill him in between the silences.

"All right then … you too," Gino said. Hanging up without saying goodbye, he sat back down at the table.

"He doesn't know where he is," Gino said.

"All that for nothing? What the hell were you talking about then? The fuckin' weather?"

"He said he'd ask around. Max is like a cockroach, and he needs money to live. Charlie thinks he'll end up back at the farm eventually."

"So go down there then. Find him."

"Okay, boss," Gino said. Neither he nor Tony made a move to the door.

"*Now!* What is this, an old-age home or something? Go find Max, find the fuckin' dad—do something, for fuck sakes," Frankie erupted before grabbing the racing program and swatting at Tony.

"Let's go, Tony," Gino said.

When they walked out, Gino could smell the sulfur from a factory a few miles north. He could also hear the sound of a slow train rattling by. Gino revved the engine, and the headlights of his Buick Le Sabre lit up the night. They passed the truck terminal and the slaughterhouse, then got onto the turnpike headed south. After an hour—Gino unable to wait for the calzone that Tony wouldn't shut up about—they turned off the highway and picked up some burgers. They sat in the car eating.

After a few moments, between loud openmouthed chews, Tony said, "You know, Gino, I'm gonna get made one day." Apparently Tony was not aware that there was no "made" in this particular gang, and he'd missed the fact that the hierarchy came to a full stop at Frankie, with him being the lowest on the chain, and only Gino in between. Granted, they had done their fair share of extortion, bribery, prostitution, guns, drugs, robbery, and murder, but they were hardly the Cosa Nostra.

"So how's your book going, Gino?" Tony said after wiping his mouth with a napkin. Then he slurped his soft drink. Gino hated that Tony actually knew he had a creative side, as he'd made the mistake of telling him once when he'd asked what he was scribbling in his pad.

"It's all right. I don't want to talk about it," Gino said, throwing his trash out the window.

For a while after he'd told Tony about it, Gino humored him with a few choppy paragraphs just so he could get some feedback, but lately Gino was going through some creative challenges. He was trying to figure out if the dirty cop gets whacked in the joint or if they keep him alive so they can beat him and bugger him every day. He was also wondering how they would torture Johnny the rat bastard, by peeling him up with a scalpel or burning him alive with a blowtorch. Gino had been the kid in grade school who drew pictures of burning houses and bloody tableaux, which caused his teachers alarm. But sometimes he was capable of showing his sensitive side, as depicted in the meandering stanzas about some girl Maria whom he had fallen in love with in Italy. Hardly a pilgrimage to his mob roots, his trip was merely a two-week guided tour with Asian tourists, blue-haired septuagenarians, and of course the Italian tour guide, Maria—beautiful Maria.

The night was pitch-black when they turned off South DuPont Highway. It took approximately ten seconds to drive through the town core. They passed the post office, pub, barbershop, and VHS movie rental store all in the blink of an eye, and then were back into almost complete darkness. After they'd driven east for a few miles passing smaller properties hemmed in by trees on either side, the countryside finally opened up. Gino pulled over to the side of the road and pressed the interior light button on the ceiling. The car lit up inside.

"There's a map in the glove box. Get it for me, all right?"

"Sure, Gino," Tony said and handed over the map. Gino spread it open and held it up to the light.

"Route 309. Yeah, 309; it's up here. County road. It's the next left. Better call Frankie, let him know we're here. See how he wants us to handle the situation."

Gino got out of the car, taking a big stretch and a deep breath of fresh air. If at Pistol Farms Gino couldn't get that real sense of country, he most certainly could here. Unlike the sulfurous breeze from the backwash of Secaucus, the air here was crisp and cool. The stars were bright and clustered in the sky. Besides the night creatures warbling away in the cornfields, there was complete silence—until Tony got out of the car.

"Ahh, that feels good. Christ, that feels good," Tony said, taking a leak on the other side of the road. Gino paced around a bit, no doubt thinking of poetic verse to describe the scene—wishing Maria were right there with him. He took his phone out of his pocket to call Frankie.

"We're just about there, boss," Gino said.

"Good, good," Frankie said on the other end.

"What should we do?"

"See if anybody's home."

"Yeah, and then?"

"If the old man's there, tell him what happened. Tell him his fuckup son cost me a lot of money. Tell him we need one hundred large to cover our losses. Tell him if he doesn't have it, we'll take the farm instead."

"And if he doesn't have the money and won't sign over the farm?"

"Put a beating on him. But don't off him. We might need him yet."

"Okay, boss. I'll check in after," Gino said. Then he hung up.

"Tony, let's go," he said. Both men got into the car.

They turned left on the county road. After passing a few properties, Gino turned off the headlights and rolled slowly into the farm. There were no other cars around, and just a few lights were on in the farmhouse. Gino parked the car. They both got out and walked toward the door.

"Psst," Gino whispered, motioning for Tony to follow him around the side of the house.

They crept around silently, peeking into windows. After circling the entire farmhouse and seeing nothing but empty rooms, Gino walked up to the front door and rang the doorbell. No answer. Gino got back on his phone.

"Boss, no one's home. We could just wait for him. We did come all this way."

"That won't be necessary. We can do better than that," Frankie said, "Go to the barn. If you see Nitro, I want you to take him."

"How are we supposed to move him?"

"Figure it out. You're in horse country, aren't you? Is there a trailer around? If not, I'm sure you can pinch one from another farm."

"Okay, will do, boss."

"And one more thing."

"Yeah?"

"Burn it down."

"You sure, boss? That's going to attract a lot of attention. And what if the old man signs over the farm? Won't we want to keep the barn?"

"He's not going to just give us the farm." Frankie sighed, as if his top henchman was being completely naïve. "Burn the fucker down."

"Consider it done," Gino said and hung up the phone.

"Hey, Tony," Gino called out to Tony, who was sitting on the hood of the car. "Let's take a walk to the barn."

Gino told Tony the plan. Then he spotted a horse trailer next to the barn.

"That's one problem solved," Gino said. He walked into the barn and turned on the lights.

The horses began making noise as Gino and Tony walked down the stalls. There was Ace McGee with his long gray whiskers, and Roundaboutway, who was flapping his gums. At sixteen hands, Nitro, who was by far the tallest, stood like a watchman over the barn, curious about what the two men were doing there.

"There he is," Gino said. They stood in front of Nitro's stall.

"Look at him, just standing there like he's better than us or something. I wonder what Frankie has in store for him. I've never had horsemeat before. Bet you he'd be good with some ketchup and potatoes," Tony said.

"All right, shut up for a minute. Let's go back into town and get some gasoline from that station off the highway. No half measures on this one. Boss says burn it down, so we burn it down."

Tony followed Gino out to the car. They drove back up the county road and back to the highway.

When they returned, they set the gas cans outside the barn and then went inside to collect Nitro.

"Looks like a tack room over there," Gino said. "Go find a halter and a lead, and let's get him ready."

Tony went looking for the equipment. He noticed the small bedroom across from the tack room.

"Hey, Gino, looks like they actually got someone living in here. Must be that trainer, Halladay," Tony said. He then proceeded to rifle through Clarence's dresser for any valuables.

"Quit fucking around. Let's get out of here before anyone gets back."

Tony emerged soon after, holding up the equipment proudly. After all, horses were a distant third on both men's skill sets after murder and racketeering.

"I'll open the stall and you get in there and hook him up," Gino said, clearly not wanting to tangle with Nitro, who had his ears pinned back and was stomping his foot.

When Gino opened the door, Tony walked around to the front of the horse carefully.

"Hush now," he said, trying to calm him down. "You're a good boy, aren't you? ... Yeaaah, everyone wants you, right? You're a winner. A real racehorse, huh? You're coming with us back to Pistol Farms. I think you're going to like it there."

When it was clear that Nitro wasn't ready to cooperate, the animal in Tony came out. He bullied the horse until he was able to secure the halter.

"Okay, let's get him out," Gino said and ran over to the barn door.

"Here, here. I'll take him. You hitch the trailer," Gino said once they got to the car.

"Take it in slow," Gino said, while Tony reversed to line up the car. The red brake lights lit up Gino and Nitro in an amber glow.

"Good," Gino said, halting him.

After Tony hitched the trailer, he took the horse from Gino and walked Nitro up the ramp.

"Let's light her up," Tony said when he was done with the horse. He rushed over to the gas cans.

"Hold on a minute there, smoky," Gino said, stopping Tony before he did anything stupid, like burn them both alive.

"Just sprinkle it around like you're watering daisies, all right?"

"What, you think I never torched a place?"

"Yeah, yeah, I know. I've heard the stories," Gino said while he splashed around his area of the barn, knowing full well that Tony was an accomplished arsonist.

Sensing danger, the horses began to whinny. The smell of gas permeated the barn.

"Okay, let's go," Gino said, when they were finished emptying their gas cans. "Ready for the fireworks?" he said. When they were far enough from the barn, he lit his cigarette and then threw the match down to ignite the fire. The gasoline caught like a candlewick, and the blue and orange line of fire raced toward the barn. Both men watched as the fire quickly spread and the barn became engulfed in flames. As the blaze intensified, so did the sound of the horses' whinnies, which could be heard above the crackling of the fire. Despite all of Gino's atrocities, it was a sound he could never get used to. Most men whimpered as they got nearer to death, he thought, but horses' screams were bloodcurdling. He did not want to be there when they finally went silent, a silence that in many ways was louder than their cries, so quickly they got back in the car and set out for Pistol Farms, while behind them the fire lit up the country night.

CHAPTER 12

"Wake up," Anna said to Bucky, gently rubbing his thigh. Bucky had slept for most of the ride, while Anna drove him back home in her fully loaded white Jeep Cherokee.

"Look over there," Anna said, pointing at the fire in the distance.

Bucky rubbed his eyes, then shook himself awake and sat taller in his seat.

"Oh my God. That looks like—"

"It's coming from the same area as your farm," Anna interrupted him.

"Do you think?"

"These guys you're dealing with, are they capable of something like that?"

"Capable? That's practically their MO."

"Well, let's just wait until we get closer before we jump to any conclusions."

"Yeah, good idea," Bucky said, even though he knew that was the exact area where his farm was. And given the space between the properties, it was unlikely it could be from anywhere else *but* his farm.

He reached into his jeans pocket to pull out his phone and call Carl. No answer. He rolled down his window. Instead of the familiar country smell of manure and fresh-cut hay, the smell of smoke invaded the car. He looked up at the blaze, straining his neck so he could see it through the windshield. The smoke, now billowing from the structure, was darker than the night, blotting out the stars.

Moments later a fire truck, *the* fire truck of Harrington's volunteer firefighters, was up behind them and screamed by with sirens wailing, the lads in the truck serious-looking with their axes and gear, ready to slay the blaze.

"Oh my God, Anna, what if Dad and Clarence are in there?"

"Don't worry. I'm sure it's fine. Everything's going to be fine," Anna said, trying to comfort him.

"What about the horses? What about Nitro?"

"You're getting way ahead of yourself," Anna said. But as they got closer, it became apparent that this fire was not in fact in Sussex or Salisbury; it was there plain to see roaring in the night. At least it wasn't the farmhouse, Bucky thought, his fear for Carl somewhat allayed. But what if Clarence was trapped in the barn?

When they pulled in, Bucky got out and made a pathetic-looking limping run with one arm dangling, wincing with the pain from every step, looking every bit a madman, before he was restrained by the volunteer fire chief, Sam Bonk—vacuum salesperson by day. Bucky had never seen him in this capacity before, and thought he looked strong, brave, and ageless, as his bald head was covered by his fire helmet.

"I can't let you go over there, son," he said, holding Bucky back, using his full girth, which, by the light of the fire and given the gravity of the situation, seemed to Bucky like pure muscle. Bucky tried desperately to reach past Bonk, but he ended up just burying his face in his shoulder.

"Noooooo!" Bucky wailed, pounding Bonk's chest. "Whyyyyyyy?" Bucky said, knowing full well that he was the cause of this, that his actions had most likely ruined the farm. They had taken their blows the past few years, but this? Bucky was sure they would never recover. The farm was on the last of its nine lives, and was already living on borrowed time and assets, thanks in large part to its main benefactor, Roy Callaghan, whose prized racehorse that he'd financed and partnered with Carl on had now officially been cremated.

Bonk handed Bucky off to Anna. He went limp. As she held him, his tears and drool were dribbling down her neck. She was the one thing that separated Bucky from the dirt. She remained patient while Bucky alternately sobbed and smelled the back of her neck and behind her ear.

When Bucky pulled himself together, he stood helplessly watching the fire burn away. He noticed Cole walking over in his fireman's outfit. He seemed taller and was wielding an axe. If Bonk looked heroic in uniform to Bucky, then Cole looked like a veritable Superman or Captain America. Bucky perked up as much as he could, and looked up at Cole, whose face was black with soot from fighting the fire.

"Jesus, Buck. What happened to you? What's going on?"

"It's a long story," Bucky said, not wanting to have to explain himself to Cole in that moment, especially about Nitro. Could Cole really separate his duties as superhero firefighter and lender with the same magnanimity?

"Hi, honey," Cole said, leaning over to give Anna a kiss on the lips. "Glad you made it back from New York okay," he said without a hint of suspicion or jealousy. Anna had told Cole she was going to New York because she was worried about Bucky, and also to see some friends, so that much was clear and probably nonnegotiable. But if Cole was showing internal signs of the same heart condition Bucky had—that same torrid, frenetic love, the paranoia of losing Anna over and over, the fear that she might blow away as wistfully as a dandelion spore— then he didn't show it. That said, did they really need to kiss right in front of him? Wasn't that overcompensating? *How much longer can she keep up this façade?* Bucky thought. He looked to Cole, who stood with authority, almost presiding over his land.

"When'd you join the firehouse anyway?"

"Oh, been a few months now," Cole said.

That's funny, Bucky thought to himself, *about the same time I left for New York. Does Cole have more time now that he doesn't have to worry about me stealing Anna?* Bucky and Anna had shared a moment at his apartment, and now that Bucky had a taste again, it would be that much harder for him to walk away. The irony of seeing Cole there in uniform was not lost on Bucky; while Cole was risking his life trying to douse the flames, Bucky was igniting an old one. And as much as Bucky had tried to deny it, those feelings were never far from the surface. He realized that moving to New York hadn't allowed him to forget or move on. It was just a Band-Aid to plug a gushing wound that would probably never heal.

While the three of them stood there, the roof of the barn caved in and a plume of smoke mushroomed up like an atomic bomb. The firefighters all took a few steps back. Bonk waved Cole back over to the fire.

"I'd better get going, guys. I'll catch up with you later."

As Cole walked away, Bucky wondered why he hadn't mentioned anything about Nitro. Did he even know they were stabling him there? Or perhaps he thought they kept him in New York? Regardless, with Cole as a direct conduit to Roy, it wouldn't be long before Roy knew. And what would be the fallout? Bucky was sure that Carl didn't have the money to pay Roy back, so did this mean he would have to hand over the farm? And who knows what the cops and insurance company might say about the whole blaze, once they determined the cause to be arson.

Carl's truck pulled into the farm. Bucky turned around and held his hand up to the headlights.

"About time," he said to Anna, and then hobbled over to the car.

Both Carl and Clarence got out of the car. Unlike Bucky, who had run over and would have gone right into the blaze if he'd been able to, both men stood silent, watching in awe as the firefighters fought the crackling blaze. A tear rolled down Carl's cheek. Clarence's lip quivered.

"Where were you guys? Where have you been?" Bucky said, barely allowing them the time they needed to process the situation.

"We were at the Hi-Dee-Ho," Carl said, not even looking at Bucky, "for dinner."

Before Bucky lashed out in frustration, he realized that Carl and Clarence still had no idea what had happened in New York. How were they to know the gravity of the situation? From their perspective, Bucky thought, they had just won a big race at the Coliseum, and now with a horse that qualified to race in the Breeders, things were about to get a lot better. In fact, just moments ago, they'd probably enjoyed a good steak as they laughed and drank and thought about all the ways they would spend the purse money.

"My horses," Clarence said. "My babies."

"Nitro," Carl said, staring straight ahead into the abyss.

Bucky didn't know what to say. He couldn't play the soothsayer and tell them that everything would be all right, because he didn't believe it. In fact, Bucky believed things could still get much worse. Clarence and Carl walked away from the car. Anna came over and gave Carl a hug.

"Hi, dear," Carl said, putting on a strong face. He kissed Anna on the top of the head.

"I'm sorry," Anna said.

"It's okay," Carl said, stroking Anna's hair almost as if it was he who was doing the consoling. "Everything's going to be fine."

After Anna let go, the four of them stood still and silent, watching the firefighters douse the blaze. Ashes fell down like snowflakes.

After dealing with the fire department, the local newspaper, and his higher-ups, JP Marshall, the ginger-haired police officer, walked over in his leather boots, cop hat, and blue-and-gold breeches. He was tall and slight, and walked with his abdomen thrust forward as if he had been a stadium hawker and years of carrying a heavy beer tray had forever changed his posture.

Bucky remembered JP as the kid who'd once squirted milk out of his nose in the cafeteria, and once shit his pants and ditched his briefs in the woods, where they were discovered with his name tag. He said it was a Boy Scout thing, but the abuse he took was painful and enduring. JP pulled Carl aside.

"Any idea what happened?" he said, swaying in his cop belt and digging his thumbs into the front of his pants.

"No idea. No idea at all," Carl said. "We were out for dinner, and then we came back to this scene here."

"How many horses you have in there?"

"Three."

"That's just a shame, isn't it? I'm sorry. We all know how much you love the horses. Hopefully they went painlessly."

"More like screaming in the night. Have you ever heard a banshee wail?"

"No, sir, I haven't."

"Well, that's the sound of dying horses."

"However they went, it's tragic. We'll meet with the fire marshal tomorrow and might come by another time to ask some more questions. In the meantime, you know where to find me," JP said. He walked back to his cruiser. Bucky was happy he hadn't approached him, in fear he would have to explain what happened to his face, which might arouse suspicion. He also thought it was better at this point that he hadn't told Carl, because under questioning who knew what he might reveal.

"What happened?" Carl said stone-faced, without looking at Bucky. It was obvious that Bucky had something to do with it, because now he'd shown up with two black eyes and a railroad of stitches crisscrossed over his face, and the barn was burned to the ground. It was a question that Bucky knew was in the offing. As much as he'd prepared to answer it, he could barely face his father. It was so far from who they were, from what Carl had raised him to be.

"Max got into shit with these guys. They call themselves the Caruso gang, from Pistol Farms. I agreed to fix Nitro in the elimination dash."

"Max … of course," Carl said, pausing. "Pistol Farms." He thought for another moment, with his thumb and finger to his chin. "But we won."

"No we didn't, Dad. We lost. Look at this," he said. They both looked at the crumbling fire log of their lives as it smoked and hissed.

"You fixed to lose?"

"Nitro was easy money, so they had the one-two taken care of. I was only supposed to show. Would have been a good payday for those jackals."

"I guess they did that to you as well," Carl said, not even having to look at Bucky for him to know his father was talking about his kicked-in face and body. Bucky thought to himself that he would accept that beating again for not only his barn to be restored, but also his life, at any stage. He'd remembered those flashes between blows: one of his mother looking down on him angelically; one of jug-eared Bobby in his Yankees cap licking an ice cream cone; and one of Anna. Of course, how could Anna not appear in his dying visions, whirling around in a feathery boa and blowing sparkle kisses off her hand into the golden sunlight.

"Yeah, Dad. They got me pretty good,"

"I'm going to kill those guys," Clarence said, his voice deep and sure. There was no question he meant it.

"No need for that, Clarence," Carl said. "We'll tell the cops everything."

"Are you crazy?" Bucky said. "What am I supposed to tell them, that I welshed on a race fix for my mob friends, so they decided to come over for a barbecue? What'd you say to JP, anyway?"

"I told him I didn't know anything—which I didn't. Now I do. They'll be coming back. So will the fire marshal. We can tell them what happened then."

"Maybe we should think about it," Clarence said, still in his sinister voice, wanting to exact revenge by any means *but* the law.

"Yeah, Dad. Listen to Clarence. Trust me. These guys will not stop until either they get their money back or one of us is dead, if not all of us. And I'm sure they don't like rats. I don't want to end up in a ditch with a tail coming out of my mouth, if you know what I mean."

"We gotta beat them at their own game," Clarence said.

"You're not being helpful, Clarence," Carl said. "We're not criminals. They are."

"What does it take to get you mad, old man? All these years you've been letting Max run wild, getting into all kinds of shit, and now this, this is his masterpiece. And you, Bucky? I haven't even started on you. What the hell are you doing agreeing to fix races, trying to bail *Max* out, of all people?"

"Not like I had a choice. He was into it with Bernie as well, so I was worried he wouldn't let me keep the stable anymore if I didn't do it. I figured it was just one race. If I did it, then maybe they'd just leave us alone."

"But you didn't do it," Carl said.

"No. No, I didn't," Bucky said, as if he had to remind himself.

"That's right, Son, you didn't do it. You haven't broken the law yet. These guys at Pistol Farms are scoundrels, and the *only* thing that will make them stop is if they're all behind bars."

"Or if they're dead," Clarence said, looking blankly ahead at the steaming pile of waterlogged barn, now a cemetery for his beloved horses.

"Let's just, let's keep our heads, all right, guys? Tomorrow, the sun will come up like it always does, and we'll figure out a way to get through it."

"Whatever, Pops."

"For once I agree with the boy," Clarence said. "There's gonna be a reckoning."

Before Carl could say anything further to dissuade Bucky and Clarence from striking back with a vengeance, Cole came back over. His jacket was off, slung over his shoulder. His shirt was soaked through with sweat, and his chest was bulging beneath the suspenders.

He must be lifting weights these days, Bucky thought, as he sized up Cole, almost waiting for another member of the fire department to come over and crown him with a baseball cap reading WORLD CHAMPIONS and pop a bottle of champagne to celebrate their victory over the fire.

Does it even matter that it was my farm, Bucky wondered, *or is it just another blaze to him?* Perhaps Cole was subconsciously happy about this tragedy, and better yet that Anna had been here to witness it. That way, she could see that Bucky literally had nothing left to offer her.

"That's about it for tonight," Cole said. "Fire's out. I talked to Bonk, and he said the marshal would be over tomorrow. Investigating the cause of the fire is above my pay grade."

"But you're a volunteer," Bucky said, unable to resist throwing in.

"I'm sorry, Carl, Clarence," Cole said, nodding at them both, ignoring Bucky's petty jibe. "Anyway, I best get going," he said, looking over at the other volunteer firefighters, who were fraternizing by the truck as they loaded their equipment.

"Anna, you good?"

"Yeah. I'll make my way home later. Thanks."

"Okay then," Cole said, "I'll see you guys."

Bucky watched Cole walk back to the truck, the reflective gear on his pants lighting up his every stride. He was happy to have Anna back to himself now; the one good thing in all of this was that after all these years, he finally seemed to be making progress again. Then, perhaps feeling a little more entitled than he should have, still not grounded in the reality that Anna was a married woman, married to his oldest and supposed best friend no less, Bucky moved closer to her and put his arm around her. Anna pressed into him. Feeling her warmth and reception to his touch, Bucky wrapped his other arm around her in a tender embrace. Just at that moment, while Bucky held Anna as tight as he could and the two rocked from side to side, Bucky looked over Anna's shoulder and saw Cole sitting in the fire truck. The two men locked eyes for a split second before the door slammed shut and the fire truck rolled away.

After everyone had cleared out, Anna helped Bucky to the farmhouse. Carl and Clarence came in soon after. It was already late, so they all had just one commiserative drink around the kitchen table. Then Bucky draped his arms around Anna, and she helped him up to his room.

"Here, sit down," Anna said, pulling the sheet back.

Bucky sat on the edge of the bed, and let out a yelp when he bent down to try to take his shoes off.

"Let me do that," Anna said. She popped off both his shoes and swung his legs up on the bed.

While Bucky got comfortable, Anna walked over and switched off the light. Then in the darkness, she stood by the bed and stripped down to her bra and panties. She slithered into bed as close as she could to Bucky without touching him. Then she emerged from beneath the covers and said, "Don't get any ideas," and gave him a peck on the cheek.

"No, of course not. We're just sleeping, right?" Bucky said, acting surprised at the very notion that she'd even suggest anything might happen.

"Yes. We're just sleeping," Anna said, not feeling all too convinced. She told herself that just this time if Bucky made a move, she wouldn't resist him.

Sure enough, it did come. It was in the predawn. Anna could feel Bucky trying to find her lips in the darkness. First he kissed her temple. Not seeming to care he had missed his mark, he kissed her again in the exact same spot, and then kissed the side of her nose, and then the peak, before finally finding her lips. Anna didn't resist. She welcomed his impassioned kisses, brushed his bangs away, and looked into his eyes. There was always so much pain and yearning in Bucky's eyes. Even in the half-light she could see his torment as he stared at her unflinchingly, trying to say everything without uttering a word.

Bucky moved closer, kissing Anna's neck and chest while she lay still. It had been a while since Cole had kissed her like that. He was good. Yes, Cole was good, and that's what Anna liked about him. He didn't have the same stench of death that she or Bucky had. He was pure, if not simple. And after Bobby had died, his family offered Anna a stability she couldn't get with Bucky, or in her own home between Judith's early-morning mimosas.

Since Bucky had moved to New York, Anna couldn't help but think what her alternate reality might be if she'd married Bucky instead of Cole. The two men were so different. Bucky had spirit because he needed to. For him it was survival, whereas everything was more or less already in place for Cole. That was the big difference in who they were. Bucky was hardscrabble and independent—he had to hack through the jungle of life with a machete—while Cole sucked from the family teat and did it well, even thriving. If Anna had stuck with Bucky all those years ago, would he be in this situation right now? in this farmhouse? in this bed? Would his face and body still be checkered with cuts and bruises? For the first time, Anna realized that if Bobby hadn't died, she probably would have married Bucky despite Judith's objections that he came from a poor family, that he had nothing to offer, and that they would probably spend their whole lives on food stamps. It was a story she had been hearing her whole life, because Judith, smart enough to see what was happening with the trio since the onset of puberty, had repeated her affinity for the Callaghans, and often made a point of mentioning how much Roy had made when he sold off his auto parts business. For Judith it would be the equivalent of a royal intermarriage.

While her mind wondered, Anna couldn't help but enjoy Bucky's soft kisses. Soon enough she could feel his hard-on poking in her side. While Bucky became more aroused, his hands began to wander, soon ending up on her panties, where he pressed the cotton fabric into her fold and moved his fingers around in rhythmic circles. Even though she gave herself a pass, she still had her doubts about crossing that sacramental line. But Bucky was persistent. Soon he peeled off her underwear. He then lay on top of her like a dead weight, kissing her softly, his hot tears landing on her cheek like a burning plastic bag. He sank his head further into her nape, inhaling her scent, and then traced a long line up her neck with his tongue, sucked on her earlobe, and rubbed his thumb softly across her forehead and down her cheek. And then, just like that, for the first time since college, Bucky was inside her.

CHAPTER 13

Max looked out the window in his room at the Diplomat Motel in Atlantic City.

There was an ice machine by the office, and small tables with dirty ashtrays and broken plastic chairs outside the rooms, which faced each other in a quadrangle. There was a sign marking the year-round pool out back, which was permanently closed, and two picnic tables by a makeshift horseshoe pitch. It was about eight o'clock. Some college kids had just pulled up and were unloading their bags from the trunk of their car. To Max they looked like an aberration. They were happy and laughing, excited about hitting it big at the casinos. One wore a varsity letterman jacket, and the other two wore T-shirts, cargo shorts, and flip-flops. Max tried to remember a time when he was like that, but he couldn't. He had never been like that. It seemed to him that the second he shot through the birth canal, there was only misery and betrayal. By the time he was their age, he had already been a part of two different families, until he was taken in at the farm. He remembered the second family, who on the first day of meeting him were all smiles, hugs, and kisses, and by the end were on the phone with the social worker pleading to return Max like they had been sold defective goods.

The Diplomat was as much a home as anywhere for Max. It was a dive motel a few blocks off the strip where budget travelers laid their heads on the lumpy pillows and prayed they wouldn't be murdered in their sleep. He had stayed there many times on his sojourns. Always looking for a quick getaway, Max had a whole bevy of preferred shitholes in any place that had booze, gambling, and prostitution. The Diplomat was one of them.

But more than that, Max had a special connection to Atlantic City. It was where he and Marge Tate had taken their three-day honeymoon. He remembered looking out at the Atlantic Ocean from the Ferris wheel on the pier with her. He couldn't have realized in that moment, but it was the crescendo of their romance. After that, it crashed down like a tsunami. And what other direction could it have gone anyway? You would think that two degenerate gamblers and alcoholics would be the perfect match, but it was just the opposite. They didn't even make it to the end of their wedding night before ending up in a tangle on the floor, wrestling for the last airplane bottle of vodka from the minibar.

Max laughed to himself while thinking about his honeymoon. Sometimes he came back, not only to relive the moment, but also with the secret hope that Marge might be doing the same, that maybe, somehow, someday, he would run into her again. That was the one common denominator with all of the towns he went to. There was a history of him and Marge together, be it on a quick drive through, a weekend getaway, or a booze-infused bender when they fought and fucked and gambled. For Max, going to Atlantic City was like tempting fate, or walking by one of his childhood homes and trying to peek inside the window.

Max hunched over the table by the window, and did a line of coke. He rubbed his nose, looked in the mirror, and wiped the white residue off his nose. Now he was ready to go. Leaving the motel with a bottle of Wild Turkey in a brown paper bag, he cut his way through a parking lot to Pacific Avenue. He passed a pawnshop, a massage parlor, and a couple of boarded-up buildings, until finally the casinos emerged like pyramids in the desert.

The columns at Caesar's stood like the great fabricated engineering marvel that they were, artificial like everything else in this town, including dreams. Max approached like a plebeian entering the gates of Rome. Once inside, he knew exactly where to go—to his favorite blackjack table in the back. After sitting down, he looked around the table at the vaguely familiar faces. There was a dapper midthirties Spanish guy who wore a neck scarf and played with his chips like it was an art form; a gray-haired Chinese lady who had nothing on the table but who kept pulling hundred-dollar chips from a ziplock bag in her purse; one guy with dead eyes, a thick jaw, and a weather-beaten face who, judging by the calluses on his hands, Max guessed was a laborer; and then probably the most normal-looking of the bunch, a middle-aged family-looking man with thinning brown hair, wire-frame glasses, and a pink Lacoste shirt. To Max, it seemed like the same people, at the same table, the last time he was there. Could they have been there all this time? They were the ones who existed after the tourist mass peeled away, the dregs of society who played through the night, people who had already given so much to the house that there was no going back.

"Chip change. One thousand," the young dealer said aloud, peeling Max's bills off the table and replacing them with chips. He had light blond hair blow-dried straight, and a concave nose that looked as if it had been squeezed permanently into place by a thumb and index finger.

"Grandma's fresh-baked cookies," he said to notify the pit boss that he'd gotten a tip. He tapped the chip and put it aside in his private stash of tips from other satisfied gamblers. He dealt a new hand. The cards came out on the smooth surface. Max, liking his three and eight, watched the other hands dealt around the table.

"You should double down," the preppy man from Anytown, America, said. Max stared a cold hard dagger through him. In Max's experience, there was one guy like that at every table, someone who told you how to play your hand and didn't shut up about it when you made a mistake.

"I'll double down," Max said and pushed more chips into the pot.

"As you wish," the dealer said. Then he hit him with a two as his final card, giving him thirteen.

The dealer dealt out the rest of the table, and then landed on himself.

"Okay, everyone ready?" he said, working whatever abysmal repartee he could with the gamblers before he took their money. Then he turned his card to reveal another eight.

"Eight and eight, sixteen," he said and then hit a five, to give him twenty-one. The whole table groaned. Max had just lost two hundred dollars and hadn't even been in the casino for two hands. As he continued losing, it made him even more reckless. How many hands could he lose in a row? Eventually the dealer would have to bust.

As Max dug in, his strategy finally started paying off. He went on a hot streak. For a while, it felt like he couldn't lose. Even the Chinese lady started paying attention to Max, nodding every time he played a good hand. The preppy family man stopped telling Max how to play as he himself got buried, most likely wondering how he would come up with his next mortgage payment or how to explain it to his wife.

With no clocks or shadows in the casino, it was impossible to know the time. Max was caught in the center of a gambling vortex. While throughout the hall people shuffled in and out—there was the odd cheer from the craps table, and the even odder sound of the slot machines hitting pay dirt—this table of gamblers diligently faced off against the dealer like they were the final holdouts of the Alamo. Sitting there slumped in his chair, Max had no idea about the farm. And how could he? One of the things that Max loved about casinos was just how cut off he was from the outside world. Any thoughts of Bernie and Frankie failed to penetrate his cerebral cortex. He sat there oblivious to everything except for the next card coming out of the dealer's hand.

It was finally Max's bladder that made him get up from the table, so he asked for a mark and made his way to the men's room. After doing his business, he went outside for a smoke and was surprised by the low light of daybreak. Had he been playing that long? The streets were wet, and the sky was dark purple. There was a street sweeper cleaning and buffing the sidewalk. The smell of a rubbish fire somewhere blended with the smell of the ocean, making the air both sweet and acrid. There were a few birds and bums. Overall it seemed to Max like the city had some kind of incurable disease.

Max flicked his cigarette into a hedge and was about to go back in when he felt his phone vibrating in his pocket. He reached into his jeans and unfolded the receiver. Before he could say anything, there was a frantic voice on the other end.

"Max! Max! Are you there? Is that you?"

"Baker?"

"Yeah, Maxi. It's me."

"Do you have any idea what time it is?"

"About 5:30 a.m.," Charlie said.

"Well, what the hell, man? Did you shit the bed or something?"

"It's an emergency. Have you talked to anybody? Where are you? You know that Frankie's looking for you, and so is Bernie."

"I figured as much. That's why I'm here."

"Where's here?"

"In the middle of fuckin' nowhere," Max said, even though he was surrounded by garish buildings and billboards, and a tourist population at rest, about to rise and take over the city like a marauding army.

"We need to talk."

"What's going on?" Max asked, knowing that people were looking for him—wanted him dead in fact—but doing his best to prolong his sense of unreality before having to face the situation.

"Listen, Max, I wanna come and see you. We need to talk. Where are you?"

"Whose side are you playing, Charlie? Last time I checked, the Big Macher had you in his back pocket."

"I'm playing all sides. That's why we need to talk. We can help each other."

"Help each other?"

"Yeah, Maxi. I have a plan."

"Oh, great."

"Where are you?"

"I don't want your help. I'm doing just fine," Max said, knowing he was anything but fine.

"Maxi," Charlie said, "I have a plan, a plan that can make both of us a lot of money. You do like money, right? I'm talking lots of money. No more chump change. I'm talking about real cabbage here—stacks."

"Go on."

"Not over the phone."

"I'm in Atlantic City," Max finally blurted out, the lure of money far outweighing the need for any more secrecy.

"I'll be there in three hours. Stay put. Where are you staying?"

"The Diplomat Motel."

"Isn't that a dump?"

"See you soon," Max said. Then he hung up and went back into the casino.

When Charlie Baker arrived, it was just past eleven in the morning. He pulled in front of Max's room, got out of the car, and peeked through the window to see Max passed out on the bed. After Charlie had pounded on the door for a few minutes, Max finally stirred and let him in, then collapsed back onto the bed.

"Took you long enough," Max said, rubbing his forehead.

"Got here as soon as I could," Charlie said.

Behind Charlie was another man who'd entered the room. Tall and sickly looking, he wore a brown suit and horn-rimmed glasses. His dark hair was parted neatly on the side, and he had a slightly crooked nose. Max didn't know what to make of him. If he had to guess, he'd say he was a shylock or a tax collector—either way, something to do with money or banking. Definitely not the usual crowd Max was used to being around, at least outwardly.

"Who's the stiff?" Max said.

"Max, meet Harold. Harold, Max," Charlie said.

After primping himself and admiring his rockabilly sideburns in the mirror, Charlie sat in the chair by the front window.

"Okay, so now that I know his name, what the fuck's he doing here? What the fuck are you doing here, stiff?" Max said, turning to Harold, who stood there timidly like he was being bullied on his first day of school.

"Here's the deal, Maxi," Charlie said, getting right down to business.

"Wait a minute, wait a minute," Max said, holding up his hand to stop Charlie. "Let me get myself together," he said. He lumbered over to the table where Charlie was sitting, his immense presence making the room seem too small, and then picked up the rolled dollar bill and did a line of coke from the table like an anteater.

"Whoo-whee!" he said, the coke quickly entering his bloodstream. "That's better." He plugged his nostrils and shook his head from side to side. "Want some?"

"Don't mind if I do," Charlie said, rolling up his sleeves to reveal his blur of botched tattoos.

"Where'd you get those done anyway?" Max said, unable to ignore Charlie's forearm, which looked like it had just been dipped in ink. "Your tattoo artist should be shot."

"In the joint," Charlie said, and then he did his line. "Kapow! That's good stuff, that's good stuff. Now let's talk. Harold, you going to join us?"

Harold came over meekly and sat perfectly erect at the table. Although he was sweating profusely, he did not so much as loosen his tie or unbutton his shirt. You could see the sweat through his jacket, almost as if he were drowning in it. Perhaps it was his penance. It was running down his face, slowly dribbling past his temples, and trickling down to a puddle beneath his palm on the table.

"Gino called me. Frankie's looking for you," Charlie said.

"That's yesterday's news, pal."

"They either want to string you up by your balls or cut your throat—it's dealer's choice. But I got you."

"You don't 'got' anything, Baker. What the hell do you think this is? You a bounty hunter now or something? And besides, I think we both know who would win if it came to fisticuffs."

"I didn't mean it like that, Maxi. Will you just listen to me?"

"Go on," Max said, crossing his arms.

"I tell Gino that I found you, and I bring you back to Pistol Farms with a gun to your back if I have to, and ..."

"Are *you* fuckin' nuts?"

"Hold on, Maxi."

"This better get good. Quick, Baker."

"All right. Well, Harold here was my cellmate in the can. He got kicked out of MIT. He's a computer genius, and he's got this plan. You want to take over, Poindexter? I can't explain this shit."

"It's called the Y2K protocol," Harold said, now speaking confidently as the subject matter expert.

"Did you know that Pary-Tote processes all of the betting from the windows, wagering terminals, and OTBs, then sends the information back to the track, where they post the handle on the tote board?"

"I'm listening."

"Well, I work there. I can open multiple wagering accounts in different names. So you place a bet, and I'll pluck it from the terminal before it transfers over. I add a few zeros and send the information back to the track. You'll be holding thousands of dollars' worth of tickets, all for peanuts. Catching on?"

"How's that even possible?"

"It's a glitch. They're overhauling their systems for this Y2K patch, and this is the last chance before all of the mutual companies step up their security."

"Welcome to the new millennium, man," Charlie said. "I told you he was a genius!"

"This can be our fuck-you to progress," Max said.

"You're seeing it. You're finally seeing it, Maxi."

"But why do you need me?" Max asked, wondering how he fit into this elaborate scheme.

"Nitro."

"What about him?"

"Well, he won the qualifier, didn't he? He'll be running in the Breeders."

"Yeah … and?"

"We still need a winner, and it's the biggest race of the year," Charlie said.

"I got nothing to do with that horse. And you think my brother, *or my nephew*, would agree to that? You saw what happened last time."

"Oh yeah, about that. Tell the kid I'm sorry for what happened at Bert's. It was Gino and Tony who dealt most of the blows; I just had to make it look believable."

"Well, that doesn't matter. It's not happening."

"Listen, Maxi. You tell Frankie that you'll help him fix the Breeders, and in exchange this whole thing is over—you're square."

"I don't know, Charlie. And besides, everyone knows me at the track. How am I supposed to cash out those vouchers when I'm persona non grata around there?"

"I got inside guys at the windows and counting room. Fuck, I even got the pit manager. It's bombproof, Maxi. Once the race is over, you cash out your vouchers from the machines and crash the windows."

"And Frankie? How do you know he'll go for it?"

"We go see him now. I'll tell him I ran into you and brought you in. That's when you tell him you're going to talk to Carl and Bucky about the Breeders."

"Will that be before or after he knocks my teeth out?"

"I have a solution for that as well."

"You got an answer for everything, don't you?"

"Get your shit together and meet me out front."

"Okay, Charlie. I'll trust you on this one. If things go south—"

"They won't."

"If they do …"

"We gotta go, Max. I'll meet you outside."

Max scoured the room. Since he hadn't changed from the white shirt that highlighted his every roll, there was nothing to gather, so he closed the door, leaving the mess of garbage and drug paraphernalia behind. He followed Charlie and Harold outside. One of the college kids was slumped in the plastic chair outside their room. He had vomit on his shirt and in a pool beside him. A car peeled out of the lot, and a plume of dirt enveloped Harold, who started coughing.

"Am I following you?" Max said to Charlie, while he got in the driver's side of his Cutlass.

"No, no, I'll go with you. Harold will follow us to Secaucus, and park at the Dunkin' Donuts while we meet Frankie. You can drop me off there afterward … and oh, my solution for Frankie not giving you a beatdown? I take a few shots at you. Make it look believable. I tell Frankie I saw you, taught you a lesson, and here we are … you know how it goes."

Max let out a deep breath, swung his legs back out of the car, and leaned over on his knees.

"You're serious," Max said. By his tone, it was obvious he knew he was, and more importantly that it was a good idea.

"Trust me, it'll be way better than what Frankie will do to you."

"Well, fuck it then. Let's do this," Max said. He got up and kicked his legs and shook his arms out like he was a boxer warming up before the starting bell.

"Give me all you got, shit brick."

"I was a bronze glove in the joint."

"Okay, not everything. Just enough to make it believable. Now do it!" Max said. He pounded his chest and slapped his forehead a few times.

Charlie sized up Max standing there like a bull in a bullring. Then he wound up and socked him in the mouth.

"Fuck!" Max said, doubling over and then spitting blood into his hand.

Harold watched the event unfold from the sidelines. At the sound of Max's scream, the college kid finally stirred, looking over at Max and Charlie, who were squaring up in the parking lot.

"Is that all you got, Baker?"

"Don't worry about it. We're friends," Charlie said to the college kid.

"We're friends, we're friends. Isn't that right, Maxi?" he said. Then he threw a vicious left hook to Max's right eye.

"Christ! Oh, ow, ow, ow, you fucker. You can at least tell me when it's coming. Fuck! Fuck, that hurt! Asshole! Okay, that's it," Max, said. He raised his hands, still somehow on his feet.

"Sure you don't want one more?"

"Let's go," Max said, his blood now running down his chin onto his shirt, and a rapidly swelling shiner developing above his eye.

"Here, take this," Charlie said, as he handed Max a handkerchief he had crumpled in his pocket. "I'll call Gino and tell him we're coming."

Max dabbed at the blood on his lip and eye and then wobbled a bit as if not feeling the full effect of Charlie's punches until now.

"You drive," Max said. He got into the passenger's side and reclined his seat as far as it would go.

"Pistol Farms!" Charlie said, turning the key in the ignition. They peeled out of the Diplomat Motel, leaving the college kid in awe of what he had just witnessed, and the Latino cleaning woman to brace for whatever horrors would be left behind.

CHAPTER 14

The morning after the barn had burned down, Bucky awoke to see Anna looking out the window in his bedroom. She was draped in a bedsheet, and the smell of her hair was still fresh on the pillow beside him. As much as waking up with Anna would have made Bucky ecstatic under normal circumstances, there was still the underlying pain not just in his ribs, knees, and head—pretty much everywhere—but also in the forlorn knowledge that outside there was no more barn or horses, and ultimately no more livelihood or future for the farm.

"You're still here," Bucky said, wiping the sleep from his eyes.

"Of course I am," Anna said, turning around to face him.

"Thought maybe I was still dreaming. What time is it?"

"Just past ten."

"Guess I don't have to rush out and feed the horses."

"I'm sorry, Bucky," Anna said, distraught after looking out the window at what used to be the barn.

"How bad is it?"

"We'll help you rebuild. It'll be just like new. Better, in fact. We can build extra stalls, a bigger room for Clarence, and ..."

"Stop, Anna. It's okay."

"I mean it."

"I know you do," Bucky said. He grimaced as he pushed himself up the headboard.

He knew there was more trouble ahead. No way was this Frankie's final play. And if that had been just his warm-up, what was he planning for the main event?

"How are you feeling?" Anna said, picking up her jeans and shirt off the floor and starting to get dressed.

"It's hard to describe it, but I imagine it is like what Evel Knievel must have felt like whenever he missed a landing."

"Sounds like a lot of pain."

"Just talking about it makes it hurt more."

"So we won't talk about it then."

"Do you want to talk about anything else?" Bucky said, hoping this might lead into a discussion where Anna declares her undying love for him, announces she has finally decided to leave Cole, and says she is open to a life far away from Delaware. After all, if one good thing could come of this, then it might be worth it. Maybe this was exactly what the stars and the universe had always had in store. Maybe it was kismet. Bucky asked himself if going through all the events of the last few days again meant he could be with Anna. His answer was yes, he almost certainly would. Other things he would also consider sacrificing: cutting off a finger (not his index, but one of his other, less useful fingers), going on a hunger strike, enduring waterboarding, and consenting to low-grade cancer, as long as it was treatable. He would sacrifice the barn, the horses, his body, and of course his lifelong friendship with Cole.

"I *do* want to talk about it, Bucky," Anna said, "But I need some time. Can you give me that? It's confusing. I never thought I'd be in this place. How could I have known that choosing between you and Cole was going to be a lifelong thing? Maybe that's one of the reasons why I married him, just so the decision was made and I could finally move forward. I'm tired, Bucky—tired of all the what-ifs."

"I understand," Bucky said. "Take all the time you need. But what are you going to tell Cole about last night?"

"The truth."

"The whole truth?"

"Most of it …"

"Okay, maybe I'll talk to him as well," Bucky said, thoughtful for a moment about what he might say to his oldest friend regarding his wife's infidelities, and the future that he was planning for both of them together.

"Maybe you should just let me handle it for now."

"You might be right."

"Might be?"

"You are. Of course you are," Bucky said. Then he added, "It's too bad we're not polygamists."

"Seriously?"

"That was a joke."

"Not funny," Anna said. Then she walked over and gave Bucky a kiss on the forehead. "I best get going," she said.

"So soon?"

"I'll check in later."

"Bye, Anna," Bucky said. From his lips the words *I love you* almost came out, but they didn't. Not this time. Anna had opened the door, and for once Bucky realized it might be best just to tiptoe through it, as opposed to kicking it wide open, kind of like luring a fish with gentle pulls of the rod, instead of trying to heave it over the starboard side, only to find an old sneaker or rubber tire.

When she left, Bucky found himself alone again, with nothing to offset the anger building inside him as the reality of their situation set in. This was the first morning since he could remember that he didn't have horses, or horse-related duties to attend to. Somewhere, the Caruso gang was plotting their next move, and here they were on the farm stripped of their livelihood and dignity, defenseless as their prize racehorse and barn lay in a heap of ashes outside. Something had to be done. Something had to be done that was quick and decisive. The Caruso gang had to go.

Bucky swung his feet over the edge of his bed, put on his jeans and T-shirt, and then hobbled his way over to the closet. He reached in and pulled out his shotgun that he'd safely stowed away for times just like these. He ran his hand along the barrel, and then nestled the stock into the crook of his elbow and slowly made his way downstairs. He was surprised to see Anna still there, and by how normal it seemed for her to be sitting around the kitchen table with Carl and Clarence. She was facing the stairs, so she was the first to notice Bucky as he brandished his firearm like Yosemite Sam. "Oh my!" she said, with her hand to her mouth, which caused Carl and Clarence to immediately turn around to face him.

"Son," Carl said, standing up from his chair.

"That's what I'm talking about," Clarence said.

"That's not the answer," Carl said. "Sit down and let's talk about this."

Bucky laid the shotgun down across the table and then went to the stove and picked up the kettle.

"This fresh?"

"It's not bad," Clarence said, taking a sip of his own coffee, seemingly never more proud of Bucky than at this moment.

"Good morning, everyone," Bucky said, once he'd sat down at the table. "Anna." He nodded.

"The boys insisted I stay for a coffee," Anna said.

"Glad you're here," Bucky said, almost like he was just seeing her, like she hadn't just crept down the stairs after staying the night.

"Are we going to talk about this, or are you just going to shoot everyone you see?" Carl said.

"Think I might go with option B on that one, Dad."

"You want to go to jail for the rest of your life?"

"It'd be three squares a day. Might be more than you'll be getting around here," Clarence said.

"He's got a point," Bucky said, winking at Clarence and then taking a sip of his coffee.

"Maybe you can talk some sense into him, Anna?" Carl said.

"You need to think about this, Bucky," Anna said. She looked down in horror at the shotgun on the table. "This isn't you."

"People change," Bucky said.

"There's a solution, a better solution. We just need to find it," Carl said, scratching his temple.

"Eye for an eye," Bucky said.

"And a tooth for a tooth," Clarence quickly added, the two of them never so close in lockstep than at this moment.

"I'll come see you in prison, then," Carl said. "Just remember to keep your back to the wall, and don't drop the soap in the shower."

At this Clarence burst out laughing. When he saw Anna and Carl looking at him with blank expressions, he tried to muffle it with a cough.

"Well, what do you want to do, Dad? Let them get away with it?"

"No, we just—we can't sink to their level, that's all."

"If you come up with something better, let me know. Otherwise, me and good ol' Patricia here will pump them all with lead."

"Still calling her Patricia after all these years, huh?" Clarence said.

"You don't change a horse's name when it gets older, do you?"

"I guess not," Clarence agreed.

Just then the sound of a car could be heard outside the farm. Bucky stood up with his shotgun, and walked over to the window. He could see Roy Callaghan driving though the dust in his white Cadillac, with Cole sitting on the passenger side. Something told Bucky this wasn't just an ordinary father–son outing.

"Looks like Roy and Cole have decided to pay a visit," Bucky said. He put the shotgun down to the right of the door and then brushed off his face, his hair, and his clothes, almost like he was doing his best to wipe off the smell of Anna before her inquiring husband came around. He looked at Carl, who seemed just as nervous.

"What are we gonna tell them?" Bucky said to Carl, realizing that for him, this quandary was now two-pronged, because he would have to answer not only about the horse but also, possibly, about Anna. Surely it would be obvious to Cole once he had one look at her tousled hair, easy demeanor, and sweet postcoital smell.

"The truth," Carl said. "They got every right to know about what happened to Nitro, so let's try to work this out together. It's the only way, Son."

"He's right," Anna said. Looking at her, Bucky wasn't sure which truth she was referring to.

Before there was a chance for any further discussion, Roy and Cole were at the door. Bucky let them in. Right away Cole looked around for Anna, spotting her sitting casually at the kitchen table with Clarence and Carl. Bucky greeted them both cordially, like it was normal for Anna to stay over at Bucky's and to sit around so casually with her faux in-laws in the morning, and led them into the kitchen. When he tried to lock eyes again with Cole—perhaps to convey that same telepathy they'd shared the night of the fire—Cole looked away. Cole sat next to Anna and put his hand on her arm. Carl brought over an extra chair and put it at the end of the table for Roy.

"Have a seat, have a seat. It's good to see you both. Just not under these circumstances, unfortunately," Carl said.

"Carl," Roy said, taking a deep breath, surely about to launch right into it.

"Nitro's dead," Carl said, before Roy could continue.

"I figured. Cole told me about the blaze, and I didn't see much of the barn left when we were pulling up. I'm sorry, Carl."

"I know you are, Roy. Let's do what we gotta do to make this right."

"What happened?" Roy asked, before going into any terms, which were sure to be substantial.

"It was my fault," Bucky said before Carl could put a spin on it and somehow make it seem like it was his own responsibility. "The Caruso gang."

"What? Who the fuck is the Caruso gang?"

"I got mixed up with them through Max and Bernie. I was supposed to fix the qualifier, but I didn't do it. This was their revenge. They tried to send a message—which they did."

"I don't know what to say here, guys," Roy said. "I guess, first, that

I'm disappointed, Bucky, that you'd even get involved in that kind of thing. I've known your father a long time and ..."

"I didn't have a choice, Roy," Bucky said. "It was Max. He bet the farm, so to speak."

"Max, of course," Roy said.

"It's always Max," Clarence said, like it was old hat already.

"Look what they did to him!" Carl said. He pointed to Bucky, as if he needed to highlight the horror show that was his face.

"I want to fix this," Bucky said, clenching his fists, "with blood. We need to go to Pistol Farms."

"Whoa now, son," Roy said, putting the brakes on Bucky's plan. "These people sound dangerous. Look what they're capable of."

"There's no talking sense into him," Carl said. "Pulled out his shotgun and everything."

"Patricia," Clarence said.

"Patricia?" Roy repeated, looking confused.

"Yeah, that's his shotgun's name. Patricia," Clarence said, looking at Roy, who was unamused, and holding up his finger to Bucky.

"We cannot solve this thing with violence. If these guys are professionals, if this is what they do for a living, then we'd be getting into the wrong pissing match."

"What should we do then?" Cole finally spoke up.

"The fire marshal's coming over later. I guess we'll just tell him what happened and get the cops involved," Carl said.

Bucky and Clarence both shook their heads, still seeking vigilante justice.

"No cops," Roy blurted out.

"What? Why?" Carl asked him.

"I think it'd be best not to get the cops involved," Roy said, without getting into detail about *why* they shouldn't involve law enforcement like any ordinary citizen would.

"What about the insurance?" Carl said.

"Ahh, about that,"

"Here we go," Clarence piped up.

"Let's just say that Nitro's sire isn't 'supposed to be' who he is, and that the guy I acquired him from, well, he didn't get him from the most honest means either. Call it the case of a missing load."

"What are you trying to say exactly, Roy?" Carl said.

"We stole Nitro's sperm from Louisiana Rampart. We brought the wrong mare under cover at the stud farm—long story—and ended up with Nitro. The sire that we have Nitro listed to is a winner for sure, but not like this."

Bucky looked over at Carl, who sat still, seemingly in shock about what Roy had just revealed. Imagine that, Roy Callaghan, former president of a successful midsized automotive manufacturer, Roy's Carbs—and father-in-law of the woman Bucky wanted to rip out of the arms of his son—was no better than a common criminal. For Bucky, this was sweet vindication. And that he'd revealed it in front of Anna—even better! Carl wasn't rich, but at least he'd come by what he had honestly.

"I've also been having IRS issues. Man, those guys are nosey," Roy continued, just when Bucky thought he was done with his disclosure. "I just don't need the attention right now."

Finally! Bucky thought. *It's out there for all to know that the seed money from Roy Callaghan's enterprise was planted with criminal hands.* Roy was a phony, phony, phony. Bucky hoped that Anna saw it too.

"So what do you want to do, Roy?" Carl asked.

"Well, first, and I'm sorry for this one, old friend, but I'm going to need title to the farm."

Before Carl could object, Roy continued. "There's no time limit here. You can stay as long as you want, but until you find a way to pay back your share of Nitro, as stated here in the agreement," Roy said, pulling an envelope from his inside pocket and sliding it across the table, "I'm gonna have to proceed with this. You can get it back anytime. But, just, it's a lot of money. I hope you understand, Carl?"

"Of course, I do," Carl said, reaching across the table for the envelope.

"Like I said, stay as long as you like. My lawyer will call you in forty-eight hours to go over the details. As far as the cops and insurance is concerned, you don't have to tell them anything. Nitro was training over at my facility, *right?* Tell him Clarence burned the barn down with a cigar or something, or better yet Max—that one's more believable—and we'll work it out between us."

Bucky looked at Carl. His face was ashen, and the dark pouches beneath his eyes looked sadder than ever. It seemed that there was not much left of Carl, that this whole situation and the constant financial pressure had aged him.

"Okay, Roy. We'll do it your way," Carl said, shaking his head, "and I don't care about the money, or the farm. I just don't get—what I don't get is ... that horse is worth at least half a million, Roy. He was murdered, set on fire by a bunch of cowards. I just hate the thought of them getting away with it."

"Oh, they won't get away with it," Clarence said, dusting off his shoulder. "No siree ..."

"That's right, Carl, they won't," Roy said with authority. "You gotta trust me on this one. Things could be a lot worse. Let's just ... we'll figure it out. Give it some time, Carl. Nothing hasty right now." Looking at Bucky, Roy added, "That includes you too."

"Agreed," Carl said. Then he stood up from the table. Roy and Clarence followed him to the door. Bucky, Anna, and Cole were slower to get up, looking at each other around the table. If they were still kids, Anna would probably have had chocolate milk foam on her upper lip, and Cole would be wearing that dumb straw hat that Bucky remembered. If they were kids, they'd still be the three amigos, charging through the meadow of their youth, one for all. Unfortunately, they were not still kids, and the situation they now found themselves in was anything but child's play. Who would be first to mention last night's sleepover? Or did it even need to be mentioned? And if so, should it be brought up now, in the rubble of the Whalens' shattered enterprise? There was a split second before Anna would shuffle off with her *real* husband and her *real* father-in-law. Bucky wondered if Cole would say something, or if he should say something.

Perhaps this was the time Anna had been waiting for. It could be more of an intervention where they all held hands and Anna calmly announced her decision to leave Cole.

"Sorry, guys, that you have to go through all this. You know we're here for you," Cole said, clearly for show, and in the same conciliatory tone as Roy's, no doubt learned behavior from the man who had just successfully maneuvered the farm out of Bucky's father's hands, probably his plan all along. What was he going to do, pave over it and build a minimall or condos? Bucky's anger welled up, before rationalizing it with his recent escapade with Anna. But Cole didn't seem to be angry. Perhaps he'd learned that jealously is a goat, and to prove his security he had to go to even further reaches, going so far as offering up Anna like she were Christmas cookies left for Santa, sure they would remain uneaten.

"Thanks, pal. I know you are," Bucky said to Cole, just because he knew he needed it, that they all needed it.

"We'll get it sorted," Cole said casually, and with a finality that irked Bucky. Of course *you'll* get it sorted. You can *sort* through anything when you have the resources, when it's not you. Bucky often resented Cole's lack of adversity. It seemed he barely experienced a stroke of bad luck or a rainy day. He had never mourned a family member, and when he was growing up, luxury items seemed to magically appear; like the regulation-sized arcade games in his basement, or the hot red Mustang presented to him on his sixteenth birthday. When they were kids, Cole would always win at things like who could spit further or, from a standing position, who could get more piss into a bottle. Cole was the one who would find money in the streets; would beat Bucky on sports bets; who could throw farther and hit longer; and who was better-looking by a fair stretch.

Cole and Anna got up. Bucky followed them to the door. The moment of confrontation that Bucky expected never came. While Roy, Carl, and Clarence stood outside talking about a horse named Lula Bell Jones, Bucky felt Cole's hand on his shoulder. Bucky turned to face him, and just like that, his perfect sky-blue eyes turned to ice, his voice deepened, and his chest crossed the social barrier between them.

"I saw you with Anna last night. Not to mention your little slumber party. Better not be getting any ideas."

"Relax, nothing happened," Bucky said. When it came to Anna, battle lines needed to be drawn. He felt like saying, *Things have changed, pal. You stole her from me; I'm stealing her back,* but he didn't. *Any decision must seem to come from Anna, so be cool,* Bucky told himself as Cole leaned closer and raised his finger—the flicker in his eyes now a blaze.

"Stay ... the fuck ... away from her. Got it?"

Anna looked on nervously, an obvious party to what had just unfolded, and looked pleadingly at Bucky not to overreact.

"You're being paranoid, old buddy. Anna's yours. She married you, not me."

"I suggest that once you get all healed, you stay up in New York."

"Don't worry. Never said I wanted to stick around here, did I?" Bucky said, looking at Anna. "Besides, we got business."

"Let's go, Anna," Cole said, like they were playing a game of red rover.

Anna followed Cole, before remembering that she had left her Jeep there overnight. So instead of getting in, she gave him a kiss on the cheek and said she'd see them back at the farm.

Roy took the wheel and waved goodbye, while Cole sat stone-faced, looking straight ahead on the passenger's side. Bucky watched as they peeled away. Given the new revelation of Roy's misdealing, he now saw Cole more clearly as his father's right-hand man, his stooge, his petulant protégé whom he had just successfully coached on the subtleties of how to wrangle away your best friend's farm; Cole was the beneficiary of his father's ill deeds, sure to be bequeathed a vast sum and admired with his father's same esteem without ever having to hang his own shingle. As Bucky watched them leave, he couldn't control his resentment. Once the Cadillac pulled out, Bucky watched the back of Anna's head bob away as she followed them in her Jeep, hoping that maybe for a moment, just one split second, she might look back, or even turn around—but she kept on going.

CHAPTER 15

"Smells like shit," Max said when he woke up. He looked around, for a moment confused by the change in scenery. It was midafternoon, and the Manhattan skyscrapers in the rearview mirror looked to Max like ghosts in the smog. They had just gotten off the New Jersey Turnpike and passed the slaughterhouse, and were driving east toward Pistol Farms.

"Welcome to Secaucus," Charlie said. "We'll be there soon. Maybe we should go through our spiel."

"Spiel? What spiel?"

"The spiel where you try not to get both of us killed."

"Oh, that," Max said, staring ahead through the window. "Well, what do you want me to say?"

"I guess just tempt him with the offer of one more fix, and see if he takes the bait."

"So no script?" Max asked. "I was looking forward to being fed lines, like when one of them Broadway actors forgets his line on stage and calls for a line. '*Line!*' Like that."

"I won't be feeding you lines, Maxi, and for that matter, I cannot appear to be complicit in anything that you say. I apprehended you. Check that: I kicked the shit out of you and then apprehended you. We're not friends on this one. You gotta remember that."

"Okay, Baker, I think I got it."

"Good," Charlie said. Then he turned off the main road and onto a smaller one, where rocks and gravel bounced against the underside of the car. He rolled to a stop in front of a metal gate with a No Trespassing sign.

"Just follow my lead," Charlie said, before getting out to open the gate. Max nodded, fearful now that he might take a beating worse than Bucky had, or might not come out alive.

When they both got out of the car, Charlie pushed Max like he was a warden trying to direct his inmate.

"Hey!" Max said, turning around to face Charlie.

"We're on," Charlie said and pounded on the door.

After a few moments, Tony appeared at the door. He was wearing a tucked-in black T-shirt that showed off his sinewy arms, and black jeans with a silver studded belt.

"Weeeeell. Looky what we have here," Tony said. "Come in, come in. Welcome to Pistol Farms," he said, as if they'd just walked into the Red Roof Inn and were about to be greeted with hot coffee and a continental breakfast. Charlie pushed Max through the door. Max stumbled in front of Frankie and Gino, who were sitting at the table.

"Gentlemen. It's nice to see you," Max said, as if he hadn't just cost them thousands of dollars and a trip to the Breeders. Gino got up from the table and walked up to Max.

"Have a seat," Gino said, digging his fingers deep into Max's collar while guiding him to the chair across from Frankie. Max winced from the pain and looked at Frankie, who looked to him like a grenade had gone off in his eye. Max imagined Frankie was a real villain, like from the comic books or James Bond movies, and that the angrier he got, the more the color in his scar would change from red to purple overload, and maybe even smoke would come out of his ears. Max looked up at Gino and Tony, who stood on either side of him like bookends, and knew there was no turning back.

"You fuckin' stink," Frankie said. "Looks like Charlie here gave you a couple love taps, didn't he? Good job, Baker." Charlie nodded proudly.

"Listen, Frankie," Max began to say. Before he could finish, Frankie slammed his hands down on table.

"Don't 'Listen, Frankie' me. You were supposed to do something. You were supposed to guarantee me something, but nooooo. What does he do?" Frankie said, looking at Gino and Tony. "He doesn't deliver his fuckin' end. So you know what I ought to do? Start by chopping off every one of your big fat fingers, and then let Tony here hammer a nail into your left nut." At this, Max couldn't help cringe. He knew it was a real threat when Tony sidled up and acknowledged his willingness to do such a thing.

"C'mon," Max pleaded, desperate for at least one line of defense.

"*What* did I just fuckin' say?" Frankie shot up from the table. Now Max was sure his scar was reaching purple overload.

"I'm sorry," Max said. It was enough for Frankie to take his seat and collect himself from his hurricane gale of anger.

"It's gonna take more than sorry," Frankie said, calming himself down by massaging his rings and then spreading his hands and connecting his fingertips. "A lot more than sorry."

Max braced for whatever his reparations might be.

"Your farm. It's mine now."

"What? *You can't* ..."

"I can do what I want. I can do anything."

"Can't you just start with something small, like a tractor? Besides, I only have a share in it. You gotta take it up with my brother and the kid."

"Oh, don't worry. I think they'll come around," Frankie said. He laughed with Tony and Gino.

"Besides," Max said, sensing that now was his opportunity to strike and doing his best not to look at Charlie, "I can do you one better."

"Oh yeah?" Frankie said. "Humor me."

Max enjoyed Frankie's curiosity like a magician who fails to reveal his trick—for what could it be? *Do I have property in the Bahamas? A couple of sports cars? Surely he wouldn't want my shitty Cutlass.* Then he came out with it. "Nitro."

"Nitro?" Frankie said, spinning the gold and diamond ring around on his pinky finger. "What about him?"

"He'll be running in the Breeders."

"Ya ... and?"

"We can do something."

"What do you want to do?"

"What we didn't do last time."

"With Nitro?"

"Yeah, with Nitro," Max said, wondering to himself when Frankie had become so thick.

At this, Frankie could no longer contain himself and burst out laughing.

"You idiot. We got Nitro."

"You what?"

"We burned your barn down and took your prize racehorse. I guess news doesn't travel so fast in the Whalen clan."

"You son of a bitch," Max said, barely containing his urge to spit in Frankie's rusty eye.

"Settle down, settle down," Frankie said, surprisingly not angered by Max's name-calling, and showing a willingness that he was ready to talk. Max couldn't help but think for a moment about his brother and Bucky, and his parents who had taken him in with nothing to gain. The one thing that had bound them all was now burned to the ground.

"Anyone hurt?" Max asked, holding his breath for Frankie's answer.

"Don't worry—your brother and everyone's okay. The rest of the horses got it. But Nitro? I suspect they all think he's toast."

"What good is a dead horse?" Max said, seizing the opportunity to come up with an angle. "You can't race a dead horse. I'll tell you what, Frankie, let's bring him back from the dead. I'll get them back their horse in exchange for one final fix in the Breeders, and we'll all be square."

While Frankie thought about it, Max added an exclamation point, to really translate it into Frankie's language.

"It's a million-dollar purse."

Frankie's face lit up, and Max, like an old salesman, could tell that instant that he'd gotten him. Frankie nodded to Gino to sit down, and Tony followed. They all hunched over, waiting intently for Frankie's response. After a further pause, Frankie deliberating now just for show, he finally said, "I like it. I think we can do something with that."

"How do you want to play it?" Max asked.

"A perfect trip," Frankie said, this time without hesitation. "Wire to wire. There's no reason why that horse can't do it, and I don't mind giving him some help."

Gino and Tony nodded approvingly. Max, careful not to overstep his bounds or look directly at the volcano that was Frankie's eye socket, said, "Good idea, Frankie. Really good idea. Let me talk to the boys on this one. I'm sure they'd like to make it happen."

"Max," Frankie said, "you don't understand. You fuck this up, you're dead. You're dead, your brother's dead, that snot nose fuckin' prick Bucky is dead. The whole enchilada. Got it?"

"Yeah, I think I got it. Pretty clear."

"You're lucky I haven't killed you already. This goes south and Tony here is going to disembowel you."

"We'll make it work. I promise you."

"One last thing. Tell your brother I'm also going to need half of the purse money. Call it a courtesy for screwing us on the last race."

"I'll talk to him," Max said. "I mean, yes, Frankie of course. We have a deal."

"Good. Now get the hell out of here. And take a shower, would you? Boys, show him the door," Frankie said. Tony and Gino burst into action.

"Thanks, Frankie. You won't regret this," Max said while Gino and Tony dragged him out by his armpits.

"Baker, you stay here a minute," Max heard Frankie say, before he was tossed outside and the door closed behind him. When he composed himself, Max listened for a scuffle or gunshots, anything, but it was quiet. He wondered if their charade had worked or if Charlie was being interrogated inside. Not wanting to stick around to find out, Max got in his car and peeled out. He hoped that Charlie wasn't in danger, and rationalized his hasty departure by convincing himself it was more believable to strand him there. They weren't friends on this one, after all. And besides, the sooner he got back to Harrington, the better.

Max relished the thought of surprising Carl with the information that Nitro was actually alive, but he knew it would be hard getting him in on a fix. And what if Carl actually agreed to it and it didn't work out again? He was used to letting his brother down, but to cause his certain death would be more than he could bear. And the kid? Who knew what the kid will do. If Frankie went out of his way to ensure he won, would Bucky intentionally lose to make a point? Max's stock with Bucky had never been lower, and to ask this of him, he knew, would draw some ire. Then there was the bigger picture with Charlie and Harold. How could Max be involved in two major scams in the same race? This was not on the level of anything he had done before, and it meant serious prison time if he got busted.

If it worked out, maybe it would be a good life in Panama, Max thought, as there was no way he could stick around. He pictured himself drinking a cold beer in some expat bar next to a tattooed pirate, when Marge Tate walks through the door. Funny that he could never find her down any US highway. There she'd be just as vivacious as ever, with her foul mouth and stringy blonde hair. As he drove along the turnpike, he remembered one time on their way back from Florida, Marge promised him a blowjob every hundred miles. She'd damn near completed the task before he swerved into a guardrail, fishtailed, and did a one-eighty, finally coming to a dead stop face-to-face with a big rig, whose heads-up driver had seen trouble ahead and was able to avoid catastrophe. If Marge hadn't almost killed him on the road, she would have done it at the bar, as she was both the best and the worst as a drinking partner. Pound for pound she was a dynamo, and could keep up with Max until she couldn't anymore, which was when things got sloppy. Max knew he'd never get over her, because no one had ever loved him like that, or at all for that matter.

Besides Marge, of all the actors in the charade of Max's life who had come and gone, it was his birth parents whom he wondered about the most. What would his life have been like had he never been abandoned? What were his parents like? Maybe they were good Christians. Maybe they were rich. Where did they live? What did they do? Did they have more children? Were they drug addicts? Why did they give him up? Why? Why? Why? There was a time when Max actually thought about tracking them down and asking them in person, but he knew they'd probably take one look at him and realize they'd made the right decision.

As Max drove along, he couldn't help but wonder where it all went wrong. When did the money dry up? *How did I piss it all away? I could have been a millionaire.* He remembered his heyday when he had expensive watches and jewelry. He even owned a '76 Corvette that he'd lost to a royal flush, and a fur coat that he'd left in a diner.

To say he was a spendthrift was an understatement; Max was downright reckless with his money. It seemed he had forgotten all about the perils of abject poverty, as there was no more need to scrimp and save when the money came in so easy. Then came Marge. Over the course of their short marriage, he'd peeled thousands off his bankroll to support her. Thinking about it now, Max realized that he'd never known where most of that money went. Maybe she was socking it all away, and finally had saved enough to buy a bungalow somewhere. Maybe she went back to Encinitas, where she said she was from, although she'd never taken him home to visit.

While Max reminisced about the good old days, he felt more than just a tinge of sadness. What he felt was an overwhelming urge to drink, so he pulled off the next exit and bought a bottle of Jim Beam. With the bottle on his knee, it got easier as the miles opened up. The sky dimmed, and the clouds stretched across the late-afternoon sky like a glowing white shag carpet. His belly felt warm and fuzzy. His face loosened and his mustache twitched. Soon it would be time to play Jesus and bring Nitro back from the dead. He hoped he could do it—the resurrection. He hoped Carl and Bucky couldn't see the seam that was splitting inside of him. He'd never felt like that before. He was glad for the whisky to numb his senses, because as he got closer, he knew there was something more pervasive and nagging. Somewhere along the way the stakes had become too high, and now, after a good payday, it was time to get out for good.

CHAPTER 16

Bucky and Clarence were sitting outside in the twilight by the burned-out barn. Around the perimeter of the structure was a trail of damp soot that the firefighters had trampled and left big boot marks on the day before. The air still smelled of smoke and death. They had brought over two chairs from the front porch, and were drinking beers and talking about the horses like it was an Irish wake.

"Ace McGee, that damn rascal, would bite me in the ass and then smile at me after," Clarence said.

"Nitro was something else," Bucky said, "Man, did he fly."

"He ran a good mile, and was always on the bit," Clarence said.

"Who, Nitro?" Bucky asked.

"No, Ace McGee. He was bombproof, that horse."

"Yeah, Ace McGee was okay. Old, though. Kind of how I'm feeling right now," Bucky said. He hugged his arms together, clutching himself in the grip of both the physical and emotional pain that enveloped him. It had been just a few days since the Crossroads, and hours since the barn had burned down and he'd slept with Anna. Bucky wondered how so many life events could have unfolded in such a short period of time. He had been thinking about Cole's not so subtle request that he stay in New York. Under normal circumstances it would be his pleasure just to get into his car and go, maybe leave a smoke trail behind him, but now it felt better to be at home. Carl and Clarence were really all he had, and it had taken him all those lonely nights in New York to realize it. But he couldn't stay in Harrington for long, and he knew it. Even if Anna did leave Cole, was she just going to hop farms, become automatically plugged into a new family with its nuances, tragedies, and dying bloodline, doomed to failure and with nowhere to go but down? How could she possibly leave a compound equipped for her every need and take up on a scant farm mortgaged to the tits, in escrow to her father-in-law, who would be less than thrilled with her betrayal of Cole. No, that wouldn't work. But perhaps knowing now that Roy was a crook—that's right, c-r-o-o-k—might make leaving easier on moral grounds. But what did morals count for these days, anyway? Not much. Adultery was still adultery, not to mention it had been committed with his supposed best friend's wife, which was something that Bucky was also grappling with. How could he carry on beneath the sun in Harrington in the daylight hours— where mothers push their babes in strollers, and the shopkeepers sweep their storefronts, and all the world is there to witness their love as they hold hands and run through sprinklers? Perhaps it would be their dirty little secret and they would escape to Rehoboth on weekends and make love at night to the sounds of the dying waves. A new life of lies and deception awaited!

No, I couldn't do it like that, Bucky thought to himself. *If I were to marry Anna, it would have to be done the adult way. I would have to talk to Cole, and maybe even ask Walter, Anna's wisp of father, whatever remnants are left of the man after thirty-five years of marriage to Judith and the death of his sweet son, Bobby. Surely I could appeal to him,* Bucky thought, as he was the lesser of two evils, and usually listened while he smoked his pipe and reeked of erudition. So perhaps Walter would give Anna away and she and Bucky could do a semiformal wedding, something not too difficult for Cole—maybe give him a silver card holder with his name inscribed on it to help ease the pain of the long, lonely life he was now certain to endure. *Whatever the wedding, or perhaps no wedding at all—even eloping would do … And why does eloping sound so extreme for lovers in flight anyway? Not like it's illegal,* Bucky thought. *Maybe we could just call it going away and never come back. Perhaps Anna would be okay with a life without buying the best*

clothes and items so casually without concern for cost, and revert to a life
of price checking and late-night couponing at the kitchen table. But would
Anna go with him? That was the question he kept asking himself over
and over. And if she did agree, where would they go anyway?

"The colt, the fuckin' colt, those motherfucking cocksuckers."
Clarence, who apparently had been talking the whole time, spat and
then threw his beer bottle into the fire pit.

"Don't worry, Clarence—there'll be a reckoning."

"A reckoning? I like that. What should we do?" Clarence said.
Then he sat back down in his chair.

"I haven't figured it out just yet."

"Something nasty. Let's go Waco on them. Something to make
those punks suffer like my babies did when he burned them alive.
Maybe we should burn *them* alive, or bury them alive. Cut their
throats. Blow them to pieces with Patricia."

"You have no shortage of great ideas, Clarence, that's for sure."
Bucky laughed. It was the first time he'd smiled that day. As much
as Bucky liked the idea of violence, what Carl and Roy had said had
finally gotten through. He knew it would be better to find another
way to get even. They were outgunned after all. Plus, Bucky had never
murdered anyone and didn't want to go to prison. But what could
they do?

As Bucky and Clarence sat and spitballed ways to get even with
the Caruso gang, they heard a rumble in the distance. When Bucky
turned to look, wincing from the pain in his ribs, which seemed to
have been the bull's-eye for Tony's truncheon, he saw Max's Cutlass
swerving down the road. Bucky leaned over and grabbed his shotgun.

"Well, looky what we have here," Bucky said, standing up from
his chair. Max turned the corner and entered the farm. He pulled up a
few meters from where the barn used to stand. When Max opened the
car door, Bucky noticed a whisky bottle fall out. He heard Max swear
as he struggled with the seat belt over his girth while the car interior
kept beeping, until Max cut the ignition.

"I came as soon as I heard," Max called out.

Bucky cocked the shotgun and pointed it at him. "What do you know about this?"

"Whoa, whoa, Nephew," Max pleaded. With his hands up, he treaded carefully as he walked closer to Bucky and Clarence. "I come in peace."

"You're fuckin' drunk," Bucky said.

"No ... I'm not drunk. Just had a taste, is all. Now put down the gun, would you?"

"We're done with you, Max. Since your friends burned down Clarence's quarters, he's taking your room, so you'll have to sleep in the trailer, or go wherever it is you disappear to all the time," Bucky said, feeling somewhat better now, even righteous. He lowered the shotgun to his side.

"You're forgetting I own a third of this place. And besides, I have good news."

"Don't want to hear it."

"Oh, I think you'll want to hear this. It's about Nitro."

"Let me guess, you found the perfect urn?" Clarence said.

"No, no, I didn't ... but good one," Max said, pausing a beat, trying to stretch out the suspense of the information he withheld, which to him was akin to revealing that Elvis or Amelia Earhart were both still alive and well.

"Out with it," Bucky said, running out of patience and tempted to raise the shotgun again. Maybe he'd just go over and butt-whip Max instead of blowing a hole clear through him.

"He's alive," Max said, standing there self-satisfied, hardly looking trustworthy with his fat lip, shiner, and disgusting shirt with sweat, dirt, and bloodstains. He hitched up his pants by the belt and waited for their reaction.

Clarence and Bucky were both caught somewhere between disbelief and astonishment. Max stood waiting for them to say something, perhaps to heap praise on him, but after a few silent moments of both men looking at him, he finally added, "He's at Pistol Farms. Alive and well."

"You know this for sure?" Bucky said, the reality of the situation finally dawning on him.

"I just came from there. Where do you think I got this shiner from?" Max said, obviously pleased with the mileage he was getting out of Charlie Baker's handiwork. "And besides, you see the horse trailer around anywhere? They must have used it to tow away Nitro."

Clarence and Bucky looked at each other, both still too deep in the fog to have noticed the missing trailer until that point.

"Did you get proof of life?" Clarence asked.

"Proof of life? What the hell do I look like, a CIA operative? Nitro's alive."

"What'd you do, Max?" Bucky said, waiting for the rub, tempted again to flex Patricia's cold steel in Max's direction.

"I didn't do nothin'."

"Yeah, right," Clarence said.

"Let's go and tell Pops, then," Bucky said, still trying to contain whatever hope or excitement he had over the prospect that Nitro was still alive.

When they got to the back of the farmhouse, the three of them walked in through the back door, and into Carl's office, where he was asleep with his head on the desk.

"Wakey, wakey, Pops. We have a surprise visitor," Bucky said.

"Hi, Brother," Max said when Carl looked up, confused as to the sudden urgency that now pervaded his small office.

"Apparently Nitro is still alive," Bucky said. When the words came out, he could see a dim light flicker in Carl's eyes.

"What's this you say?" Carl said, still drowsy, reaching for his ledger, perhaps to make it look like he had just been busy.

"You heard me. Max just came from Pistol Farms and says Nitro's alive."

Carl looked at Max. "Is it true?"

"It's true," Max said.

"Did you see him?"

"No, I didn't see him," Max said, looking at Clarence, "but they got him."

"How do we get him back?" Carl asked.

"The Breeders."

"Don't even say it, Max," Bucky said, knowing what was coming next.

"All you gotta do is drive him," Max said, "to win this time."

"And if I lose?"

"You won't lose."

"There are no guarantees in this sport," Carl said to Max.

"Frankie says he'll give you some help. It'll be a perfect trip."

"Christ, is there anyone in this sport that's not corrupt anymore?" Bucky said, shaking his head, wondering who else was in on it with Frankie.

"I agree with Bucky. This one stinks," Clarence said.

"What are our options?" Carl said. He then pulled out a cigar from his top drawer and stoked it to life, the match quickly burning down to his fingers. It seemed to Bucky that his father was not yet ruling out whatever it was that Max was scheming up.

"I'll tell you what our options are," Max said. "We fix the race and get Nitro back, or the farm gets divided up like a turkey pie in Ethiopia."

"I hate both of those options," Bucky said.

"So do I, Son, but it's just ... I don't know." Carl sighed. "Maybe we should get Roy on the horn, let him know about this latest development. It's mostly his horse after all."

Before anyone could object, Carl picked up the phone, punched in the numbers, and put it on speaker. After a few rings, a woman's voice answered.

"Hi, Mary-Ellen. Carl Whalen here. Roy around?"

"Oh, hi, Carl. He's around somewhere. Let me get him for you," Mary-Ellen said. Then screamed at the top of her lungs until Roy picked up.

"Roy, it's Carl. I'm here with Bucky and Clarence … and Max just showed up. We got some news for you. It's about Nitro."

"Hi, Carl. Everything go okay with the inspector?"

"He bought the story."

"That's good. We'll figure this out, Carl."

"There's something else," Carl said, looking across at Max as if to say, *If this is a joke, time to fess up right now*, but Max didn't budge. "Turns out he's alive. He didn't get killed in the fire."

"What? What do you mean? How in the hell?"

"He was kidnapped."

"What are you talking about, Carl?"

"Same guys who burned down the barn scooped up Nitro. Now they want to make a deal."

"How do you know?"

"Max."

"Fuckin' Max," Roy said. Everyone in the room looked at Max, who raised his hands like an athlete exaggerating his innocence in front of a referee.

"I guess it doesn't matter. He's alive; that's what really matters. Now, what do we have to do to get him back?"

"Something that I'm not especially proud of, old friend," Carl said. From the expression on his father's face, Bucky could tell just how much he meant it. "We need to fix the Breeders."

"Fix the Breeders! Are you crazy?" Roy belted out on the line.

"It's not as bad as it sounds," Max said, perking up, and sitting on the edge of his chair so that Roy could hear him better. "He's just gotta win, and Frankie's going to make sure there's nothing but daylight."

"That's just … that's just rotten, is what it is," Roy said.

"I know, Roy," Carl said, "but—"

"Would this mean we get Nitro back?"

"Absolutely," Max said. "But there's one more thing."

"Holy shit, Max," Bucky said, with his head in his hands.

"Frankie's going to need half the purse money," Max said with his elbows crossed, ready for the blowback. Bucky was relieved that it wasn't an organ that Frankie demanded.

"That's a joke! No way. That's my horse, and *I* have to give *my* money away to those gangsters?" Roy squawked on the line.

"Roy, Roy," Max said, "you don't understand. That's it. There's no negotiating here. If we want Nitro back, that's the deal. Frankie's gonna help us win, and he wants more action on it. It's our only play."

From the silence on the phone it was clear that Roy was thinking about it.

"We're going to need to see the horse first," Roy finally said.

"Of course," Max said. Bucky, who until then had been in utter disbelief that this whole thing was happening again, looked up brightly from his hands and his disillusionment.

"I'll meet with Frankie. Get me a sit-down, Max. I'll do the deal, and bring Nitro back to Roy's farm," Bucky said.

"Son," Carl said, looking at Bucky with his weepy eyes. Bucky didn't budge.

"Roy? How do you feel about all this?" Carl said, looking at the phone console as if it were Roy's person.

"Well, I'm not thrilled about this entire situation. Let's just be clear about that. But if it's our only option, then it's our only option."

"Seems like it is," Carl said.

"Then let's do it," Roy said. "And no guns. Got it, Bucky?"

"Of course," Bucky said. He was now calm and clear-eyed, without the usual strain he carried in his forehead and between his brows.

"Good. Let me know how it goes," Roy said, and then he hung up.

"It's on, boys!" Max said.

Carl sat back and took a few quick sucks on his cigar, blowing out a thick cloud of smoke.

"You know this isn't a good thing you've done here, Max."

"This is the last time, Brother. I swear," Max said, in what was the closest thing to honesty or sincerity he could muster.

"I hope so. And I don't know if Bucky told you, but we put Clarence in your room. That's just how it's gotta be right now. The trailer's outside, or you can sleep on the couch."

"I can find my way, big brother. You know that," Max said. He turned to Clarence. "Don't get too comfortable. You don't wanna know what I did on that mattress."

"I could only goddamn imagine," Carl said. Max grunted as he hauled himself up and out of his chair.

"Tell Frankie to meet me alone at the Crossroads next Tuesday at eight, and to bring Nitro," Bucky said to Max.

"Got it. Now, if this is all done, then I best get going. Can probably still make it to Dover for the ninth. See you, boys."

Bucky was happy that Max was quick to go, as he could finally have the discussion with Carl and Clarence he had been waiting for. Only after Bucky had watched Max lumber toward his car through the office window did he prepare Carl and Clarence for what he had to say.

"Dad, Clarence. As I was sitting here listening to Max and Roy, all of us trying to figure a way out of this … It seems like we've been going backward ever since I moved to New York. It wasn't supposed to be like this. And to be honest, if I stay up at Speedway, this shit's just gonna keep on happening, if not with Frankie, then with Bernie. And if it's not them, it'll be someone else. That's why … I was thinking about it, and then it came it to me. The only way to get out, to *really* get out, is for me to wear a wire." He paused. "I'm going to wear a wire. Let's bust these assholes. Up to this point, we haven't done anything wrong. No way I'm going to keep doing this. The way I see it is, they'll probably end up killing us anyway, so let's do it right."

Bucky looked at Clarence, who, from the flaring of his nostrils, still seemed to have vengeance on his mind, whereas Carl sat up from his chair and looked straight into Bucky's eyes.

"I like it. I think it's a great idea."

"Good, Dad. You know I'm not like those guys."

"Of course not."

"How do we do it? Going to take more than that Hasbro detective kit I bought you for your tenth birthday, y'know."

"I'll talk to JP. He was here for the fire. We can confide in him."

"You're going to trust that gingerbread cracker with this?" Clarence said.

"I know he's not Magnum P.I., but I don't know how this works. I don't think you just call the FBI or stroll into HQ bursting with this information."

"Magnum? I don't think that yokel could Scooby-Doo himself out of a telephone booth, let alone bust a plan to fix the stakes," Clarence said.

"I agree with Bucky," Carl said. "He'll know what to do. Besides, we could use some discretion here."

"You got something better, Clarence?"

"You know what I got."

"Well, that's not happening."

"I guess it's settled then," Carl said, as if to announce he had closed the book on it.

"Fine, have it your way," Clarence said, finally agreeing, much to Bucky's relief. Bucky would need everyone on board, and if it backfired, then they were all dead. What could go wrong? Bucky didn't doubt Frankie's proficiency to influence the results, so why not just race for daylight with Nitro? He was a winner after all. Was it wrong that he had more confidence in Frankie holding up his end than in JP coming up with a sting? If he could just get Frankie on record, then maybe they wouldn't even let the race go off, and not have to risk the safety of the horses or drivers. Then maybe Frankie and his thugs would all get thrown in jail. Bucky could keep driving and it would clean up the sport. Besides the barn and the horses, the other thing lost in all of this for Bucky was his love of driving, everything from that first tug of the line to that feeling of racing down the homestretch. It was a joy that he needed to reclaim, and if it meant a having sit-down with Frankie Fingers, then he was prepared to look the devil in the eye.

CHAPTER 17

Over the next few days, Bucky got the rest that he desperately needed, and was finally ready to do something he'd promised himself he'd do between bouts of lucid dreams and semiconsciousness—tell Cole about him and Anna. There was nothing left of him to beat down, so why not just face it? Whatever happened with Anna and Cole would be between them. It would likely still be Anna's decision, as it had always been, and since right now her love pendulum swung back in Bucky's direction, why not take a calculated risk? Sure, Anna would object, but at least it would get things out into the open, and not like the last time when Cole walked in on them. No, this was way better.

When he went downstairs, Clarence was singing "Ain't No Sunshine" over the stove. The room smelled like grease and the smoke that billowed up from the frying pan and wafted out the small kitchen window. Carl was reading the paper. It seemed to Bucky that his father was more content now that Clarence was living there. Not only could Clarence cook a mean breakfast, but also he provided company for Carl and was handy around the house. Until now, it had been a test of wills between Bucky and Carl to see who would do the dishes, take out the garbage, or do the laundry. Clarence was one who took initiative, so now things actually got done.

"Special salami and eggs comin' up. You hungry, boy?" Clarence said, turning in midflip when he heard Bucky enter the kitchen.

"No, I'm all right," Bucky said.

"Fine. Have it your way."

"Morning," Carl said. "How you feeling? Where you in a rush to? Want a coffee?"

"No, I gotta go, thanks. Mind if I borrow your truck?" Bucky asked Carl, since his truck was still up in Yonkers.

"Fine. Keys are by the mirror," Carl said, pointing to the credenza in the hall.

"Great, thanks," Bucky said, quickly scooping up the keys. He was off before any further questioning.

While Bucky drove over to Cole's farm in Carl's green jalopy, he wondered how to break the news. Should he lead into it, perhaps obfuscate the facts with sentiment and half-truths, or just come out with it? Here he was betraying his oldest friend yet again, when Cole had only ever been loyal and trustworthy. He was steady Cole who had taught Bucky how to shoot a BB gun and throw a curve.

Thinking about it, for all the times growing up Cole had stuck up for Bucky, offered him money, or invited him to ride his horses, he'd never asked for anything in return. He didn't deserve this betrayal. They both loved this girl who was caught between them, whose affection just happened to fall on Bucky first. Perhaps it was what had made Cole and Bucky brothers at the beginning. Their shared love of Anna propelled their friendship forward. They were like her two guardians, making sure she had no other suitors, or even very many girlfriends, as Cole and Bucky would stymie anyone's request or imposition.

It was in the pale that followed Bobby's wake and burial, after all the food was eaten, the guests gone home, and the grass grown over his grave, that Anna started to pull away from Bucky. Judith ardently blamed him for Bobby's death, and made Anna promise not to see him anymore. Cole seized this opportunity to become closer to Anna, and their once magnificent triumvirate had begun to dissipate. It became Anna and Cole or Cole and Bucky. Very rarely was it Anna, Cole, and Bucky all together. That was the period for Bucky when he remembered waiting and waiting, for the phone to ring, for a knock on the door, for something, anything, to happen. How could Anna just stop being his girlfriend? For all the pain that Anna had caused him, Bucky wondered, if he had the opportunity to go back to that Independence Day many years ago and not befriend the little girl who'd stood before him with her knobby joints, gangly legs, and honeycup ears, would he take it? It certainly would have made his life easier up to this point. Perhaps he and Cole would have continued being best friends, taken trips to Vegas, maybe even gone to a Super Bowl together. Maybe Bobby would still be alive.

When Bucky arrived at Anna and Cole's farm, there was a foreboding silence. No one answered the doorbell of the farmhouse, and there were no groundskeepers or farmhands buzzing about like usual. He hadn't even broken the news to Cole, but already he felt as if he were at a crime scene. Suddenly, the long, painful squeal of a horse from the barn broke the silence. Bucky limped as fast he could. When he got to the barn, he stood languidly to catch his breath for a moment before walking in slowly, afraid of what he might find.

"She's having contractions," Anna said, looking up at Bucky when he opened the stall door. She was wearing a blue bandanna, a vet apron, and long rubber gloves.

"Is she okay?" Bucky asked, kneeling down beside Anna.

"I think she's all right. It's mainly the foal that I'm worried about. It's already late, so we'll need a clean delivery."

The mare thrashed her neck and whinnied. She was covered in sweat and straw. Bucky could see the exertion in her face as she strained through another contraction and then lay back down, breathing heavily. Anna was alert and in complete control of the situation. She had a medical kit and forceps to the side, and looked intently at the horse for any signs of danger. With every contraction, there seemed to be a new depth to the animal's pain. After the contractions finally ceased and it seemed there would some respite for the old girl, Bucky noticed the white bubble emerging from her vulva. Soon after, her water burst, and the birthing process began immediately. Anna kneeled at the mare's opening. When the hooves finally appeared, Anna reached in to help guide the foal. After a few gentle pulls, Anna let the mare compose herself before her next mighty push. The horse strained and pushed harder, this time the foal budging just a little. To pass its shoulders and torso would require one mighty heave.

"Might need your help if it doesn't want to come."

"Sure, sure," Bucky said, leaning in across from Anna.

"Let's see how her next push goes. We'll both just pull if it's coming." Soon after that, the mare grunted, recoiled, and then let out a mighty wail. Her foal was coming out, so both Anna and Bucky pulled as hard as they could. When the stubborn foal finally plopped onto the earth, the weight sent Bucky flying back into the hay, and Anna onto her back. They watched in silence for a moment, looking for the horse's first breath while they in turn held their own. When finally the foal came around, Bucky and Anna stood up and hugged each other. The mare lay there exhausted. After a few minutes the foal staggered to its feet. She was a dark brown filly, and her hair was matted and wet. Bucky and Anna watched as the foal sniffed around her mother.

"She's skinny," Anna said.

"Not the prettiest either," Bucky added. He could tell already she had a short neck and questionable conformation. Her eyes were bulbous and wider apart than most horses'. Her nostrils seemed too big and her muzzle too small.

"What should we name her?" Anna asked, bestowing the honor on Bucky.

"Hmm," Bucky said, with his finger to his chin. "How about Matilda, or Tilly? Lady M, Ruby Bluesday, Chelsea? Wait. What time is it? What day is it? I always have such a hard time naming horses."

"C'mon, Bucky."

"Her whole career depends on it."

"Chelsea. I like Chelsea," Anna said.

"Chelsea it is then!" Bucky said, relieved that the name game hadn't gone on any longer.

Anna put her arm around Bucky. They stood there like two proud parents. With Anna so close, Bucky could only think about spinning her in for a long, deep kiss, but that was not what he had gone there for. Would he have to tell Cole about that as well? *It would be innocent enough,* he thought. They were just lost for a moment and couldn't contain their excitement. Bringing a life into this world is a profound experience. Perhaps he could explain to Cole that it was just a three-off. But did he really have to explain everything he ever did with Anna? If he were to just gloss over the details, then this would be but a trifle in the grand scheme of things. While he stared into Anna's eyes, the sliver in her iris like an iceberg adrift in the ocean, he fought back the urge to kiss her.

"You know, Cole is away at a sale today," Anna said. She put her hand on Bucky's chest.

"Anna, really, I ..."

"We have the rest of the day to ourselves."

"I came here to tell Cole about us."

"About us?"

"Yes. About us."

After Bucky's confirmation that it was indeed them they were talking about, everything went silent. Bucky felt the vacuum not just in the air but also in his chest as the whole world seemed to collapse all around him. It was an empty silence, a petrifying silence, the silence that lingers in the middle of the day when no one else is around.

"Not ready to own up to the fact you're in love with me, Anna?" Bucky said, his voice cracking with the sudden fear that what she might say next could devastate him. It had always been the plan to ask her to leave with him, but Bucky didn't think it'd be now. The plan was to tell Cole first, but was Anna ready to go to that next level? It was hardly a delicate transition. *Anna, fly away with me tonight. Paris, London, Rome!*

"Let's start over somewhere, Anna," Bucky said, not just to fill the rendering silence, but also to pressure her before she cast more doubt. "It can be anywhere. Anywhere you want. It's not right to do this to Cole. You've always loved me more. I know it. I told you back then that I'd love you forever, and I meant it."

After Bucky laid bare, he took a breath and stood back to look at Anna. She took off her bandanna and shook her hair down to her shoulders. When she untied the apron, Bucky admired her neck and shoulders beneath her tank top. He loved her armpits, and wondered why of all things her armpits, but it was the perfect crease and was smooth and feminine. He remembered the faint smell when he'd buried his face into her left armpit when they lay together, and couldn't wait to try her right side.

Anna put her bandanna and apron next to the medical kit. They both watched for a moment while the foal took her first milk.

"It's amazing how they just figure it out, isn't it?" Anna said in a moment of levity, not yet answering Bucky's question, which dangled before him like a million setting suns. Anna led him out of the stall. In a burst of sunlight and fresh air, they walked over to the paddock. She had not yet outright dismissed the idea, which was a positive sign, and different from her usual upbraiding at the mere suggestion, and here he was planning a whole life together, a life away from Delaware. Maybe they would even have a few cows and chickens somewhere. There were endless possibilities, but it all depended on one thing. Bucky wasn't sure if Anna's silence was to revel in her imagination about what their lives might be like together, or if she was trying to figure out a new and unique way to reject him.

"I should tell him," Anna finally said. "He's my husband."

"Does that mean …?"

"It doesn't mean anything, Bucky."

"Well, yes, of course it does. It means everything."

"I'll tell him what happened."

"And?"

"You need to slow down," Anna said.

"Aw, Christ."

"Bucky. It's just … this is a lot. Think of what you're asking here."

"Well, I'd hoped you'd be as excited about it as I am. You tell him about our affair, and I can tell him we're leaving."

"Affair!"

"Well, that's what this is. Are you not seeing this, Anna? Is it just me?"

"You make it sound so … scandalous."

"I want it to be official, Anna. I don't want to do this behind Cole's back, or anyone else's."

"Let's just think about this," Anna said, turning her face to the breeze and closing her eyes for a moment.

"So you're happy just fucking? Is that what you want, a good lay once in a while?"

"That's not what I'm saying, Bucky. We just … I need to digest everything. Maybe we just wait until the stakes are over. Then we can figure it out."

"I guess nothing's changed then, has it?" Bucky said, revealing years of frustration, constantly waiting for Anna to come around. She was always elusive in her ways. Anna had become a master of giving him just enough, just enough to always keep him waiting, a safety net if things didn't work out with Cole.

"Me and Cole have built a life together," Anna said, "and it's hard to just walk away from that."

"To walk away from the money."

"*What?*" Anna said.

"You said that you and Cole have built a life together. You both have rich parents. Money and money equals more money. I know what you have. All the things I never had. How much is enough? Will you ever just follow your heart? You do know that Roy is a shyster?"

"Now you're just being ridiculous."

"Must be nice always having a plan B."

"Is that what you think you are to me?"

"C'mon, Anna, just be honest with yourself is all I'm asking."

"It's not about the money."

"It's always about the money."

"This is about you and Cole and nothing else, and any further suggestion is downright insulting."

"I'm sorry, Anna," Bucky said, backing off. Perhaps it wasn't what he necessarily thought about Anna but how he felt about himself. It can be hard to shake off the poor man's stigma.

"You know how I feel about you."

"Well, I don't always. I wonder about that a lot."

"There's nothing that you need to know that you don't already. It'd been a long time since we've been together, and now I remember what it felt like, or how it feels … I dunno."

"Do I satisfy you better?"

"Don't be a pig," Anna said. "You know what I mean."

"Yes, Anna. Of course I know what you mean. It's like a spring day or Niagara Falls; it's like everything and anything. Just fuckin' love me, Anna."

"You know I do," Anna said. She held up Bucky's face. They kissed in the open before Bucky pulled away and wiped his mouth.

"Yeah, I know you do. That's just part of the problem."

Before Anna could say anything else, Chelsea and the mare pranced out from the barn and out to the paddock. The foal was playful, while the mare seemed to be trying to impart her first lessons.

"Would you look at them," Anna said, in what Bucky suspected was yet another conversation changer. For Anna, it seemed that every time things got serious, she'd steer it back to friendship mode, the safety zone that only Anna seemed able to traverse. For Bucky it was a constant, whereas Anna had this whole other life, a life of regular lovemaking and companionship. It was a life that Bucky longed for, but at what cost? And what were the guarantees? *Maybe Anna leaves me when I'm old and infirm. Maybe at that point Cole is the better shuffleboard player, or can dab his bingo card quicker. Perhaps living a life alone would be just as rewarding. There will be no hair clogging the sink, no makeup on the counter, no visible maxi pads in the trash can or forgotten flushes. I will have more money and time, and when traveling will never have to pay double occupancy. I can careen in and out of restaurants and bars like a ghost and be forgotten. I will learn some tricks from Max to see how he slithers by, take up with girlfriends and floozies, and learn about life on the road. Maybe that is the trick, to keep on moving on so that the past never catches up to you. She loves me, she loves me not. There are only so many petals on a daisy. Will they come around, or get washed away like words carved into the sand?*

"Don't they just get under your skin?" Anna said, still in awe of the filly who had just learned how to run. The mare was chasing her along the fence.

"Yeah, they sure do," Bucky said flatly, sensing now that the transition was complete. He could bring up their "situation" again now, but it would be at his own risk, and he wouldn't likely convince her to uproot her life and depart immediately into the unknown anyway. Of course she would be pragmatic and take her time to think about it, Bucky tried to convince himself. He had already waited his whole life, so what was another week until the stakes were over? Maybe by that point, with Frankie and his men gone, he could stay in New York and Anna would move in with him. *It's not much, but it'd be a start, and if I worked hard and got the drives, then maybe we could move out to the Catskills. That's what life could look like,* he thought. He took a moment to savor the sweet smell, before realizing he was on his friend's grounds, with his friend's wife, staring out at their vast acreage. Bucky had thrown down his last volley, and didn't expect anything more from Anna when she leaned over and pulled him in by the loophole of his jeans.

"Look at me, Bucky," Anna said to him while he was doing his best to look away. "Everything's going to be fine. We're going to work this out, I promise you," she said, dispensing yet another nugget of hope to Bucky, who finally relented, and this time gave into her kiss, which in his best estimate lasted at least ten steamboats.

CHAPTER 18

The police station was in a red brick building in the middle of town. Bucky was waiting in the reception area, and across from him was an obese man in sweatpants he recognized from the track. Another guy was holding a bloody cloth up to his forehead, and next to him was sitting what looked to be an exceptionally old prostitute, easily over seventy, her red lipstick smeared on her ashen face, and her black cocktail dress disheveled like a dirty napkin. For Bucky it was always confounding where all these people came from. For such a small city, there was no shortage of miscreants. He wondered if they treated the drunk tank more like a Super 8. Max had been there many times. Bucky wondered if they should have his portrait on the wall.

"Bucky Whalen," the tired-looking woman at the front desk called over in a nasal drawl, "Officer Marshall can see you now." Bucky got up, and walked around the front desk and into the back office area. JP was still on a call. He waved Bucky in while he finished up.

"Okay, honey … right. Cracker Barrel. Can you tell Jennifer to remember to bring our CorningWare? Great … love you too …" While Bucky waited patiently for him to finish, he looked around at some of the pictures on JP's desk. There was one of his two twin girls, just as red-haired as their father; a sunset picture of him with his wife, both wearing bracelets from the all-inclusive resort where they'd honeymooned; and one of him with two of his friends proudly holding up a marlin.

"Bucky," he said, when he put the phone down. "So nice to see you.

I've been meaning to call and check up on things. How are you? You look terrible. What happened to your face?"

"Thanks, Officer Marshall. I'm okay."

"Bucky?"

"Yes, sir?"

"Cut the shit. We grew up together."

"Okay, JP."

"Better," JP said. "Now tell me why you're here."

"I need your help," Bucky said. It was a statement he never thought he'd utter from the day he'd first found out that JP was entering law enforcement. JP listened intently while Bucky told him the story behind his injuries, and what had happened at the barn and to Nitro.

"Quite the pickle," JP said, when Bucky was done. "Quite ... the ... pickle," he repeated, tapping a nickel on his desk. Bucky wondered if that's all he had to say about it.

"It is. But I think I've got a solution," Bucky said. "I've got a sit-down with Frankie Caruso, and I'd like to wear a wire. I can nail these guys."

JP let out a deep sigh, as if he was thinking about how much work this would create for him. Bucky could tell by the stack of papers and new arrivals that he was already overloaded, and here he was with a plan to bust a fix on the biggest race of the year. It was hardly a small favor. Bucky could tell that slowly the thoughts were churning in JP's brain.

"Bucky, you know that's way out of my jurisdiction. The race is in East Rutherford, and we're in Delaware. It's a federal crime. I can get in some serious shit just for listening to this," JP said. Then he got up from the desk and paced around.

"And Beth and me are planning a trip to Bear Mountain with the girls. Not sure if I can get wrapped up in this sort of thing right now."

Of course, that's what Bucky had expected at the first pass. With the mention of JP's wife, he couldn't help but remember that back at the high school prom she'd left with Davey Robinson instead of JP, and as Davey tells it, gave him the five-knuckle chuckle on the fire escape. JP was always a little bit weak, but this weak? Surely there must be some semblance of a man beneath the badge. Bucky knew he wasn't leaving there without something.

"Think about it, JP. This is like a promotion on a silver platter. When's the last time you did something that mattered? This will put your name up in lights."

"I like to think I do something that matters every day," JP said. He stood still for a moment, perhaps questioning the notion, counting how many vandals or drunks he had arrested over the years. While JP took a harder look at what he'd done during his career, Bucky wondered if it amounted to an existential crisis. JP sat back down in his chair, swiveled around, looked out the window, and then at the stick drawings he had on his wall. When he turned to face Bucky again, he suddenly shot up from his chair and left the office. Bucky, able to see him talking to the chief of police through the open blinds, was trying to read their lips and looking for any body language that might indicate the operation had been green-lighted.

When JP walked back into the office, Bucky couldn't wait for him to sit down before asking, "What'd the chief say? Did he like it? Are we a go?"

"Oh, I didn't talk to the chief about this," JP said, sitting back down.

"No?"

"Fuck no. Are you kidding me? We were talking about the Hens. They got a great fullback coming up this year."

"So you got up from your chair and ran to talk to the chief about football?"

"He likes when I engage him in sports talk."

"Oh, Christ, JP. I'm sorry, Officer Marshall. When are you going to grow a pair?" Bucky said. He regretted it immediately, thinking he had gone too far. Maybe JP could even cuff him for it.

"Listen, Bucky. First of all, I don't appreciate that. I don't have an easy job. I am a law. Enforcement. Officer. Have you any idea what that entails?"

"Yes, I do. I'm sorry. I know that what you do is very important."

"Thank you," JP said. He put his elbows on his desk and let out a deep breath, his chin resting on his hands.

"But I do wonder sometimes if I could do more."

"That's right."

"I've stamped enough paperwork to last both our lifetimes."

"Free yourself!"

"Then when the twins arrived, it just became about them, and me, and Beth, you know. It sure would be nice to do something exciting again. Might even help with the romance."

"Of course it would. Of course it would ... Detective," Bucky said, teasing JP, who was clearly taken aback at the mention of it, his copper eyes lighting up while he gazed into the future.

"Detective ... I like that," JP said. Then he got up and sat awkwardly on the corner of the desk, facing Bucky.

"This isn't NYPD. We're a small department. Only so much we can do here."

"So you'll help?"

"I don't even know if we've got the equipment."

"But you'll look for something."

"Beth will murder me if we miss Bear Mountain. And the kids? Have you ever seen *The Shining*? Real devil's spawn, I'm telling you. I mean, they're my kids and I love them, but Key-rist, they can be scary sometimes. And my in-laws are coming in the week after, and I have the fund-raiser coming up, and then the ..."

"JP, JP," Bucky finally interjected, because he could see that he was beginning to short-circuit. "Everything's going to be fine. You won't miss Bear Mountain, I promise you."

Bucky wasn't sure if JP had taken his word for it or if he had run out of fatal outcomes, but finally he seemed to relax.

"This is what we'll do," JP said with unexpected resolve. "I'll see what kind of recording equipment we have. We'll get them on tape, all right?" Then he picked up a squeeze ball from his desk and started pumping away furiously. "I got a couple of guys up in Jersey, Parker and Jonesy—bureau guys. We'll make the tape and get it in their hands. They'll know what to do with it."

"That's great, JP! Officer Marshall ... Detective Marshall! Thank you!" Bucky said, leaning over to shake his hand.

"No problem. It'll be just like the movies," he said. Out of everything else that had come out of JP's mouth that day, that was the thing that worried Bucky the most.

On the evening of the sting, Bucky was waiting for JP inside a motel room a few miles from the Crossroads. He went into the bathroom with its stained tiles and mildewed shower curtain and turned on the faucet. The tap sputtered out brown water that smelled like rotten eggs. Bucky reluctantly cupped it in his hands and splashed some on his face. He then reached for the dirty hand towel, wiped down his cheeks and neck, and stood for a moment staring into the mirror at his mangled face and bloodshot eyes. He looked like a cardboard cutout, a stranger in his own clothes.

"What are you doing?" he said out loud, tempting the ghost in front of him to answer. Unable to face himself any longer, he went back into the room. There were cigarette burns and stains of every size and type all over the orange rug. There was a piece of plywood that separated the box spring from the mattress. When Bucky plopped down on it with a thud, he grimaced in pain. There was a water stain on the ceiling, and a fly trap hung beneath the chandelier. Bucky watched as a fly bounced off the light bulb a couple of times and then landed on the sticky trap, never to move again.

He picked up the greasy television converter, which didn't work. His only other entertainment was the Bible, which stood out like an incubus on the veneered side table.

Suddenly a set of headlights lit up the room. Bucky got up slowly, and peeked out the curtain and barred windows. JP got out of his silver K-car and looked around nervously. Bucky let him in before he could knock.

"You're late," Bucky said to JP, who looked decidedly less authoritative in his I Love Orlando shirt showing off his hollow chest and long, skinny freckled arms.

"Sorry, had to drop off the kids at a playdate. You're gonna love this," he said, as he pulled out a small device from a paper bag and held it up between his thumb and index finger.

"*This* is the M909. Voice-activated, and small enough to stuff in your crotch. I picked up a mike that we can run up your pants and through your sleeve."

"What if they shake me down?"

"You'll be fine."

"And if I'm not?"

"I'm strapped," JP said, lifting up his pants leg to reveal a .45 in his ankle holster.

"That's reassuring," Bucky said, not knowing himself if he was being sarcastic.

JP pulled a roll of duct tape and a long wire from the bag, plugged the wire into the recorder, and pressed Record.

"Testing, one two, sibilance. I'm the one, the man with the gun. I like that! Anyway, by now I'm sure this thing is on and picking up every word just fine, but it's always good to test, so I'll just say one more thing if I can." JP burst out into song: "*Mooooon River, wider than a mile, I'm crossing you in style ...*"

Before he could finish, Bucky's nerves were finally shot.

"Fuck sakes, man!"

"Sorry. My father always used to sing that song," JP said. He rewound the tape and played it back. "Seems to work all right. Now take your shirt off."

"Good thing I wore long sleeves," Bucky said, while he unbuttoned his shirt.

"Jesus, these guys really did a number on you, didn't they?" JP asked once Bucky's bruised body was revealed.

"They certainly did take their liberties."

"Put this down with your boys," JP said, handing Bucky the recorder. Bucky held it in his hands for a moment, impressed by the weight and size of the device, and then stuffed it into his underwear.

"Now just stay still," JP said, rolling the first layer of duct tape around Bucky's torso.

"Not so tight." Bucky winced.

"Almost done,"

"I can barely breathe."

"Sorry, pal. Now hold out your arm."

Bucky did as he was told, and JP rolled the tape around his arm like he was taping up a hockey stick.

"I think that's enough. Thanks JP," Bucky said, thinking about how much it was going to hurt when he pulled it off.

"Looks good," JP said. Then he bit off the end of the tape, and passed Bucky his shirt.

"You sure you're ready for this?"

"Ready as I'll ever be."

"I'll be outside in the parking lot. If something seems fishy, I'm on it like Dirty Harry."

"No! Don't go there. You might be recognized."

"Even in my civvies?"

"Listen, it's a popular drivers' spot. Some of them might know you. People talk. Just stay cool. Last thing I need is for you to go in there with guns blazing."

"Okay, Bucky, but I'm telling you—"

"Don't. I'll meet you back here with the cassette as soon as we're done."

"You're the boss. Good luck."

"Thanks," Bucky said. Then he left for his sit-down with Frankie Fingers, resigned to whatever fate might befall him.

When he pulled into the parking lot, Bucky was relieved to see it was filled with cars. *It would be much harder for Frankie to murder me in a crowd,* he thought. When he drove around back, he noticed a few horse trailers parked in a row. He parked alongside them, and then went one by one, trying to spot Nitro. Finally on the last one, when he climbed up on the tire and peeked in through the grated window, he was met with Nitro's eye staring back at him like a black-and-red globe.

"Hey, boy," Bucky said to the horse, who didn't seem as happy to see him. He stomped and swung his hindquarters against the side of the van.

"Don't worry. I'm gonna get you home," Bucky said, thinking for a moment how easy it would be to just take him now and disappear into the night.

Inside the Crossroads there were different groups scattered in the din. There was a group of drivers whom Bucky recognized, a table of midforties guys in golf shirts, and some regulars sitting around the bar. As Bucky scoped the room, he spotted Frankie in a booth in the far corner. When Frankie saw Bucky walking toward him, he waved him in like a king with his gilded hand. Bucky felt the weight of the moment increase with every step forward. He casually covered his crotch, and thought about how he used to conceal all his teenage hard-ons, deciding that this would be no different.

"Sit down, sit down," Frankie said, once Bucky got to the booth, and pointed to the seat across from him beside Gino.

"I thought the deal was to come alone."

"I don't drive that fuckin' trailer. You see me driving a trailer?" Frankie said, waving a finger in front of Bucky.

"Don't worry. We're not going to hurt you," Gino said. "Unless we have to. Right, boss?"

"Settle down, Gino," Frankie said. "He's my bulldog, kid. You gotta understand that. He comes everywhere with me."

Maybe it isn't so bad, Bucky thought, feeling the recorder in his underwear, *because now I can get Frankie and Gino on tape.*

"Let's just cut through the shit, Frankie. You almost killed me, you burned my barn down, and you stole our horse. Let's get this over with," Bucky said, placing his miked-up arm casually on the table.

"My, my, aren't you confident as a peacock?"

"We made a deal," Bucky said, not bowing to Frankie's intimidation. "You give us Nitro back, and I'll ride him in the stakes, which you plan on fixing to ensure our victory."

"Very good, Bucky. *Very* good. There's one more thing, though."

"What is it?"

"Half of the purse money. Did your uncle mention that?"

"Yes, he did. It's part of the deal. How do you plan on doing it? I should know if I'm driving," Bucky said. He waited while Frankie looked at him closely—his mangled eye like the sewer for all his evil pouring over him—until he was unable to take it any longer, and looked down at Frankie's rings.

"It's going to be a perfect trip—wire to wire. Only three drivers aren't in on it yet, and I got that taken care of."

"So you just 'take care' of anybody who won't go along with your plan?"

"Is it your business? Don't make it your business," Frankie said. "But if you must know, that Phillips guy won't be showing up. He's going to trip over a crowbar on his way to the race. And the other guy, the French guy … what's his name?"

"Boucher," Gino answered quickly, as if he were the register for all of Frankie's forgotten thoughts.

"Yeah, Boucher. I bribed the trainer to overfeed his horse."

"And the others?"

"You're going to like this one. Hot 2 Trot is a Lasix horse, so let's just say he'll be getting a special injection."

"Do you really need to do that? There's other ways, you know."

"He'll be okay. Just a little hitch in his giddyup is all."

"Just please think about it," Bucky said. For a moment he thought about debating it further, but it wasn't the time to push Frankie more than he had to. He got what he needed, and with any luck the feds wouldn't let the race go off anyway.

"The horse is out back," Frankie said. "Gino will give you a hand. Don't fuck me on this. You know what happened last time."

"Yeah, I still can't piss standing up."

"Good. So we understand each other."

"As long as *you* understand that I'm racing to win, but that still doesn't guarantee victory."

"My dead nonna could win if we dug her up and put her on a horse," Frankie said. Bucky wondered if it was possible that Frankie had actually *killed* his nonna.

"After this is done, I'm out," Bucky said. "No more. Take your money and your thugs, and leave us alone. I won't do this again. Not with you, not with Bernie, not with the fucking pope if he asked me to. Got it?"

"Just get the fuck out of here. I'll kill you *after* the race, okay, kid?" Frankie said. Bucky could tell that he meant it—would probably even enjoy it.

Bucky got up slowly from the table. After a few steps, Gino gave Bucky a shove. Bucky staggered only slightly, discreetly made sure his package was still intact, and walked toward the door with a smile on his face and one thought on his mind—*gotcha!*

When Bucky got back to the motel, JP opened the door.

"So? So? You're here, right? You're alive. That's a good thing, I guess. How'd it go? Did you get it?"

"Everything went well. I got it. Should be more than enough to put Frankie away for a long time," Bucky said. He reached into his crotch and pulled out the recorder. "Here you go. Don't mind the funk on there."

"That's great!" JP said. He took the recorder from Bucky and then wiped it down on the duvet.

"Let's give it a listen," he said. He rewound the tape and pressed play. JP's voice was the first sound to emit from the recorder, belting out "Moon River."

"Not bad, huh?" he said to Bucky after listening for a moment. Then he fast-forwarded to where the conversation started. As they listened, JP could hardly contain his excitement. He held on to every word. When finally Frankie revealed his plans for the race, JP got up and pumped his fist like he was a baseball umpire calling a runner out at home plate.

"Got 'em!" he said, springing toward Bucky and giving him an awkward unreciprocated hug.

"We got 'em, we got 'em, we got 'em," he said. He continued to carry on while Bucky stood there nonplussed, waiting for JP's moment to be over with.

"You know what this means?" JP said, clicking open the recorder. "This is going to guarantee my place on the force, maybe even a promotion." Just as he said that, he jerked out the cassette. A spool of the tape came whizzing out.

"What! What'd you do, JP?"

"I didn't do anything," JP said, holding the recorder in one hand and the cassette in the other, with the long spool of tape still connecting them.

"Gimme that," Bucky said. He took away the recorder before JP could do any further damage. "I've got a pencil in the car," Bucky said. Then he stormed out, returning shortly after with a stubby green pencil from the track.

"This is how you do it," Bucky said, first delicately picking out the jam, next straightening the crinkled tape, and then inserting the pencil into the circle of the cartridge and spinning it around. "Just like my old Genesis tape, easy does it," he said. And then when the tape had completely wound, he reluctantly gave it back to JP.

"JP, please don't fuck this up, okay?"

"Of course not, of course not. We did it. We did this together. Don't think you won't be recognized for it either."

"I don't want to be recognized. Just promise me, JP. Promise me you won't fuck this up."

"I promise," JP said. He stood straight, giving a Boy Scout salute. "I will not fuck this up," he said, which brought Bucky no comfort. Little could he have known that it was already too late.

CHAPTER 19

On the day of the Breeders, Bucky was watching the earlier races from the grandstand. He was sitting on a picnic table, wearing his baseball cap, and remained a silent observer to the scene playing out in front of him. Of course he wasn't in his colors, as who knew who might *actually* handicap him. He was there to meet JP's guys Parker and Jonesy, who wanted to meet up with them because of JP's critical error. The day JP took the tape to the bureau guys' tiny shared office in New Jersey, when they ran the tape there was not so much evidence, but JP belting out not only "Moon River" but also other Broadway hits, like "Memory" and "Don't Cry for Me Argentina." Every time they hit the fast-forward button, there was a new one. JP was mortified. He'd made the tape the night before Bucky's sit-down. His wife, Beth, could even be heard singing backup vocals on some of the numbers. They figured they'd just tape over it, so why not have some fun? But somehow the crinkled tape had formed a medley of JP's greatest hits. As the men stood around while the recorder played on the table, JP looked at Jonesy, who looked at Parker, who looked back to JP and said, "What the fuck are we supposed to do with this?" And that's when they figured it'd be best to try to bust the Caruso gang on race day. Parker and Jonesy were going into the field. It wasn't part of the original plan, but with no tape, and nothing to go on, they had to let the race go off, or else they'd go down as goats if they were wrong.

Bucky watched the railbirds who were scattered in the track apron, the excitement increasing with every race closer to the main event. One man tugged at his child's arm and then yelled at the boy when he dropped his hot dog. One lady wore a peacock-feather hat, and her friend was in a wide-brimmed yellow hat with what looked to be a fruit basket on top.

There was a band playing clanky tunes, and a group of teen boys bouncing along with the music and pointing at girls they would never talk to. Bucky watched it all happen, and thought to himself that it was a world that had escaped him, a generation gone. *There are certain things you can't get back,* he thought.

Bucky admired the horses as they pranced by for the post parade with their equipment jingling, each one seeming just as capable of winning as the next.

He recognized most of the drivers and wondered if they were all in on it. Had they gathered before the race like his favorite wrestlers, Tito Torpedo and Ricky the Loon, to discuss the outcome and how they would make it look real? Fortunately, tonight, Bucky didn't have to make anything look real. He just had to go for it and head for daylight.

When the race started, everyone on the rail began yelling at the horses and drivers. In the middle of the race, JP and the bureau guys emerged from the fray and stood in front of Bucky at the picnic table.

Bucky was relieved JP had not shown up in uniform or another tourist shirt. Instead he was dressed normally, in a navy blue suit and yellow tie.

"Bucky, glad you're here," JP said, shaking Bucky's hand.

"This is Jonesy," JP said, nodding to the federal agent, who was in aviators and a long black trench coat. He had wavy blond hair and sculpted cheeks and was well over six two. He was lean and strong-looking. Bucky thought he could pass as an officer from the Great War or at least an actor playing one.

When JP introduced Bucky to Parker, they shook hands. He was just a few inches taller than Bucky, but thick with a dark brush cut. Bucky couldn't help but notice a hardness in him, like he had seen some *real* shit. He noticed his huge biceps through his black bomber jacket. Parker stared hard at Bucky while he gripped his hand like he was choking a fish.

"You see anything yet?" JP said, looking happy to be part of the big boys' club with Parker and Jonesy by his side.

"Nothing yet, and I gotta get back to the paddock soon. Sorry I can't ID anyone for you."

"So ... the leader, Frankie," Jonesy said, taking off his aviators and scanning the track apron, "he's got a scar?"

"Yeah, a big ugly one. But don't tell him that. During the qualifier, he was standing right about there," Bucky said, pointing to where he recalled first seeing Frankie's icy glare. "And where you find him, you find his minions."

"Don't worry; we'll get them," Parker said, his jarhead face blunt and sturdy.

"Anywhere else we should look?" Jonesy asked, putting his aviators back on, ready to dive into the mission.

"You can check the lounge upstairs. Sometimes they do their dirty business up there and then come down to watch."

"We'll check it out," Parker said.

"Good. Is that it? I've got a drive. Time to fix the biggest race of the year. Thanks for that, JP ... sorry, Officer Marshall."

Both Parker and Jonesy also looked at JP, obviously disappointed with his gumshoe operatics. While all the focus was on him, JP, unable to stand it, said, "C'mon, guys, it was an accident!"

"Yeah, yeah," Jonesy said. "Let's go, Parker."

Just as Parker and Jonesy turned to walk away, JP called out, "I'll stay here!" But his voice was drowned out by the cheers and curses as the current race came to a finish.

"Find them and end this," Bucky said to JP, and then he disappeared in the crowd and made his way to the paddock.

—————o—————

"Nice of you to show up, boy. Only the biggest race of your life," Clarence said to Bucky when he spotted him coming out of the change room.

"I'm here. Wouldn't miss it for the world," Bucky said, feeling better now that he was in his colors and that the race would soon be at hand. They walked together through the paddock, looking at a few of the other horses. When they were close to Nitro's stall, they saw Carl sitting outside it studying a racing program. When he saw Bucky and Clarence, he got up and walked over purposefully, almost like he was trying to prewarn Bucky about something. But before he could do it, it was too late. Cole and Roy came up from the other direction. For a moment Carl looked like an air traffic controller trying to avert a head-on collision. Everyone had been there that morning at the farm; they had all heard Cole's warning shot and knew the backstory.

"Hey, Bucky," Roy said, making a show of coming over to shake his hand. Cole, avoiding eye contact with Bucky, handed Carl a coffee in a paper cup. At this point, the tension between Bucky and Cole was palpable. Roy was quick to seize the moment. "Well, how about we leave these boys alone?" After a pause, he said to Carl, "Got any of those stogies on you, old man?" Carl seemed delighted by the suggestion. Clarence joined them as they walked away. After a few steps, he turned back to flash Bucky a wink and a smile. Bucky watched them go and was desperate to call out, to get a lifeline from somebody, but they all couldn't seem to get away fast enough. This was the last thing he needed on race day.

Bucky still hadn't seen Cole since his outburst, and he'd made sure to steer clear until Anna had told her husband about the affair. How would Cole react if he actually knew what happened? Would he resort to violence? Should they just bare-knuckle it in the street to see who finally got her? What would be the cost of this? There is always a cost.

Still not engaging Bucky, Cole stepped into the stall and stood next to Nitro in the crossties, stroking his neck and mane. *What is going through his mind?* Bucky thought as Cole's hands traced the muscular lines of the horse's hindquarter.

"He looks good," Bucky said, hoping his intro would lead into a conversation about anything other than Anna.

"Yeah, he's ready," Cole said. Now it seemed to Bucky that there was some kind of transference going on between man and horse, because how could they both be so calm while inside being ready to explode? "Don't know what they were feeding him over there, and he still seems a bit spooked, but he's ready. Ready as he'll ever be," Cole said, surprising Bucky, who'd begun to wonder if he'd get more than a few words from him, but here he was actually talking. They were talking. Anna must not have told him. Or had she?

Then before he could stop himself, in an attempt to relieve the guilt that he'd tucked away so neatly, Bucky came out with it. "Listen, Cole. I'm sorry about this. About everything."

Bucky hoped Cole couldn't detect the smoke bombs he was throwing to hide what he really felt bad about but wasn't sure if he could mention it yet. "Bringing you guys into this. It was my fault. Everything's my fault," Bucky said, now awash in real guilt as he looked at Cole, who seemed small and vulnerable next to the horse. What would he have left if he lost Anna, besides the mansion, the full stable, the sports cars, and the high-end farm equipment? Did all that stuff matter anyway? Who would Cole be without her? It was a feeling that Bucky knew all too well, as he had been living it in the long, painful intervals. But Bucky was trained now. He had mainly the teenage memories to repress, where infatuation could be confused with love and every moment seem like a flare that bursts in the night. Maybe that's what Cole had that he could not provide—real-world love, the kind of love where you wait for someone in the hospital no matter how long it takes and what the diagnosis. Cole had been there to plug the hole when Bobby died, and in subsequent years he had been the model partner and friend in crisis. He knew Anna in a way that Bucky might never. He had lived with her, really loved her. He didn't mythologize her or think of her as some perfect creature without bad habits or private ailments. He knew her dreams and most of her secrets. Even with everything he had, Cole was still a better man. There was no way Bucky was kicking in doors on the volunteer fire brigade, or pretending to like his mother-in-law.

"You know what—it's fine, Bucky. It's fine," Cole said, turning away from the horse and looking at Bucky. *Does he mean everything is fine?* Bucky wondered.

Cole obviously didn't know about the affair, and what Bucky really wanted to say was sorry in advance. *Sorry for ruining your life. Sorry for taking the only thing you ever loved away from you ... but, well, now you know how it feels, and there is plenty of alcohol and drugs you can take to numb the pain.* If ever their relationship had come to a final impasse, then this was probably it.

"Good, because I mean it," Bucky said, feeling not the least bit exonerated. Cole remained fixed on him somewhat expectantly, as if to say, *Anything else?* After a few more moments of allowing Cole to stare right through him like an airport x-ray machine, Bucky almost came clean again, but knew he couldn't just yet.

"Sport's changing," he said instead. "I can see it all over."

"The world's changing," Cole added, turning back to Nitro, seemingly just as relieved not to get into it, at least not now.

"Soon this track will be condos or a shopping mall, just like out in Westbury and Brandywine."

"As long as I can keep driving in Delaware," Cole said. Bucky wondered if he'd forgotten to finish his sentence by saying, "With Anna." Perhaps Cole, too, was under a strict directive from her. Whatever it was, they were both going to find out somehow—and soon.

"Don't see why you wouldn't."

"And so we soldier on."

"Like gladiators!"

"Yeah, gladiators," Cole said. They both couldn't help but laugh.

"What else do you have going on?" Cole asked, now that he had loosened up and left the stall. He didn't seem to be asking as a follow-up to his not so subtle request that Bucky go far, far away, and preferably never come back; he seemed to be asking with genuine interest.

"Well, that seems to be the number one question right now. Just get all this shit done with and live my life. Learn how to sail. I don't know."

"Gonna keep driving?"

"I don't know what'll be left for me," Bucky said. He felt a tinge of sadness and cringed at the thought of doing anything other than racing, like selling insurance or real estate. Maybe it was time to go back to school and get computer skills. "No one likes a fixer."

"You're doing the right thing."

"Well, whatever I'm doing, it's messed up, man. I mean, c'mon, Frankie Fingers? I got a guy people *actually* call Frankie Fingers who's going to kill me if I don't win this race. Even if I do win this race, I'm probably still dead."

"You'll be fine," Cole said. Bucky wondered if he already knew that he was about to experience his own personal Hiroshima.

"At least I already know what it feels like to have cracked ribs."

"You got Nitro back," Cole said, "and I know my father appreciates it."

Of course, your father, Bucky thought to himself. *How long will we Whalens be beholden to your father, crooked founder of Roy's Carbs and horse trader extraordinaire?*

"It's the least I can do," Bucky said, looking closer at Cole now that he was beside him. There certainly was reason for Anna to be more attracted to him; it could be sickening looking at him with his bright blue eyes and curly blond hair. In Cole, he saw the face of the young boy he once knew, the kid he'd met way back when at the state fair. That was when everything was new and as of yet untarnished on life's cutting room floor, with all the other lips and assholes. They were strange bedfellows indeed, part friend and part foe. The only thing that could prevent them from being friends was Anna. It was always amazing how familiar they were in those few precious moments when they both forgot and talked about horses and sports, or the weather—anything to escape the obvious. But every time they got closer, eventually silence reigned, as there was no real bridging the gap between them. It was like no-man's-land with bullets whizzing overhead. But now, Bucky didn't know if he would see Cole again. The plan was not to. He had done enough already. And the longer he spent with Cole, the more his sentiment crept in. Before he had a chance to fight it, again he gave into his impulses.

"Cole," he said, taking a deep breath and tearing up in his left eye. He was ready to open up but was lost for words. Bucky moved closer and put his hand on Cole's shoulder. Before Bucky could utter the words, he heard Clarence shout down the hall, "Fifteen minutes to post!" And just like that the moment was gone. Soon everyone else was up behind them, and their stall became a busy hive as final preparations were on for the Breeders.

Max was waiting with Charlie in the Silver Bullet in the parking lot outside the stadium. They were both huddled around the galley table.

"When the hell are they going to get here?" Max said, referring to the two other men whose involvement Charlie hadn't revealed until just then.

"Maxi, would you just relax?"

"If shit goes wrong today, I'm dead, and so is Carl and Bucky," Max barked. Then he poured himself a shot and winced it back.

"There you go. Attaboy," Charlie said. "That'll help."

"It's a start," Max said, wiping the dribble from his chin. He'd already been feeling the ill effects of three hard days in Saratoga, and if anything this would level him out. But even for Max, he was run down, the cycle of his drinking and gambling having finally caught up with him. His stomach to him felt like an alien appendage, and his head was throbbing with addiction and exhaustion. If he could just get through this one final score, then it would be all bikinis and margaritas—maybe even Marge Tate, somewhere in Max's version of Xanadu.

Rap, rap, rap. There were three hard knocks on the door.

"Finally," Max said. Charlie got up to let them in.

"Gentlemen," Charlie said as he welcomed Jo Jo and the lounge manager from Speedway, Westing Schmidt, who both shuffled into the trailer with deep leather cases.

"Here's yours, Maxi," Charlie said, handing one of the cases to Max.

"This belong to you, Baker?" Max asked, pulling out a fluffy brown wig from the case. "I always knew you were thinning."

"Oh, I didn't tell you? We're wearing disguises."

"No. You didn't tell me. You definitely didn't fucking tell me."

"That's how it is, Max. My guys at the counters are in on it, but we gotta make it look real for the cameras, so at least those guys can play dumb."

"Anything else I should know?"

"Well, there is one more thing," Charlie said. He pulled out a wireless clipper from another case and turned it on.

"Get the fuck out of here."

"Max."

"I did not agree to that."

"Don't worry. There's a fake mustache in there. You can wear it for the Charlie Chaplin look. It's more versatile. Look at Jo Jo," Charlie said. Jo Jo paused to show off his freshly breamed upper lip while he was changing into his headbanger disguise with a long black wig and AC/DC shirt.

"I hardly would have called that blond thing on Jo Jo's lip a mustache, maybe more of a shitstache. But fine, fuck. Do it.

"I'm not happy about this," Max said, his lips barely moving, like a ventriloquist's, while Charlie sheared off his mustache.

"There you go, just like your First Communion."

"I'm not Catholic."

"Does it matter?"

"He's lapsed. Don't worry about it," Westing Schmidt spoke up, winking at Max as if to say, *I remember all those nights in the lounge—* very un-Christian.

"What I mean is, does it really fucking matter? We're about to rob a racetrack, and we're talking religion," Charlie said.

"You brought it up," Max said, pulling out a black robe from the case.

"What's this for?"

"A man of the cloth," Charlie said. "Just a coincidence."

"Maybe God really is calling the shots here," Westing said, having already changed into his white suit, shades, and fedora.

Max put his head through the robe and then put on the wig.

"There you go; now you're getting it," Charlie said, now also changed into a black tuxedo with a frilly shirt, an afro wig, and Elvis glasses.

"It looks like you're in a muumuu, doesn't it, Maxi?"

"Fuck you, Jo Jo."

"Here's the deal, boys. Listen up. We changed the locks on the handicapped bathroom on the first floor, and in here there's a key for each of you. Also your swipe cards and account codes," Charlie said, passing each one an envelope. "Place your bets, and then stay in position at the machines until after the race goes off. Then, when Nitro wins, print out a voucher and head to the windows. Come back; change; cash another ticket: wash, rinse, and repeat. Everybody got it? We keep going until it's a heat score, and then we meet at the trailer afterward. Got it?"

"And then what do we do?"

"I don't care what you do after, Jo Jo. Disappear."

"Got it."

"Good. Now everybody ready for this?" Charlie said, looking around at his Halloween band of misfits. "Readdyyyyy, break!" he said, like they were in a football huddle, and all men burst out the trailer door and snaked their way individually through the busy parking lot and into the stadium.

MIT Harold sat at his desk in his brown suit at Pary-Tote headquarters in Dover. He was looking deeply at the green numbers flashing across his computer screen, and typing away furiously while the betting data rolled in. While his coworkers mulled away in their cubicles, they had no way of knowing that their industrious and introverted colleague was about to cause a breach in the system that would make him a legend, not just in hacker circles but also in the pantheon of the greatest harness-racing scandals. It was something he took a strange pleasure in. Whoever would have suspected him? He'd had Pary-Tote marked since his first interview. It had been seven devoted years wearing a name badge and a number, towing a line that was about to snap—in grand fashion.

The trumpet sounded first call, and the drivers began walking their horses out from the paddock for the post parade.

"I guess this is it," Bucky said to Carl and Clarence, who stood by him like they were walking their prizefighter into the ring.

"Any last will and testament?" Clarence said, looking at Bucky, who was now wearing his helmet and goggles.

"You can have my alarm clock."

"That's generous. Oh! I almost forgot," Clarence said, reaching into his back pocket and pulling out a folded envelope. "This is from Anna. She found me earlier and said to give this to you. She said I should tell you to read it only *after* the race. Can you wait that long?" Clarence said, teasing Bucky by pulling it away when he went to grab it.

"I'm sure you already know what it says. Why don't you just tell me?"

"I wouldn't do that to you, would I, boy? Is that what you think of me? I bet you it's juicy," he said, just before Bucky snatched it away and tucked it into the breast pocket of his jumpsuit.

"Go time," Bucky said, hopping on the sulky and rolling away after all the other drivers.

"Give 'em hell," Carl called out after him. He stood there looking helplessly as if Bucky was off to college or going to climb Mount Everest.

It was balmy out. Bucky enjoyed the light breeze as Nitro towed him along in front of the grandstand. The evening shadows had disappeared, and insects swarmed the track lights that lit the night. He tried to spot Frankie in the track apron, but it was too crowded. He heard his name called out on the loudspeaker, and then the announcement that Barney Go-Go, driven by Wayne Phillips, was a scratch, which Bucky knew was the result of the driver's unfortunate run-in with a crowbar.

Bucky caught up with his old rival from Speedway, Jack Danby, on Blind Luck, jogging around the far corner. He couldn't resist. "Who you losing for tonight, Danby?"

"Don't push your luck, kid," he said. Bucky jogged by him before he could say anything else.

When Bucky caught up to the other horses, he thought that Faster-'n-You already looked fatigued, most likely from being overexercised. Yankee Wrangler was wearing a Murphy blind, which may or may not have been necessary. There were no depths that Frankie wouldn't sink to in order fix a race. Getting to the trainers and drivers first was probably his singular best talent. After all, he was a hard guy to say no to.

After reaching about midway of the backstretch, Bucky turned Nitro around and then began his jog toward the starting car. The other horses were falling into their lanes. Bucky was the last one in, having drawn the outside post. As they all jogged to keep up with the white Cadillac, Terry Miller, the driver on Hot 2 Trot, yelled out, "This is it! Good luck, fellas!" Bucky felt bad because Terry was an honest driver, and who knows what Frankie had injected his horse with? Then Guy Boucher piped up, "Who needs luck when you got Supersonic?" Bucky wondered just how much they'd fed his horse.

As the horses raced to keep up with the gate, the starter yelled, "*Go!*" on the roof-mounted megaphone. The Cadillac pulled off to the side and the race was off.

Bucky could feel Nitro on the bit, but since they were on the outside post, there was more ground to cover. Letting him go could tire him out. *So much for a wire-to-wire win,* Bucky thought as he fell back, watching to see what the other drivers were doing before he made his move. The first victim of Frankie's tampering was Yankee Wrangler in his Murphy blind, who instead of going around the first turn, kept growing straight and interfered with Albatrocity. Just like that, the field was narrowed to six. Bucky gained ground around the first turn and was beside Supersonic down the backstretch, who soon dropped off on a full belly and was distanced from the field.

Bucky, racing along the outside, kept an eye on Rain Maker in the pocket and wondered if his driver was in on it. His curiosity was soon answered when Danby dropped back to block him out. Both of them fell back, leaving Hot 2 Trot, Nitro, and Faster-'n-You, the last of whom was having a helluva race considering he'd already been run ragged, although now he was beginning to slow down as he huffed and grunted, before he too fell away.

Bucky cut a hard angle around the clubhouse turn. When they straightened out, it was him and Hot 2 Trot three lengths ahead of the pack. Hot 2 Trot wasn't giving any ground. Bucky wondered if something had gone wrong with the injection. The horse wasn't showing any ill effects, and the driver seemed intent on winning, even flashing Bucky a wink as he pulled away.

The crowd was in a frenzy as they screamed at the horses. Hot 2 Trot gained a length down the stretch. How could this be happening? How could Frankie have gotten it this wrong? Bucky spied the finish line coming up like a graveyard. With everything on the line, he began whipping Nitro and gave him all the line he needed. The horse ran for daylight like a true champion with heart and grit, but in the end it looked like Hot 2 Trot just might take it. Just when Bucky was resigned to his fate, five yards from the finish line Hot 2 Trot dropped dead, his momentum carrying him forward across the line.

In the pit there was an outburst of screaming and swearing. Losing tickets rained down like confetti. Max was sitting in front of a betting terminal where all the chairs and monitors are, listening to the chatter of the die-hard horseplayers.

"Three DNFs and you're telling me this sport ain't fixed?" the obese man in sweatpants said to the skinny Puerto Rican guy on the opposite side of the aisle.

"This is the last time I bet on these assholes. I'm sticking with thoroughbreds," said the old Greek.

"They're just as dirty," the Jamaican guy said, who nodded to the Slav. Finally they all agreed on something.

Everyone in the pit had something to say. They spoke over and across each other to make their points. Even the man who towed his oxygen tank around in his walker uttered, "Fuckin' mutt." The Chinaman said something that must have been a curse. Those who still had live tickets held their breaths until finally the announcement came on the loudspeaker:

"Subject to inquiry, in first place it's Nitro; Hot 2 Trot in second; and Blind Luck in third. Again it's Nitro, Hot 2 Trot, and Blind Luck. On a positive note, the driver Terry Miller seems to be okay. And let's all say a prayer for Hot 2 Trot as his experienced vet team takes him away."

Right after the winner was announced, the pit exploded into another round of expletives, while Max sat calmly in front of the machine, brushed a strand of the wig from his face, and reached into his jeans beneath his robe to take out the pad of account numbers and plastic swipe cards that Charlie had given him.

Back at corporate headquarters, Harold was staring anxiously at his screen. After the inquiry and the race was settled, there would be a short delay before bettors got paid. If his plan worked, the money would soon flow from the handle into the dummy accounts. He looked around at his colleagues and their unbearable inertia. Henrietta was clearly on a personal call, and Sal was playing Minesweeper and eating a bagel. Having stopped caring long ago, they didn't do anything about it, and probably never would. *Not me,* Harold thought. He looked at the clock on the wall and counted down the seconds to reserve his place in harness-racing infamy.

Max swiped the first card and punched in the corresponding account number from the list. The balance—two dollars. The race was final. There was no reason why he shouldn't have been paid. He hit the refresh button; nothing. He hit it again—same thing. He put both his hands up on the machine, almost like he was trying to choke it, and still nothing. He looked around at the other machines, and spotted Jo Jo and Westing Schmidt. They didn't seem to be getting paid out either. They exchanged nervous glances.

Max hit the button again, and this time the machine blipped and the balance changed to $23,675.

"Oh, baby!" Max said. His face lit up, and he stroked the machine now as if it were his pet. He then hit the cash-out button, adjusted his wig and his robe, and walked briskly over to the counter with his voucher.

He could tell that the shabby-looking young teller probably recognized him, but it didn't matter.

"Good win, sir."

"Thanks. Sometimes you get lucky."

"I'll say. Gimme a minute," he said. He took the voucher and went to talk to the pit boss, who inspected the ticket and, after a moment's deliberation, disappeared into the counting room. Soon after, the pit boss emerged with the cash. The teller then returned to his station with Max's payout and had him sign for it.

"Here you go," he said, putting the money on the counter, "don't spend it all in one place."

"Thanks," Max said. He scooped up the cash and then beelined it for the handicapped bathroom.

When Max got back to the bathroom, Jo Jo and Charlie were already there changing into their next disguises.

"How'd it go at the windows, Maxi?" Charlie said, out of his tux and into his cowboy look with fake mustache, shades, and ten-gallon hat.

"Pretty good haul. You guys?"

"Not bad," Jo Jo said, "on a two-dollar bet."

Max pulled another disguise out of the case, and put the money inside.

"How'd you know my size?" Max said, stretching out a pair of pastel blue shorts, a Hawaiian shirt, and a floppy fisherman's hat.

"It was the biggest they had," Charlie said.

"Surprised you didn't have to go see a tentmaker for that."

Before Max could respond to Jo Jo's barb, there was a knock on the door.

"*Guys, guys, it's me,*" they heard in a whisper.

"It's Schmidt. Let him in," Charlie said. Max reached back in the cramped space to open up the door.

"Where's your key?" Charlie asked.

"I lost it, but that's not important right now. You know there's some people waiting outside to use the can? They don't look happy."

"Well, they're just going to have to wait then, aren't they?" Charlie said. "So listen up. Now that I have you all together, I want you to switch up the windows. Max, you're on six; Schmidt, you're on sixteen; and Jo Jo, take eleven."

Max struggled trying to button up his shorts. He was bursting out of the Hawaiian shirt. Jo Jo put on a mesh shirt, weight-lifting gloves, and a straight blond wig.

"I'm noticing a theme here, Jo Jo."

"Oh yeah, what's that, Maxi?"

"Sure you're not smoking pole these days?"

"Whatever, Shamu ... weren't you in the Mamas and the Papas?"

"Fuck you, Jo Jo. I swear."

"Why don't you just cut the shit and blow each other already?" Westing Schmidt said, out of his white suit, and struggling to glue on a fake nose.

"Okay, I'll be last out so I can lock the door," Charlie said. "Let's get her moving."

———O———

"I don't see these guys anywhere," Jonesy said to Parker, as they stood around the bar on the third level, trying to find Frankie or his men.

"Why'd I let you get me into this anyway?" Parker said, scouring the room.

"I thought it'd be good, for both of us. Think about the news coverage when this breaks."

"Well, right now, we don't have anything."

"I don't think I can listen to 'Don't Cry for Me Argentina' again," Jonesy said, rotating a toothpick around his mouth.

"It's a good song," Parker said, revealing an unexpected soft spot beneath his Kevlar skin.

"Was a good song."

"Let's go downstairs," Parker said, running out of patience. "They gotta be around somewhere." The two of them stormed out of the bar and fought their way through down the crowded escalator to the main floor.

Max was now in his Charlie Chaplin look with a fake mustache, a baggy suit, and a bowler hat. The crowd was thicker because the bettors were trying to get their last-minute bets in. Max couldn't spot his accomplices. He was breathing heavy in the line, and nervous that things were closing in. He felt hot and dizzy, clearly unfit for any kind of sustained physical activity. He didn't know how many more trips back and forth to the bathroom he could handle, and wondered when they would shut it down.

When he got to the counter, it was the gray-curly-haired curmudgeon teller who had nicotine-stained fingers and whiskers sprouting from a mole on her chin.

"Finally a winner," Max said. He put his ticket down and leaned on the counter. Without saying anything, she spun around in her chair and got up to collect the cash. When Max walked back with the money, he stumbled and dropped a bundle. The two FBI guys were right beside him. Parker even picked up the money and handed it back to Max.

"Looks like you're having a good night there," Parker said.

"Mind your own fuckin' business," Max said, taking the money back. Jonesy put his hand on Parker's shoulder to restrain him.

"Let's go. We're wasting time. And fuck you, douchebag," Jonesy said. "He was trying to do you a favor."

After the chance encounter, Max weaved his way through the crowd. He had to fight his way through the growing line for the handicapped bathroom. Now the old man with the oxygen tank in his walker was waiting, along with a person in a wheelchair and some other seniors, who all stood around and bitched about it equally. When Max went to the front of the line, they all started yelling at him.

"It's maintenance, I'm maintenance," Max said. Then he went in and quickly shut the door. Charlie was changing alone. Used disguises were strewn all over the floor.

"I'm done, Charlie. I can't do it anymore," Max said. He sat heavily on the toilet and leaned back against the wall.

"You got one more in you, Maxi. I know you do," he said, throwing him over a bald cap.

"Seriously, Baker, I don't know if I can hold up. It's hot, and we got enough. Have you seen that line? Those geezers are going to start a riot."

"You do have a point. You see the other guys out there?"

"No, not in a while."

"Okay, I'll wait for the others and clean it up in here. I'll meet you back out at the trailer. Last one, Maxi. You got this?" Charlie said.

"Yeah, I got it," Max said, fitting himself with the bald cap, checking the mirror, and then recycling the robe for his latest disguise.

"You look like Friar Tuck's retarded cousin."

"You too, Baker?"

"Jo Jo's not here, so I had to say it for him."

"You're both assholes," Max said. Then he carefully squeezed back out the door and fought his way through the line of unruly elderly and disabled.

Max went back to the betting terminal to cash another voucher. As he walked back to the counter, he could tell that something was wrong. The bettors were demanding payment on their winning tickets. Finally the pit boss emerged from the counting room. He put both hands around his mouth and made the announcement as loud as he could.

"There seems to be a slight problem in the counting room. Please be patient. We'll cash your bets as soon as possible."

While the bettors stood around and time dragged on, and more angry people swarmed around the windows, eventually the tellers deserted their stations, running for their lives through the mob.

—————O—————

Bucky and Carl were rubbing down Nitro in his stall when they heard a loud scream from somewhere in the paddock. Carl grabbed Bucky by the elbow and led him cautiously around the corner, and together they watched as Len MacDonald, the Lasix administrator for Hot 2 Trot, emerged, hysterical, from the Lasix room.

"He's dead! He's dead!" he said. He whirled around in his white scrubs, his face a sickly pale from whatever horrors he had just witnessed.

"Who's dead? Who's dead?" Derek Carter, driver for Albatrocity, asked. He put his arm around Len's shoulder to try to calm him down. Having heard the fracas, a crowd of other horse people began to form. Bucky and Carl stayed back and watched while they all stood around, curious as to what had set off the delirious man.

"The guy who kidnapped me and locked me up in his van in the parking lot!" McDonald said, his eyes bulging now and the veins in his neck threatening to explode like a gushing oil well. "That's who!" he spat. Then he pushed away from Carter and pointed at the door.

"Okay, just calm down now. Tell me what happened," a patient Carter said, again trying to corral the man, but Len kept his distance.

"I was doing the Lasix injection when this guy snuck into the room and knocked me out with a truncheon. Next thing you know, I wake up in his van bound and gagged. I suppose he was there to mess with my horse. Oh my, Hot 2 Trot. How is Hot 2 Trot?"

"He ran a good race," Carter answered honestly.

"Thank goodness," Len said, relieved for a moment, and then continued telling his story. "When I escaped from the van, I went back to the Lasix room and noticed a horse blanket in the corner, so I pulled it back and there he was. It wasn't me. Good Lord, it wasn't me. I know how this must look. Have I incriminated myself? Am I under citizen's arrest?"

"No, no, you haven't, but we have to call the cops. Somebody call the cops," Carter said. He looked out at the smattering of people who had all witnessed the spectacle. Bucky didn't need to see the body to know who it was; he remembered that truncheon well. But who could have done this? Tony was supposed to have been the killer, not the killed. As Bucky tried to piece together what might have happened, it dawned on him that he hadn't seen Clarence since he'd given him the note from Anna. Come to think of it, he wasn't even with them in the winner's circle. Could Clarence have murdered Tony? Did he have it in him? Sure, there were pieces of Clarence's past that Bucky didn't know about, but murder? Bucky had no doubt that Clarence would never murder an ordinary citizen, but someone like Tony who was a criminal and torched a barn full of his precious horses? That certainly would be a tooth for a tooth, so it gave Bucky pause. Realizing that, and the precariousness of their own situation, Bucky looked at Carl. Without saying a word, they both did an about-face and rushed back to get Nitro packed up so they could leave the stadium as soon as possible.

"Good evening, racing fans." The stadium PA crackled. "It is with our regret that we inform you that due to security issues, all other races on tonight's card will be rescheduled. Thanks for coming out to the races, and please maintain order when exiting the building."

The crowd didn't respond favorably to the announcement of a security threat. A dozen police officers entered the hall and fanned out, trying to control the pandemonium that broke out as the first wave of people stampeded toward the exits.

"What do you think's going on?" Parker said to Jonesy as they stood in the middle of the hall.

"I don't know. Let's find out," Jonesy said. He stopped one of the officers who was attempting to direct the traffic.

"Agent Adam Jones, FBI," Jonesy said, flashing his badge. "What's going on here?"

"Apparently they found a body in the paddock. Got nearly the whole force here to lock this place down."

"Thanks," Jonesy said to the officer, who quickly disappeared in the melee.

"What do we do? Do you think it's related?" Parker said to a much calmer Jonesy.

"Of course it's related."

"Should we call it in, tell them what we know?"

"We're in a bad spot on this one. We fucked up—bad," Jonesy said. The panicked crowd streamed between and around Jonesy and Parker, as if the two agents were standing in the middle of the great wildebeest migration.

"So, what should we do, help these guys out?"

"I think we oughta do what everyone else is doing and get the hell out of here."

"What about JP? Maybe he's got some intel down in the track apron."

"Fuck JP. If he hadn't messed that tape up, none of this would have happened to begin with. Let's go," Jonesy said. Parker followed him through the crowd.

Still in his bald cap, Max slipped through the police cordon. As he ran like a hunted beast back to the trailer, he saw a helicopter flying overhead. *That's it,* Max thought to himself. *It's over. It's always the last job where they get busted in the movies.* After making it to the first row of cars, he stopped running, put the bag down, and lit a cigarette, believing it would actually help his breathing. He was sure he was having a heart attack, so he leaned on a car. After a few puffs, he looked around and saw other people scurrying in the parking lot, so he gathered himself and walked at a brisk pace to the trailer. He was the first one back. After a few minutes, Charlie, Jo Jo, and Schmidt finally appeared.

"Where have you guys been?"

"Have you seen it out there? It's a dragnet," Schmidt said, taking off his green visor hat and peeling off his fake nose.

"We're fucked," Max said, peeking out the small blinds, trying to spot the helicopter in the sky.

"Take it easy," Charlie said. "As long as we're cool, we'll get out of here."

"Didn't think it would have blown up like that," Jo Jo said. He pulled out a stack of bills from his case and fanned his face. "It's like they called in the National Guard."

"Maybe we were set up," Schmidt said. The three other men looked at him curiously.

"Who the fuck do you think set us up?" Charlie said, as if it was a personal affront. "And don't you think they would have taken us down by now?"

"Well, I don't know. Something doesn't make sense."

"We weren't set up," Max said. "They ran out of money at the windows. I saw it. The pit boss came out. When he made the announcement, everyone went crazy."

"They must have known they'd been robbed; otherwise, there would have been enough from the handle to pay out the bettors," Jo Jo added.

"The pit boss promised me he'd hold off as long as possible, but at some point he had to go up the chain."

"Yeah, the point where we cleaned 'em out," Schmidt said.

"Well, whatever happened, let's get the hell out of here. Hand over the keys, Maxi. I'll drive," Charlie said, holding out his hand for the keys.

"What? You're not driving my car, Baker,"

"You're a mess. Look at yourself," Charlie said to Max, who sat flaccidly, drenched in sweat at the kitchen table.

"What if they ask for your driver's license at the gate, genius? What then? They come back to inspect the trailer and find these jokers and stacks of cash."

"You may have a point."

"Let's get going then," Max said. After doing one more shot of whisky, he slid out from the table.

"Sure you're good to drive?" Charlie asked, wincing as if it were him who'd suffered the systemic abuse of body that Max had.

"Don't worry about it, Baker. I'm a professional," Max said. He slammed the door behind him and got into his Cutlass, which was hitched to the Silver Bullet.

There was already a lineup of cars waiting to exit and a police roadblock at the front gate. Max waited nervously, inching ahead in line, rehearsing what he might say if questioned about the robbery. *A heist? Here? At the Big C? No, sir. Wow, that's really ... unfortunate. Don't know anything about it. You'd have to have some balls for that, right, Officer?*

When finally it was Max's turn, a large black police officer leaned down and looked at him. "Driver's license and registration."

"Sure, sure," Max said. He opened up the glove box, which sprung loose all kinds of junk like a jack-in-the-box. "Here you go, Officer," Max said, handing over his documents after rummaging through the compartment.

"Are you a horseman?" the cop said, looking around the interior of Max's filthy car and then back at the trailer.

"Yes, yes, I am. An owner, actually. Just came up from Delaware. My horse ran in the fourth. He won tonight. Didn't think he had it in him, but he did all right. Time for a good steak or something. Haven't had one of those in a while. Just trying to get out of here to beat the traffic, but that didn't work out so well, heh, heh. Something going on? Everything okay?"

"Quite the shiner you got there."

"Oh yeah, that." Max chuckled. "Just an accident on the farm. Kind of embarrassing, like giving a rake to Larry, Curly, and Moe. Anyway, it's okay now. Thanks for asking."

After a few silent moments, while the cop studied Max's license and insurance, he finally handed it back without looking at him.

"You can go," the cop said, waving him through without any further questioning.

Max felt a wave of relief pass over him. Speeding down Stadium Road toward I-95, he kept looking up to see if the helicopters were following him. He noticed the media vans racing toward the stadium. He turned on the radio and was surprised to hear the broadcaster announce, "This just in. In addition to a murder, there are reports of a robbery at the Coliseum." *Murder!* Max was shocked when he heard the news. *Who has been murdered?* he wondered. *Could it have been Bucky or Carl?* Everything had gone according to Frankie's plan, so there shouldn't have been any bloodletting. No wonder there was such a commotion. If he were to be fingered in the robbery, would that mean he would also be tied to the murder? Would he go to Sing Sing or Attica? Would he get shivved in the laundry room or in the yard? No, jail wasn't the place for Max. Whatever the fallout, he knew one thing for sure—it was time for him to disappear.

CHAPTER 20

Bucky and Carl dropped Nitro off at Roy's farm. When they got home, the Airstream was grounded and there was no sign of Max or Clarence. Since the sting had failed, Bucky wondered if there would be any justice for Frankie and Gino, and if JP, Parker, and Jonesy would bail him out if he were under suspicion. Maybe it was time to come clean with someone else, other than JP, who wasn't incompetent, or else go to the papers.

At least we won, Bucky thought, *so in Frankie's eyes we have done our part. But with all the heat on, is Frankie just going to appear on our doorstep asking for his share of the winnings? Certainly I can't be expected to rush out to Pistol Farms with a bag of cash.*

"Oh shit, Pops, you better come look at this," Bucky said to Carl, who was rifling through the junk drawer in the kitchen like a crazed old man.

On the news was the harness beat reporter, Ronnie Vincent, live from outside the Coliseum.

"This just in. Pary-Tote headquarters in Dover is reporting an anomaly in their system, a possible breach just days before the rollout of a security patch called the Y2K protocol. So if the allegations of race fixing, robbery, and murder weren't enough, now we have a cyberheist to add to the intrigue. It's a fast-developing story. Some folks around the grandstand are already coining it the 'Millennium Handle'—"

"This isn't going away, Pops," Bucky said, looking fearfully at the television. "The commissions are going to want to know about this, the cops. You think with this kind of coverage they're going to just let it go? And worst of all, not only are Frankie and Gino free somewhere, but also we owe them money. It's never good owing those guys money. Not to mention I'm sure they'll have some questions about who killed their paisano."

"Turn it off, turn it off, Bucky. What the hell are we supposed to do?" Carl said, waving his arms bewilderedly, his age and frailty never so apparent to Bucky as in that moment. It was the first time Carl had ever turned to him to ask what was next. It was always Carl who had one last trick in the bag, usually in the form of a bright young filly, or a last-ditch effort to ward off starvation, but there it was—he was out of options. *Does this mean I am responsible for making all the decisions around here now?*

"Maybe if we just think rationally," Bucky suggested.

"Rationally? I don't even know what that means."

"Just breathe."

"Breathe?"

"Yeah, do this, with your arms," Bucky said, demonstrating controlled breathing. "In … out. Relax, Dad. We'll figure it out."

"Do you think it was Max?" Carl asked.

"Of course it was Max."

"And Tony? Who the hell could have killed Tony?"

"I don't know. That's what I can't figure out. Could it have been Clarence?"

"What!"

"Dad, I haven't seen him since the race. Isn't that unusual? When's the last time we didn't see him in the winner's circle? If there's one person who would kill that dirtbag, it would be him."

"He's not a killer, Son."

"I know, I know … but I wouldn't blame him."

"Whoever did, I'm sure they won't get away with it. And we have the law on our side. At least I hope we do. We do have the law on our side don't we?"

"It's a bit of a gray area."

"I see."

"At least I can explain everything … if I have to. I was really hoping that would be the end of it, but really it's just the beginning. Better go get Patricia, I guess."

"Not this again."

"Who knows what's coming?" Bucky said. He went upstairs to retrieve his shotgun.

For the next few days, Bucky and Carl sat on the front porch of the farmhouse waiting for something, anything, to happen. Instead of Frankie, the cops, or the feds, there was barely a breeze. In the quietude, they sweated, looked out at the broken landscape with the burned-out barn, and tried to figure out what was next. Sure, they had won the race, but because of the outcome and the day's events, there was sure to be further inquiry. Since Clarence wasn't around, it was the longest Bucky had been alone with Carl since he'd been a kid. He remembered the last time because they'd been at an auction in Kentucky and went out for BBQ where there was a steer's head at the entrance. It was the type of place where if you finished your meal, you won a T-shirt and got your picture on the wall. That had been right after Delores had died. Bucky recalled how without any warning or apparent provocation Carl had broken down and started sobbing at the table. That was over twenty years ago, but it seemed like Carl still carried that pain as if it were yesterday.

Now, with so much uncertainty hanging over the farm, Bucky wasn't sure if Carl could carry on. If he were a normal man in a normal industry, if he worked for DuPont or GE, he'd be well past retirement age and would have a nice pension, some savings, and years of early bird specials to look forward to. Instead, because of the situation Bucky had forced him into, now he would probably have to work until his last dying breath—or go to jail. There were only so many times

Bucky could apologize. He did just that as they sat on the porch, staring out at the bleak future.

Bucky wondered how he could possibly leave Carl alone now that Clarence had disappeared. Even more disconcerting was that Carl was still looking to his son for direction. Had the point already come in his life where he became his father's caregiver? Would he soon have to install a stairlift, and handrails in the shower? Would he have to wipe the dribble from his father's chin and wipe his ass? Was that what he was sticking around for?

He thought about waiting for Clarence to return, or going to look for him, but by that point it was obvious that Clarence had disappeared for a reason. Bucky turned over all the options in his head—go back to New York, settle things with the authorities, rebuild the barn, go to college, work on a resume—but it wasn't until after he opened up Anna's letter that he came to a decision.

He had been carrying the letter around like Atlas, with the weight of the world on his shoulders, waiting for the perfect moment to open it up so his future would be revealed. He'd kept it in his back pocket and ruminated over it, feared it. It had been lodged there like an unclaimed lottery ticket or pocketful of broken glass. The last time he'd placed that much importance on a piece of paper was when he'd waited for his fortune from Zoltar, the fortune-telling machine on the boardwalk in Rehoboth, where he remembered announcing to Anna and Cole, "This ticket, this is the ticket to my life. Whatever Zoltar says, so shall it be done."

To this day he could not remember the fortune, but he could still recall the disappointment, and Anna and Cole both laughing and pointing at him. *Was it really just me way back then? Was I always destined to lose? A future foretold because of one night on the boardwalk so long ago?* That's how it felt most days, waiting around, waiting for the seasons to change, wondering where love was or if it existed. *Where was love all those nights beneath the flicker of my purple light bulb, when I waited days on end for the phone to ring and there was no amount of the Cure or Depeche Mode to soothe my heartache? Where was the love with all those empty miles on the odometer, and the fast-developing crow's feet in the corners of my eyes? Where was love when I went days without a friend—years, even?* All this time Bucky had known exactly where love was, and that's what had made it even harder. Love was over at Anna and Cole's place. Bucky often wondered if Anna ever thought about him during those quiet hours of domesticity. *Did she think about me on roast beef Sundays or chicken liver Wednesdays? Was there something, anything, she would have rather been doing with me?* All these years Bucky wondered at what spectrum he'd appeared in her thoughts. *How much did she really care? What would she do if I died, or better yet if I died in her honor, jumping off a building perhaps, screaming her name as I plummeted toward the earth? Maybe love is overrated. Maybe I already spent too much time waiting for love, like a ghost in purgatory waiting for final judgment.* And now finally, with a note in his back pocket with consequences much larger than Zoltar, or the origami fortunes from grade school where the future was preambled by, "My mother told me not to swear … my mother told me not to swear," Bucky felt like he was a contestant on *Let's Make a Deal*: pick right and you find love; pick wrong and you get the donkey. Unfortunately, he didn't have much of a choice. There could only be one of two doors for him to walk through, and at this point he feared them both equally.

Finally, unable to stand the torment anymore, Bucky told Carl he was going for a walk. He took his time walking to the outer reaches of their property. Across the escarpment was the edge of the next property over. Bucky remembered there was a stud that used to stand still as a statue on the elevation and stare forlornly at Summer Rose grazing in the field. He had escaped before, jumped both fences, and mounted Rose, so now the paddock was reinforced with electrical wire. After getting zapped twice, he'd finally learned his lesson. After Max had sold Rose in a claimer, the lonely stud came around every day hoping to see her, until one day he trotted off and never looked back again.

Bucky walked across the paddock and down the slope, where he unlatched the gate. He walked along a muddy path until he got to the rock he used to come and cry on after his mother had died and after Anna had dumped him. He sat down. It was a place of complete solitude, where the only sounds were the buzzing insects, distant power lines, and frogs burping and plopping into puddles. Sometimes the bugs would ravage you after it rained, but fortunately today it was sunny and silent. It was just the openness and isolation Bucky needed for a moment of this magnitude.

Bucky pulled the note from his pocket. His first instinct was to smell it, as if something of Anna might come across, like on her old Valentine's cards and the cinnamon candies he could still taste on her lips, but instead it just smelled like paper, and there was no SWAK in red lipstick or scribbled hearts on the outside.

He opened it up as if he were revealing a sacred covenant on an ancient parchment. It was a short, simple note, not the gushing proclamation of her love or agonizing rejection detailing the reasons she couldn't be with him in point form from A to Z, both outcomes that he had weighed in on equally all week. Here it was, the moment bigger than the valley and the farmlands, bearing down on him like water rising against a break wall:

> Dear Bucky,
>
> Pick me up next Saturday at 1:00 p.m. I will have my bags.
>
> XO,
>
> Anna

Bucky ran his fingers across the page and clutched the letter to his chest. At first he thought it was a mistake or typo. Had Anna accidently swapped letters and put them into the wrong envelopes, her pen pal in Long Island getting a letter saying that she never loved him and couldn't do this, etc., etc., all those things he half expected to hear, and had already heard over and over. Whatever it was, after the initial shock of it, it didn't feel as sweet as he once thought it would. Anna was his. After all the buildup, the moment he had been dreaming about his whole life had finally come. He had won, yet he couldn't shake the feeling of malaise. He looked down at the stone he was sitting on, wondering how long it had been lodged there and what had caused it to be in that exact spot. Was it formed in the big bang, or had it rained down in a meteor shower? *Perhaps the land beneath the properties had split like the continents and this rock, my rock, that had once been buried was now risen to the top?* He had sat there so many times with so much loneliness and sorrow, and now that something good had happened, the best thing in fact, he couldn't even give the long-suffering rock the one piece of good news it had been waiting for all these years. *Is this what victory looks like, victory over my best friend, and Anna is the prize?*

Looking out at the land, it was obvious to Bucky that unlike his move to New York, this time he would be saying goodbye for good. It would be the last time he would sit on that rock. For so long Bucky had been anxious to escape the farm and the memories that haunted him, but now with his certain departure, he couldn't help but feel sad over the loss of his childhood home. It was where the only memories of his mother were, and where they had lived as a family and were happy. It was where once there had been a well-stocked fridge and laughter, where he'd once had a train set, and Hot Wheels cars in a mash-up on the floor. It was the place where there had been suppertimes and togetherness—love, in short—with a woman's touch and sensibility to lighten the place up.

As the sentiment crept in and Bucky pined for the place he had not yet left, he remembered a life lesson imparted by his mother before she'd left him too soon. There was a family heirloom, a porcelain bull coated with sprayed gold, that somehow had survived a long-ago journey across the Atlantic. Carl had extolled its virtue for years. One day Bucky had been driving around the farmhouse on his Big Wheel and hit the corner of the table. The porcelain bull fell off and smashed to pieces. Knowing this, and just how important it was, Bucky burst into tears. Hearing the smash and commotion, Delores came over and looked at him with kind eyes. "It's all right, Johnny; it was just a thing. The memories don't disappear; life is made of them—nothing else matters," she'd said. And now he was leaving, worried that his memories might fade even more, with no more frame of reference, no shared space where Delores had once moved and breathed when she was alive.

Bucky went back through the paddock and walked uphill to the ridge, where the entire farm could be seen on the downslope. He could see across the valley to the other farms. Across the plain was the shadow of one giant cloud that slowly swept across the parceled land. He took a deep breath and raised his arms to feel the breeze upon his chest. He wanted to remember the earthiness, the smell of manure and fresh-cut hay. *There couldn't be a more beautiful place than this,* he thought. He put his arms down, his eyes blurry from staring into the sun, and stumbled forward on the uneven ground.

When he got to the track, he walked around and remembered one race he'd had there with Cole. Bucky could still hear the echoes as they yelled at each other and their horses while they raced for home. Bucky won that day. Cole had sprayed him in the barn to get even, and when Clarence had come along, they dumped a bucket of water on him—which did not go well.

By the time Bucky got back to the remains of the barn, it felt like he had lived the whole span of his life in that one long walk. There had been time and space for reflection, and as much as he tried to visualize what the next chapter of his life would look like, he didn't have that epiphany until he was closer to the farmhouse and could see Carl sitting alone, rocking on the front porch chair. He was glad that he hadn't waited any longer to read the letter. Saturday was in two days; there was a lot to get done before then. It was with that in mind that Bucky started walking with some urgency toward the farmhouse, and then he started running.

—O—

When Saturday came, Bucky drove over to Anna and Cole's in his Datsun. Behind him he towed the Silver Bullet. He had both windows open to feel the country air. It was just the kind of summer morning he might have expected, one designed to make him miss Delaware—everything from the rich land to the state fair where he'd had his first kiss, to Rehoboth where he remembered Anna's sandy knees and grape-stained tongue. He thought about when he used to get Astro Pops from the Harrington confectionary when he was a kid, and the public library where Delores used to drop him off with an apple juice drink box and three Oreos in a ziplock bag. It was bittersweet, his relationship with Delaware, and now that he'd made the decision to leave it, he felt a solace in his mother's words, that life was just memories. Now it was okay for him to move on and create a new life and new memories.

As he drove the last few miles, he fought off his pangs of self-doubt. When he arrived, he could see Anna standing at the end of the lane with two suitcases. She was wearing a yellow summer dress that blew against her body, showing off her perfect breasts and long legs. She waved to him, and waited for him as he parked the trailer. Before he got out, Bucky took a moment to admire Anna from afar. It was always those moments when Anna couldn't have known he was watching that Bucky thought her most beautiful. She could never have known how even her slightest movements and expressions were enough to send Bucky into a tizzy. As he watched her now, standing erect and stoic, brushing her windblown hair behind her ears, he wondered what she could be thinking as she took the final steps to leave Cole. What must it have been like for her growing up between the two men who loved her unrelentingly? To always be torn and uncertain—to refuse a love she always knew existed. Maybe she was just as damaged by it, and no longer willing or able to live with it, she had finally set herself free. What this would do to Cole, and her mother. How this would change the makeup of her life, not to mention the uncertainty with Bucky, made it a courageous act. There she stood, nose to the wind, fear, love, sadness, everything, in her eyes as she watched Bucky get out of the trailer and walk toward her.

Bucky felt a lightness of spirit; it was in these rare moments where life was defined. He felt a knot in his stomach and a wobble in his knees. The sun backlit Anna's face in a soft hue and was pretty in her hair. Bucky took her hands and looked into her eyes and the diamond sliver of her iris. There before the horses and trees, and all of eternity, he whispered softly in her ear.

"I can't do this, Anna."

When the words came out, he felt a sharp pain like a bullet ricocheting over every bone in his body. A pulse of sadness rushed through his veins. Remembering all his other sad goodbyes, he knew for sure that it was really that moment. When she let go of his hands, he took a step back and looked at her. She had a blank expression. *Perhaps Anna is the loneliest of all,* Bucky thought. It sounds easy to have twice the love, to go flittingly between two lovers, but perhaps that was its own form of torture. Then there was Bobby. Nothing could replace the loss of a sibling, and in that she was truly alone. Bucky could feel an emptiness in Anna, so he leaned into hug her, squeezing as hard as he could while she stood there limply.

"I'm sorry," he said. Then he gave her a kiss on the cheek, backed away a few steps, and walked back toward the trailer. When he got into the truck and put on his seat belt, he could see Anna still standing there with her two suitcases. Had she told Cole beforehand, or was it a fly-by-night, or in this case fly-by-day, decision, making it a swift abandonment without even the cover of darkness? Perhaps Cole was reading her letter right now in the kitchen, and soon she would need to go inside to face him. Maybe since she'd already packed her bags, she would still be determined to leave Cole, and just like their game in the swimming pool when they'd held hands and whirled around in a circle, they'd all let go and drift in opposite directions. Perhaps that was really it—the final breaking up of their triumvirate.

As Bucky drove away, he felt a strange sensation. Now, it was really settled. *Better now than in twenty years,* he thought, because given that no marriage is perfect, eventually it was bound to happen again in a weak moment. Assuming that Cole would take her back, they could go on and start a family, and this would just be a blip. Their children and grandchildren would hear rumors of one last dalliance in their great love story.

So now that Bucky's number had finally come up, and he was standing at the counter ready for his ice cream, he turned and walked away. He had waited his whole life for Anna, and when she'd finally come around, it was too late. There were times when he'd ached to see her face and to hear her voice, times when he would have done anything, in fact, for just a whiff of her cherry shampoo, but not anymore. He felt strangely liberated. He had not foresworn himself from love, nor was he destined to live alone to collect stamps or cats, whatever single people did to fill the void of their lonely lives. No. He believed there was a greater love, a love without a past, one that wouldn't leave so much carnage. He believed in a love that you could scream from the rooftops, that grabs you and shakes you, that rings you out and fills you up, that lets you know you're the *only* one.

Now with this renewal, this sudden awakening, it seemed there was a whole new world of possibility. Perhaps it was the realization that love would happen in its own time and place, and it didn't have to be Anna's, that set Bucky free. Maybe it would happen in a nightclub or restaurant, or somewhere unsuspected, like the dentist's office or the bank. *Perhaps it will just be the smile of a stranger that says,* I know you; we have done this before. *And just like that, the world would stop and the future will finally be revealed.* Bucky could already see the blur of her face, and taste her morning kiss. In a flash, there was life, bigger and brighter. *It's true,* Bucky thought, as he cranked up the radio and screamed out the window while the wind blew his hair and swirled paper particles around in the cab. *It's true that love is out there. It's what countless poems and songs were written for, and there it is, dangling in the periphery.* What Bucky now understood was that as long as he kept his heart open, it would come along in due time, and when it did, it would be like a warm blanket or like sitting on the front porch in a rainstorm. Bucky would never go as far to say he'd found God in that moment, but it was a moment when he knew that from that point forward he would not take anything for granted, no leaf or insect, no living, breathing thing. It was a time to get out of old routines, to open up and be a better man. He knew that Cole would take Anna back—of course he would; he couldn't live without her—which was another difference between them, so now he happily bestowed that honor fully and unequivocally back on his best friend, because who better? Cole was kind and generous and ran into burning buildings. Knowing that there was no one better to help ease Anna's pain, to try to help her sort through whatever confusion, loneliness, and grief she had, gave Bucky great solace. *Because, who knows, maybe there is still room to patch up that friendship.* He was steady Cole after all, and perhaps one day they could go skeet shooting or take a rafting tour down the Colorado River. All things they once swore they'd do when they were kids, they would do as older men with the long and tattered history behind them.

Bucky headed west into Maryland and soon crossed the Chesapeake Bay Bridge. When he stopped for gas in Annapolis, he noticed on the newsstand a picture of Harold on the cover of a *USA Today*. The headline read, "Cyber thief at large." In was an old picture of him, pale, pimple-faced, and bespectacled, taken from his community college called Athabasca Tech, where he'd dropped out. Turns out he wasn't MIT material after all.

There were also smaller photos of Gino and Frankie with the subheading "Still missing," as well as a few other gray boxes with question marks on them. Bucky paid at the counter, folded the paper and put it under his armpit, and headed back to the truck. With all the sensationalism surrounding the Breeders, he wondered how long it would take for the authorities to turn their attention away from the murder and robbery and start looking at the suspect results of the race. Bucky also figured it would just be a matter of time before Max's picture filled one of the gray boxes, and he wondered where he might be and whom he was working with to execute such a sophisticated operation. It was a mystery that would baffle not just him but also law enforcement, threatening to forever be in limbo like where Jimmy Hoffa was buried or who shot JR.

It was just outside of Uniontown, Pennsylvania, when Bucky heard banging coming from the back of the trailer. He pulled over to the shoulder of the road. When he opened up the door, there were Carl and Clarence, both in hysterics. Clarence, it turned out, had gone home to his sister's place to lay low after the Breeders. He'd returned to the farm to find Carl and Bucky in a frenzy of activity, selling off whatever they could and rushing to tie up all the loose ends. Clarence agreed to go with them. The night before they'd left, the three of them got incredibly drunk and talked about all the great memories they had of the farm, all the horses, and all the setting suns. While they laughed and cried, Bucky tried to get it out of Clarence if he was the one who'd killed Tony, but all he got was a wry grin and no denial.

"What's going on back here?" Bucky said as he stepped inside the trailer. After a few more panicked moments where it looked like Carl might be hyperventilating, he began practicing controlled breathing like Bucky had taught him. Clarence was still pacing and banging on the walls.

"Take a look," Carl said, pointing at the black case on the kitchen table. "It was under the divan."

Bucky approached the case slowly as if it were kryptonite, and then he peeked inside. It was three-quarters full with money, obviously from Max. Who else would have left such a stash? He must have unhitched the trailer right after the race and gone on the lam. Maybe that was his way of paying them back, or perhaps he planned on coming back for it. In a way, Bucky was proud of his uncle. He wasn't perfect—about as far from it as you can imagine—but in some ways he was human and was always generous, even if it was dirty money. If being a thief and a bandit was Max's true calling, then he had certainly risen to the top of the ranks. After all, it wasn't just anybody who could pull off a heist as great as the Millennium Handle. Max had gone for it and done something big, and now he was gone—probably for good. Bucky's memories of Max would always be overwhelmingly negative, but at times he couldn't help but see the humor in his antics. Like the time he dressed as Santa for one of Roy's Christmas parties and puked in the sack and then passed out in the Nativity scene. Or the time he spilled gravy all over an elderly woman's head at the Rotary Christmas dinner. There were hundreds of drinking stories about Max that Bucky would always be told. In his own small, pathetic way, Max was a legend. Chances are that he would never be clean, because how do you polish such a rusty spoon, but it was true he had his reasons; being abandoned by not just one but two families must have exacted its toll. And Bucky knew that in Max's heart he wasn't necessarily mean or unkind. He was just flawed—like a dented can. Max was the bull, and life was the china shop. Bucky hoped that someday he'd find a place to stumble home to.

"What now?" Carl said, looking to Bucky, as if this influx of cash might change their plan of settling down in a small town outside of Pittsburgh. Clarence originally was going to do some training, and Bucky some catch-driving through the Midwest, with the added benefit that it wouldn't look like he was in hiding. Carl would have his first taste of retirement, mentioning a small apartment he noticed for rent last time they had passed through. It was above a hardware store and was close to a pharmacy for Carl to meet all his geriatric needs as he limped his way down the backstretch.

Bucky looked down at the money and then up at Carl and Clarence, who were waiting for an answer. If it wasn't clear before that the torch had been passed, it was now. With a bag full of cash and a world full of options, Bucky scratched his head and thought to himself for a moment. And then it came to him.

"How about Sunshine Raceway?"

"Great track," Carl said.

"I got a guy down there," Clarence said, "Juan Carlos. He's a jai alai player. Would probably let us dock the Silver Bullet in his yard."

"So it's settled then," Bucky said.

"Florida!" Carl chimed in, with his finger raised.

Bucky got back in the truck and turned it around. It wasn't long before he crossed the Mason–Dixon Line into West Virginia and drove all night through the Carolinas. He was just outside Savannah when the sky was lit purple and blue, the stars struggling to shine, barely twinkling while saying their last good night. The air was softer and warmer; a fog was coming off the trees that lined the highway. Bucky was exhausted. He had been driving for sixteen hours and caught himself nodding off. He thought about taking a break and stopping at a motel, maybe a Waffle House, but he couldn't because he knew he was getting closer. He could feel the warmth in the air and in his bones. While the violet dawn turned blue and a jet's contrail painted a thin line across the sky, Bucky shook his head and gripped the wheel. With everything now ahead—life and love, free of all fears and regrets, no longer a sufferer or an old nag—he let the slow drift of the highway roll him along the endless mile.

Printed in the United States
By Bookmasters